Copyright 2022 © by Leslie A. Piggott

Published January 2022
Published by Indies United Publishing House, LLC

Cover art by Danielle Johnston

All rights reserved worldwide. No part of this publication may be replicated, redistributed, or given away in any form without the prior written consent of the author/publisher or the terms relayed to you herein.

ISBN: 978-1-64456-404-2 (paperback)
ISBN: 978-1-64456-406-6 (ePub)
ISNB: 978-1-64456-405-9 (Mobi)

Library of Congress Control Number: 2021950538

This is a work of fiction. None of the characters are real, nor are *Apothecom* or *Regulair*.

INDIES UNITED PUBLISHING HOUSE, LLC
P.O. BOX 3071
QUINCY, IL 62305-3071

www.indiesunited.net

RISING PRESSURE

by Leslie A. Piggott

INDIES UNITED PUBLISHING HOUSE, LLC

Dedication

To Brad, Abby, and Simon: you are the joy of my life. Thank you for all of your support.

Acknowledgments

This book would not have been possible without the superb editing skills of Jennie Rosenblum. She helped me mold this story into something I think all of my readers will enjoy. Thank you, Jennie!

Danielle Johnston did a tremendous job on the cover art. I sent her a watercolor image of my idea and she made it shine. Thank you, Danielle!

To Lisa and all of the Indies United group: thank you for your support, advice, and expertise!

Chapter 1

"Act natural, act natural," Dr. Emmitt Strydent coached himself as he stepped off the stage and approached the tall, copper-headed woman.

"Addison Feringer! Wow! What a small world. Who would have guessed that we'd end up at the same symposium? After all these years. I'm glad to see that the girl who challenged me for every local academic scholarship in high school is still putting her brain to good use. What are you up to these days?"

"Oh, hi, Emmitt. It's actually Dr. Fischer now. I'm married, 3 kids, have my own lab as a PI." Addison's blue-grey eyes flared as she tried to hide her offense at Emmitt's rather condescending comments. She had decided to attend the symposium after seeing his name as the keynote speaker. Emmitt Strydent had been the student she always tried to one-up in high school. Back then, he hadn't seemed so arrogant though.

"It seems like you have done well for yourself. I didn't realize you studied ion channels until I saw your name on a departmental flier. I enjoyed your talk."

"Well, thank you. It's an exciting world to be in right now. Dr. Fischer, you say? Of course. I know your work. I just never realized you were the same Addison from my younger years. A bit of a sodium channel expert, huh?"

Addison relaxed a bit when he complimented her. Maybe he was just another man that didn't realize how their vocabularies were outdated when it came to women in science.

She smiled. "I'm trying to carve a path, yes."

"We should grab lunch. Do you have time? I'd love to catch up."

She hesitated. She really needed to get back to the lab. One of her graduate students apparently needed constant supervision in order to finish his work and get to the point of writing his dissertation. She had a meeting set up with him for 1:30 that afternoon and wanted to review his scope before sitting down with him.

"C'mon. I won't keep you forever. It will be a quick lunch, I promise." Dr. Strydent extended his hand.

"Okay, I can squeeze in a quick lunch for an old friend. There's a café over by my building. Sandwiches and soup work for you?"

"Sounds perfect. I'm going to grab my rental car and pull it around. What's the restaurant's name?"

"'Santouits.' It's Greek for sandwich. I'm walking, so I'll see you there." She turned to grab her bag and headed for the exit.

"Clever. See you there." Dr. Strydent called after her, a smug grin on his face.

As Addison headed out the double doors of the auditorium, she thought back to her time in high school with Emmitt. He had been a hard worker and dependable as well as an athlete. He was the quarterback of their football team and a starting forward on the basketball team too. In their small town, everyone did a bit of everything, and he had excelled in multiple fields. She never expected to find him as a colleague of sorts in the academic world. Addison picked up her pace. Maybe she could get to the restaurant before him and look up some more background on the man. Rounding the corner, she saw the blue and white awning of the café up ahead. She'd grab a table and get to work.

As the hostess led Addison to a table for two near the salad bar, Addison pulled her phone from her bag, unlocking it. She was in the process of typing his name into the Google bar when she realized the hostess had asked her a question.

She looked up. "I'm sorry. I wasn't paying attention."

"Will your companion be here soon? Should I bring waters? Menus?" The hostess glanced around the dining area hinting at the busyness of the lunchtime rush.

"Oh yes. Any minute. Waters and menus would be great. Thank you." Addison said as she looked back to her phone screen.

Emmitt had done really well for himself. Numerous papers in high level journals, big lab at a big university; he was definitely a leader in the field. A recent news article hinted that he might be being considered for the Nobel Prize in medicine before too long.

He had discovered a protein involved with stabilizing ionic channels into cell membranes and displayed its role in regulating blood pressure. Not only that, he had taken his discovery a step further to identify an important mutation in this protein, which he named STABL. Fascinatingly, this mutation was found in the majority of otherwise seemingly healthy people that suffered from chronic high blood pressure.

Addison checked her watch and glanced around the café. Emmitt should be arriving soon, but she just wanted to read a little more about him. She went to the NCBI database and started to pull up some of his papers to see what methodology he typically used. In his talk earlier, he'd spoken in clinical terms regarding blood pressure control and less about the basic science he'd used to break down the puzzle of high blood pressure. She had just started to download his latest paper when she was startled back into reality. She quickly turned her phone's screen off as she looked up. Emmitt was standing next to the table.

"Doing some light reading before lunch?" He laughed.

Addison felt her cheeks start to flush. "Caught me red-handed. I was just reading about all your amazing discoveries. Fascinating work, Dr. Strydent."

"Sometimes I can't believe how far we've come. It's an exciting ride, for sure. But please, call me Emmitt." He beamed while taking a seat at the table. Addison realized that he still had his boyish good looks even though his hair had a few grays sprinkled in around the temples. If not for those, most people probably would have mistaken him for someone in their early 30s rather than a man pushing close to 50.

Just then, the waitress stepped over to take their order. The small café was filling up quickly and anyone could see that she was running from table to table to keep up. She had her pen and notepad up and ready.

"Oh wow! You got over here fast. I've never been here before. What would you recommend?" Emmitt said, looking at Addison.

"I always get the egg salad with tomatoes on honey wheat

toast. It's delicious. Honestly, it's what I ordered the first time I came here and I haven't tried anything else. Ryan, uh, my husband, usually orders the tuna." Addison said quickly as the waitress scribbled on her notepad.

"Egg salad it is. I'll get an iced tea too, if it's not too much trouble." Emmitt smiled.

"Sweet or unsweet?" The waitress responded.

"What? Oh right, the South and its sweet tea. That will be UN-sweet for me. Thank you."

The waitress gathered their menus and rushed off to the next table.

"Busy place. Is it always this crowded?" Emmitt asked.

"Ummm, I don't know. I usually order mine to go or Ryan picks it up. I haven't really paid attention, I guess." Addison stuttered a bit. Being around Emmitt again brought back memories of trying to match him in high school. Being female, she often wasn't taken as seriously as the boys in her classes. To be fair, most of the women in her small town were either stay at home moms or elementary school teachers. She was used to breaking stereotypes. She mentally chided herself for not having her usual self-confidence. "Anyway, tell me about your research. What questions are you trying to answer, Emmitt?"

"Still not one to mince words, huh?" He chuckled. "Well, my work started out on the fringe of ion channels. After college, I knew that I wanted to go into science research but wasn't sure what field or pathway. It seemed like everyone was heading to cancer research, and rather than be a small fish in a big pond…well you know the phrase, I'm sure. I decided to pick a relatively common disease that was poorly understood and stumbled onto blood pressure regulation. My advisor, Dr. Watt—"

"Wait, what? Dr. Watt?! As in Dr. Benjamin Watt?" Addison blinked.

"Ha ha. Yes, the one and only. He's your boss, your department chair, right? I'm surprised you hadn't found the common thread yet."

"It's a big department. He was only hired as the chair last spring." Addison explained.

"Oh, well that makes sense. It takes time to get to know the help." Emmitt winked while Addison inwardly groaned. Emmitt still had the boyish charm that had helped him gain fame and popularity in their town. She respected Emmitt's intelligence, but only barely managed to paint on a grin in response to his joke. He cleared his throat and continued.

"Anyway, as you know, Dr. Watt studied membrane proteins and blood pressure, so I set up a meeting with him and knew I'd found my home. As you also know, he studies the proteins in the cell membrane by looking at their structures. The human genome had just been sequenced, so he was looking for anything that resembled a membrane protein within the endless genes in our DNA. He looked at things like a puzzle. You know, if this piece in the membrane has this shape, then there must be something else that fits in next to it, and so on. It was brilliant! He had a whole list of proteins that I could pick from to study for my dissertation. Sometimes it feels like I won the lottery. I picked STABL because it's small, one of the last five by size on the list. Of course, that list has just continued to grow in size over the years." Emmitt spread his hands as he finished speaking.

"That's incredible. But don't sell yourself short. You've really taken STABL to the big leagues, from what I've read. You made STABL. It sounds like it could be life changing for some people."

"I sure hope so. That's what got me into research. I wanted to make a positive impact on the health of others."

"So, what method do you use to study structure? Crystallography?"

"Yes, Dr. Watt has a great system for isolating membrane proteins and then figuring out their structure with crystallography. Side note, it is so nice to talk science with someone that understands it. Whenever I try to explain crystallography to my mom, she just glazes over. I try to simplify it, you know? It's so hard to get it down to her level, though. I remind her about growing salt or sugar crystals for science fair projects, but my crystals are just microscopic and require an electron microscope to view them. She waves her hands around and changes the subject. Ha ha."

Addison laughed. "It's definitely a challenge to break things down into layman's terms. I hate to eat and run, but I've got a grad student that I need to ride herd on. He cannot stay on task. Sometimes I wonder if his unspoken goal is to break the record of longest stint as a student before defending a dissertation."

"I understand. There's always that one student, huh? Let me give you my card, so we can stay in touch. Maybe there's something we could collaborate on in the future." Emmitt pulled a business card from his coat pocket.

"That sounds great, Emmitt. I'll be in touch." Addison took his card and tucked it into her bag, while signaling to the waitress for the check.

"Please, let me pay. I took you away from your schedule. I'll take care of the bill while you get your student back on track." Emmitt waved off her wallet.

"Don't be ridiculous. We can just split it." Addison pulled ten dollars from her wallet as the waitress laid down their ticket.

"As you wish. Thanks for joining me. It was great to see you again." Emmitt said as they shook hands.

Chapter 2

Addison walked the short block back to her lab, excited at the possibility of collaborating with the Strydent lab. Her department chair would surely welcome the idea, as Emmitt was his former student, not to mention associating with someone as renowned as Emmitt could only be profitable for the lab as well as the department. Swiping her fob to enter the building, she pulled her phone out as she walked over to the elevator bay. Ryan wouldn't believe the opportunity that just fell into her lap.

"You'll never guess who I ran into today. Tell you all about it at dinner tonight."

"Sounds exciting. Hope he isn't hotter than me!"

"Where's that eyeroll emoji when you need it...love you!"

"You too."

Addison smiled as she stepped off the elevator. Ryan loved to joke around with her and always knew how to make her laugh. They kept a running banter going day in and day out. She checked her watch. She had twenty minutes before her meeting with Anthony. Time to find a way to get him on the straight and narrow.

She unlocked her office and logged into her computer. She had opted for an interior office that didn't have a window so that her lab could have windows. Most of the full professors in her department had office windows, but she figured that having a happy staff was more important. She had room for a fairly large desk, a cushioned office chair on wheels, two extra chairs as well as a filing cabinet that held most of her previous students and postdoctoral fellows' old notebooks. It was cozy, but it worked. She had several photos of her family on the walls, as well as her own diplomas.

Pulling up Anthony's file, she sighed. He was such an intelligent student, but he was SO lazy and messy. He was running through reagents and money without making any progress, but part of her role was to help him find his niche. What could she say to help motivate this kid?! He had started out promising and seemed fairly knowledgeable about the lab and the techniques. All that fell away quickly after he finished his classwork within the degree program. Now that he was just completing experiments to round out his dissertation, he barely put forth any effort.

Although, she had to admit that his lab etiquette had been pretty rough from day one. He constantly "borrowed" solutions or reagents from other lab members, usually without asking. He rarely cleaned up after himself, frequently leaving full ice buckets out on the countertop for someone else to empty. Her lab assistant, Eleanor Ritkey, was very kind and forgiving, but Addison was fairly certain that she kept many of Anthony Wydrow's blunders to herself. The other lab members were much more forthcoming in regards to his messiness and *borrowing* habits. Addison had to continually remind him that not every lab would be so forgiving, and he needed to take care of his area and prepare his own reagents. Hearing the shuffle-step she recognized as Anthony's reluctant walk to her office, she pulled out a notebook and pen for their meeting.

Anthony was an attractive young man. Addison sometimes wondered if he had relied on his good looks and charm instead of his intelligence when he was in high school and college. He was a few inches north of six feet tall with dark brown hair that he kept a little longer than average, much like a California surfer. His eyes were dark blue to the point of almost seeming to be black when the lighting was right. The twenty-eight-year-old had come to her lab from the west coast and definitely had the *take it easy* air about him.

"Hi Dr. Fish. I brought my lab notebook. I got it all organized, just like you asked."

Addison looked up to see a binder with some pages hanging out unevenly from multiple sides and stifled a grimace. She couldn't bring herself to wonder what it looked like in an unorganized state.

"Wonderful! Let's see where you are with your project," Addison smiled as she reached for the binder, moving her own notebook to the side. She opened the binder carefully, hoping not to dislodge any free papers that hadn't been successfully locked into place within the 3-ring binder. She gently flipped through the pages to where they had left off two weeks before and realized there was only one more page remaining.

"Anthony! Have you only done one experiment in the last two weeks?!" She asked, exasperated.

"Well, you see, Dr. Fish. I had planned to do more, of course. I set up an experiment for last week, but I think the power went out or something on my incubator. All of my cells were dead and floating when I went to harvest them on Thursday, so I had to scrap that idea. The page you're looking at is from my experiment this week." Anthony held his hands out, palms up, hoping for leniency.

"But, Anthony! You still need to keep a record of a planned experiment even if you don't get positive results from it—yes, even if you don't get to complete it. There is always something to learn from a failed experiment. I heard about your incubator problem. I don't think it was a power issue as no one else in the lab lost cells or experiments last week. Are you certain that you got the door completely closed when you put the cells back the day before? Small changes in temperature or humidity can result in cell death. You have to be very careful." Addison sighed. This meeting was not starting well.

"I mean, I thought I did. I'm sorry, Dr. Fish." Anthony said timidly. Addison sometimes felt like she was talking to her teenaged son about leaving dirty clothes around his room whenever she met with Anthony.

"Okay, well there's nothing we can do about that now, except try to be extra diligent from here on. You really do a great job with your experiments when you actually do them, Anthony. You aren't that far away from your next committee meeting, you know. If you really put in the work, you might have enough data to get permission from them to start writing your dissertation. You have great hands, Anthony, and you're really smart. You could make a great PI someday." She said encouragingly.

"Really? That's great to hear. I feel like I've been spinning my wheels on this for a long time and not really making any progress. PI. Wow! That acronym always makes me laugh. Like we're undercover agents, not principal investigators—scientists! Ha, ahem." He cleared his throat when she wasn't laughing. "What are my next steps? What is my research missing?"

"As I said, you have really done a good job with your project, you just need to focus on completing it. Talk to me. Tell me what story you're trying to convey with your project. Getting your doctorate isn't just about doing experiments; it's about understanding why you did which experiments as well as what the results tell you." Addison knew that Anthony understood his project conceptually, but she wanted him to realize that too. Maybe that would help him see the big picture of getting it finished soon.

"Okay, right. Ummm, it just feels kind of funny explaining my project to you when it's really YOUR project from your grant and…" he coughed in response to her raised eyebrows. "And I would be happy to tell you all about it. My project tested the hypothesis that the sodium ion channel, $Na_v1.5$, is regulated by the small protein, alpha9. When alpha9 is activated by phosphorylation, it triggers $Na_v1.5$ to open, allowing the flow of sodium ions across the membrane. If you block phosphorylation with the drug mexipres, the flow of sodium ions is decreased. Furthermore—"

"Okay, I'm going to stop you for one second. We tossed around the idea of you writing an abstract in layman's terms. You know, something that your non-science friends or your parents or your great-aunt Bertha could understand. Have you thought about that anymore? Why don't you just try it for me, really quick? It's really an important exercise."

Anthony groaned and slumped his shoulders.

"Okay, Dr. Fish. Let's see. My project studies an ion channel—wait, can I say ion channel? Okay. My project studies an ion channel that is positioned within the outer membrane of heart cells in mammals. This channel opens to allow sodium ions into or out of the cell. A lot of things are responsible for getting this channel to open or close. My advisor identified a small, um molecule? Can I say protein? Okay, a small protein that plays a significant role in the opening and closing of the sodium channel in the heart. This protein is called alpha9. My research shows that alpha9 gets turned on or activated by a process called phosphor—"

"You can't say phosphorylation. That is a ten-dollar word. It will be the beginning of eyes glazing over and your audience tuning you out." Addison interrupted.

"I was going to explain what phosphorylation is. I just hadn't gotten there yet."

"It's not necessary. While it is something *you* have to understand and explain as part of your dissertation for your degree, it is not necessary to explain to a lay audience. Continue, please."

"Fine. So, alpha9 gets activated, which results in a special signal—" Anthony paused to see if Addison was going to stop him again. "Signal to the ion channel. The activation of alpha9 causes it to, um, change shape, triggering the channel to open. The activation is not long-lasting and, much like flipping a light switch, alpha9 returns to its original shape and the ion channel closes. I hypothesized that the activation of alpha9 was a key step in the opening of the ion channel as well as one that could be regulated pharmaceutically." Anthony grinned as he finished, clearly pleased with his summary.

"That was actually very good, if you leave out the ums and the random pauses. It's important for us, as scientists, to be able to simplify our language into layman's terms. While the majority of funding for basic science labs comes from the government, from NIH, occasionally, you will come across grants from pharmaceutical companies that are not necessarily reviewed by scientists that have a firm grasp of your field of study. Also, NIH grant money is made possible because people pay taxes, but the budget for NIH can change at any time. If the people setting the budget don't see a need for your research, then the budget could decrease. Okay, okay, I'll get off my soapbox. Let's figure out which experiments you need to finish up your story." Addison said, grabbing her notebook and pen.

"Every experiment needs to be completed in the same way at least three times so that you can do statistical analysis on it. It cannot be included unless you have shown that it is repeatable. Let's make a list. You have the first experiment showing the interaction between the channel and the protein. I know you did that one several times, right?" Anthony nodded. "Okay, good. Then the experiment showing the phosphorylation of alpha9 in response to the stimulus..." Addison flipped back through the binder to count the experiments.

"Okay, I found four. You definitely used all the same solutions and conditions, right?"

Anthony shrugged. "I mean, we only use certain ones, right? So, sure. I must have."

"You really need to do a better job of taking notes on your experiments. Okay, continuing on. The next experiment was to show that you can block alpha9 activation with mexipres, our pharmaceutical regulator. Thankfully, you repeated that one enough times so we don't have to go through the headache of working with the radioactive materials again. I don't think the rest of the lab could tolerate your care, or should I say, 'lack thereof' in handling radioactive isotopes again. So, what completes this story, Anthony?" Addison looked up, hoping her young student could connect the dots.

"I need to show that blocking phosphorylation also decreases channel activity. The best way to show that is the whole-cell patch experiment again, right? I run the experiment under normal conditions, then add the drug mexipres and show how it changes."

Addison beamed. "Perfect! That's exactly the experiment that you need to do."

"I was afraid you were going to agree. Those experiments are so tedious. And it's not just three times. I have to get multiple readings from multiple cells on multiple days. It's going to take FOR-EV-ER." Anthony slumped again.

"Oh Anthony. Chin up. You've already made it this far. Buckle down. You can do this. To help you stay on track, I'm going to need weekly updates from you."

"But—" Anthony started to protest.

"No. No complaining. You know what to do. There is no reason this should take more than another few months of work. It could possibly take less. Go get to it. Eleanor can help you thaw out some new cells if you need them."

"Oh, I uh, just got some from Becky on Monday."

"Please tell me you asked first."

Anthony shrugged.

"You really need to be more responsible. Becky is a second-year student. You should not be taking reagents from her. You should be helping her, not pilfering from her supplies. You're better than this kind of behavior, Anthony. You have so much potential. In fact, there is a decent chance that I might have found a possible postdoctoral collaboration for you today. I ran into a former classmate…anyway. I can't recommend you to another lab if you continue to have such poor lab etiquette. It would reflect badly on me too." Addison admonished him.

Anthony looked at his feet. "I'm sorry, Dr. Fish. I know, I know. I'll try to do better."

"You know what Yoda says…" Addison thought as Anthony turned and walked out of her office.

Chapter 3

Emmitt drove his rental car towards the airport, easily navigating the traffic. *"Quite a change of pace from Los Angeles."* He thought. The half hour drive gave him a chance to think about his meeting with Addison—*Dr. Fischer*. The meeting could not have gone better. No way she suspected that it was anything more than a chance encounter with a former classmate. Contrary to his comments to her, he knew a great deal about her lab and their studies of the sodium channel. When *Apothecom* had told him that they needed more than just structural studies to justify a human clinical trial of the new drug they were developing alongside his studies, he had scoured the journals for a contact in the field that he could possibly manipulate. *Apothecom* was the first pharmaceutical company to respond to his proposal. It wasn't a large company, which was one reason Emmitt had selected it. His college roommate worked in the research and development department, which gave Emmitt a way to get his foot in the door. *That puny wimp thought I hung the moon. I could get him to do literally anything for me,* Emmitt thought. The new treatment would break open the floodgates in funding for his lab. It would definitely boost his already stellar chances of winning the Nobel Prize. He could already see the headlines about being the youngest researcher ever to be crowned as a laureate.

Apothecom had funded his early developmental studies of the blood pressure medication, currently referred to as XRN-12.4C, but Emmitt had already picked out the name: *Regulair*. He grinned at his cleverness. They were so close to this becoming a reality. *Apothecom* requested voltage experiments showing how his work actually regulated a channel in the heart. It wasn't enough that the animal trials had been free of significant side effects but showed great efficacy. They felt it was unethical to proceed without further knowledge of the mechanical effects in a cellular system. At first, Emmitt had panicked. His life's work hung in the balance! Did they realize what it would take to find a reliable collaborator and one that he could influence in the way he had been controlling his own lab from day one? Did they have any idea?!

Emmitt looked at his hands and realized he was gripping the steering wheel so tightly that his knuckles were white. He took a deep breath and forced himself to relax. He finally had a colleague that he could work to his advantage. It had taken some time, not to mention a nearly disastrous learning curve. He grimaced remembering how one of his first postdoctoral fellows had almost blown the whistle on his whole operation. While he and Dr. Fischer were not exactly friends from high school, he knew she at least respected his intelligence and pedigree. She would not dig too deeply into his background or question his stipulations of using all of his reagents for a collaboration. In fact, she would welcome it! Less cost for her, but more recognition. He could send in his own postdoc to run the project, claim that the person needed to develop their own system within the Fischer lab. They needed familiar tools and reagents. He found himself nodding along to his ideas and quickly glanced out the window to see if anyone was watching him. Thankfully, the traffic had thinned even more and no one was around as he took the exit for the airport and rental car return. Cruising into the lot, Emmitt felt his spirits lift. He was finally going to get *Regulair* into a trial. The timing would be perfect for the Nobel committee. The trial would be announced but not yet started, so the results wouldn't matter. His name would shoot to the top of the list.

Chapter 4

Addison shut down her computer and began gathering up her things. It was Friday, and she was really looking forward to the weekend. Her husband, Ryan, had the weekend off too. He owned his own business, a medical equipment distribution company. Sometimes, this meant that he had to navigate hang-ups between the warehouse and shipment orders. Thankfully, his warehouse manager was in charge at least one weekend every month, allowing Ryan to have some weekend family time. They had made plans to go camping with their three children in the nearby state park. The park had several hiking trails as well as some fun mountain biking trails. Their youngest son, Martin, was not the most adventurous child. He preferred computers or video games to the great outdoors, but he did enjoy mountain biking with his mom. Over the last year, they had made a tradition of biking a 10-mile trail together every Saturday morning. It was the only time that he really opened up to her and let her into his awkward, nerdy world. Martin was in the 6th grade, wore glasses that only slightly concealed the myriad of freckles all over his face, and had probably hacked into every database in the county already. Thankfully, she and Ryan had convinced him that breaking into other people's servers was not a good idea, nor was it legal. Keeping tabs on his online doings was a challenge, but he had earned their trust by helping them set up parental controls and allowing them to search his history. He even developed a new app to help parents monitor their children's activity. They shared the app with their friends and neighbors when they realized it worked better than any of the others on the market. She smiled, proud of his honesty and intelligence.

Addison locked up her office and walked towards the catwalk that connected her building to the parking garage. They had all agreed to be home by 5:30 that night so that they could get set up at the campsite before it was too dark. Martin would already be there as he rode the bus home after school. She knew Ryan would make it home on time too. The biggest risks were their two high school aged children: Joe and Olivia. Unlocking her car and sliding into the driver's seat, Addison felt herself relax as she thought about the upcoming weekend, hoping her children were equally excited about the trip.

Ryan and Addison's oldest child, Joe, was a senior in high school this year. He was still trying to decide which college or university he wanted to attend next year. Addison knew that he was hoping to be offered a football or basketball scholarship, even though he would easily earn academic scholarships at any school. He had his heart set on getting a mechanical engineering degree and had a short list of schools that he was considering. Joe was the spitting image of Ryan, having inherited his dark hair and dark eyes. Thankfully, the high school football team actually had a bye this weekend. She was glad they were going to get to spend time together as a family. The time for these opportunities was decreasing quickly.

She turned into their neighborhood at 5:20 as her thoughts turned to Olivia. Their auburn-headed middle child was a freshman this year. She ran cross country during the fall and planned to join the track team too. Olivia had fallen in love with playing the piano at a young age and was accompanying the school choir this year. Ryan liked to say that Liv was colorful in every way imaginable. Between her curly red hair and big green eyes, she was hard to miss. Her daughter was much more free-spirited than their other two children. It wasn't that she struggled academically by any means. She was on the honor roll every semester and frequently got all A's. Staying on task or schedule was a different story. Olivia did not like time constraints. She could get caught up in a book or a song or just a walk through a park without any attention to the time. Hopefully, Joe could catch up with her and everyone could be home on time. Addison pulled into the driveway, mentally crossing her fingers that she would be the last to arrive.

Their house sat on a rise at the back of the neighborhood. It was two stories tall with a sandstone exterior. They had thankfully had the foresight to have it built with three garages, so they didn't have to leave any of their vehicles in the driveway. Ryan was in charge of the landscaping and kept the yard and flower gardens in tip-top shape year-round. He loved to comment to the family about the "nicely manicured lawn" whenever they would pull out of the driveway.

"Anybody home?" She called into the house, setting her keys on the counter.

"We're all here, Mom. Don't worry. We know you're excited about the weekend. Dad's out back, loading up the camper. Liv and I are just packing up the rest of the food." Joe called out from the kitchen.

Martin came running around the corner, Nintendo Switch in hand.

"Mom! I beat the next level in my new game!! I only have THREE levels left before I beat the whole game! Look! I got a new costume for my avatar." He hopped back and forth from foot to foot in excitement.

Addison ruffled his ginger hair and looked at the screen. She would never understand video games, but knew Martin hadn't found one that he didn't like. Smiling, she said, "Great job, Dude! I think you finish off games faster and faster each time we get a new one. Looks like you reached a good stopping point. Why don't you get it saved and plug it in?"

Martin kind of frowned, but knew the rule. *No video games on camping trips.* "Okay, Mom. Dad already got our bikes loaded. Think I can beat you up the hill tomorrow?"

"I don't know, Bud, I've been working out a little more lately…" she paused, flexing her muscles.

Martin laughed and trotted down the hall to put his game away.

Addison took her laptop and bag to their home office and then quickly went to change her clothes. She pulled her hair out of her face into a ponytail, glancing briefly in the mirror on her way out of the room. Soon, they had all piled into the camper and were pulling out of the alley and onto the street. Addison relaxed and felt herself smiling. She was really going to miss having Joe around next year. She hoped that they had lots of opportunities to take little trips like this one before he headed off to school.

"So, who did you run into today at the symposium?" Ryan broke into her thoughts.

"Oh! Right. Emmitt Strydent. You don't know him. He's a high school classmate of mine. He was the keynote speaker today. Small world, huh?"

"Small world indeed. Did he give a good talk?"

"It was really interesting. You know, the symposium was organized for the *medical* doctors at University Hospital, so it wasn't really on my radar until I received the departmental email earlier this week. I saw Emmitt's name and figured it had to be him. Strydent isn't really a common name, especially paired with Emmitt."

"I wonder what the odds are that two students from your tiny high school class got their doctorate in biology." Ryan mused.

"My high school was NOT tiny. Okay, it was small, but it was 4A in the state!" Addison laughed at Ryan's familiar ribbing of her small town.

"Okay, okay. What does Dr. Strydent study? Anything of interest to you? I know you've been looking for a good collaborator."

"Actually, yes, something of real interest to me. His lab studies a small shuttling protein that helps orient the sodium channel in the membrane. He used x-ray crystallography and a scanning electron microscope to show how a relatively common mutation can result in decreased function of the channel. I haven't really read any of his papers as this is so much further upstream from my work as well as completely different methodology, but I downloaded a few to look at when I have a chance."

"That was borderline over my head, Dr. Fischer. You're saying he studies the effect of structure on function. I don't need to know the specifications. I guess Emmitt wasn't a close friend from high school? I never heard you mention him before."

"No, he wasn't a close friend. Really, we were more like rivals.

Academic rivals, that is."

"Oooh, this gets more interesting by the minute. Did you beat him out for the mathletes team or what?" Ryan laughed.

"Very funny. No, I beat him out for every academic scholarship that our school offered as well as taking the captain's position on our Quiz Bowl team." She lifted her chin and puffed out her chest.

"Ugh, Mom. Please. Don't ever talk about being captain of the high school quiz bowl team around any of my friends. I would literally die of embarrassment." Olivia responded from the backseat as Ryan's laughter increased.

"I think everyone knows that your mom is a big science nerd, Liv. BUT, if it makes you feel better, I promise not to parade my champion quiz bowl trophy around the living room when you have guests over." Addison grinned at her horrified daughter.

"You have a trophy?! Are you even kidding me?" Liv's eyes grew wider.

Addison laughed. "Well, yeah, I have a trophy. It's just a small one, though. The high school has the big one on display. As far as I know it's the only time our school ever won the State Quiz Bowl Championship. They are pretty proud of it."

"Anyway, back to Dr. Strydent. Do you think your lab could collaborate with his?" Ryan asked.

"I can't say for sure without looking at his work, but I'm optimistic. From what I heard in his talk, he is hoping to develop blood pressure medications based on his studies. I also read there are rumors circulating that he'll be nominated for the Nobel Prize in medicine this year. He has really done well for himself."

"Wow, Ad! That could be really good for you too, if you collaborated, right? Haven't you said that your lab's associations bolster your grants and how they're perceived by the funding people?"

"Whoa, big fella. Let's not get ahead of ourselves here. You are correct. The more familiar and prominent your associates are in the science world, the better reviews your grants get, and the more likely they are to be funded. The reverse is true too, though, so you have to show some discretion with whom you associate."

"Okay, enough science talk already! We're almost to the park. What are we going to do first? I'm starving." Martin shouted from way in the back of the camper.

"Well, I guess you better help unload the camper, Chief. Once we get checked in with the ranger station and pulled into our spot, we can start talking about food." Ryan told him.

"What did *we* bring for food? Are we grilling? Can I light the grill? We brought matches this time, right?" Martin asked.

"Ha ha ha! Yes, we're going to use the grill at the campsite. And, *yes*, I remembered the matches. I forgot them ONE time and you guys won't let me live it down. Was it really so bad?" Ryan feigned being hurt.

"I mean, we had to just eat the buns and cheese and raw vegetables. Thankfully the group that showed up the following day had a lighter or I would have been without protein for 48 hours!" Joe complained.

"Oh the horror." Ryan rolled his eyes. He slowed down as they approached the ranger station. They had an annual pass in the windshield, so it was really a formality.

"Let's see. I have you down for two nights, correct, Mr. Fischer?" The ranger asked, looking at his clipboard.

"Yes, sir. That's correct. Thank you." Ryan took the receipt and taped it into the windshield next to their pass. He rolled up the window and cruised around to the camper spots.

"Martin, you grab the cooler and then you can help get the grill lit. Liv? You and Joe are responsible for getting all the beds made." Ryan instructed.

"Does anyone else ever feel like Dad still thinks he's on the boat with all his Navy buds barking orders at the crew?" Liv asked, unbuckling her seatbelt.

"It's a SHIP, not a boat," Joe said in a mocking tone, mimicking the words they had heard their father use over the years.

They all laughed and set about their various tasks. Martin tried to sneak a marshmallow when he thought no one was looking, but Addison stopped him at the last second. She was slicing a tomato for the hamburgers in the mini kitchen of the camper when he climbed back inside to get the bag of s'mores supplies.

"Hey, little raccoon! Those are for later. Hand over the goods." Addison stuck her hand out.

"Ah, Mom! I was this close. Rats. Dad is almost finished grilling the burgers." Martin turned over the bag and started to step outside, then turned back around quickly. "Oops. I forgot that I told Dad that I'd grab the plates."

"I'm finished with this tomato. I'll grab them and join you. Liv, Joe—soup's on!" She called to the back of the camper. The two teenagers emerged and they all joined Ryan outside. He had set up their five collapsible chairs near the fire pit, which was just starting to really burn.

"I am not sitting downwind of that fire. I don't need to smell like a chimney all weekend. It takes forever to get that smell out of your hair, you know?" Liv demanded of the group.

"Ahh, just put a hat on. It's fine." Joe teased, adjusting his own Falcons hat. Liv rolled her eyes and pulled a chair around to the opposite side of the fire pit.

The hamburgers disappeared in record time and soon everyone was roasting a marshmallow, anticipating the familiar dessert that no camping trip was complete without. Much to his chagrin, Martin caught several on fire before toasting one to perfection. Luckily, Joe was willing to sacrifice and consume the scorched ones. They played some horseshoes with the help of a couple camping lanterns hung strategically from the nearby trees and then filed back into the camper to get some sleep. All in all, it had been a fantastic first night.

Chapter 5

The next morning, the sun woke everyone up a little before seven o'clock. Martin was already itching to go for a bike ride while Joe and Ryan were trying to talk Liv into fishing or kayaking with them. She was lacing up her shoes to go for a run. Ultimately, Joe joined Liv for a run leaving Ryan behind to make breakfast for everyone.

"Eating before biking or biking before eating, my dear?" Ryan asked Addison who was putting her own shoes on.

"It seems like the consensus is eating after, so that works for me. Are you ready yet, Martin? I can't wait forever." She said with a gleam in her eyes.

"Are you kidding me right now? Waiting for me?!" Martin said incredulously. "I've been waiting for what seems like hours!"

"Well, I guess we'd better get going then. We should be back in about 45 minutes, Ry. I'm guessing our runners will return around then too."

Ryan saluted. "Sir, yes, sir. I will have the breakfast served and ready!"

Martin laughed as he helped Addison get their bikes off of the back of the camper. "Dad just can't leave the Navy behind."

"It was his whole life for a long time. Even if he isn't on active duty anymore, part of him will always be a Navy-man. All right, are you ready to ride?"

Martin hopped on his bike and took off toward the road which had a well-marked bike lane, Addison following behind him. It was a beautiful day. The sun was shining, the air was fresh and clear, and the temperature was perfect. She couldn't imagine a better way to spend a Saturday morning.

They wound around the park, heading up the hillside towards the cliff that overlooked the river and man-made lake. It was fairly rare to see any vehicles along the road as most people preferred to be in the water rather than driving above it. Addison could already see several people floating down the river in innertubes.

Martin yammered on about the video game from the day before

as they approached the big hill that he liked to race up. Addison steered the conversation around to school and what he'd been learning about lately. It was his first year in middle school, which can sometimes be a big adjustment both socially and academically. His two best friends attended the same school, which helped with the transition. Martin was awkward and nerdy, but he also had a great sense of humor if you got to know him. His two friends, Joel and Derek, were both athletes. The three boys had been friends since preschool and were nearly inseparable. Addison was thankful that the two bigger boys looked out for her skinny son.

"Mrs. Richardson said that there's a chance I could skip advanced seventh grade math and take Algebra next year, Mom! Algebra. In seventh grade. I think she's going to call you or email you or whatever."

"You know, I think some of Joe's classmates did that. It can be a challenge, but if anyone can do it, I know you can. But first, you're going to have to beat me up this hill!" Addison clicked her bike into another gear and started pumping her legs to pull even with Martin. He could usually stay even with her until they got to the last ten or fifteen feet. Then his little legs lost steam and he would fall back.

"Today is the day, Mom. Get ready to LOSE!" Martin pedaled his bike as fast as he could, pulling ahead of Addison by a full bike length. Always the competitor, Addison pedaled harder, leaning into the hill, trying to make up the lost ground. She could almost see the little hut at the top of the hill that was part of a historic site within the state park. She was gaining on Martin and had closed the gap. Surely, he was still too young to beat her up this hill! They were both pedaling furiously as they crested the hill, but much to Addison's surprise, Martin's tire was just a bit ahead of hers at the peak. They both maneuvered their bikes to the shoulder to catch their breath.

Martin pumped his fists in the air. "Yes! I did it! I won this time! Guess you better spend a few more hours at the gym if you wanna keep up with this *specimen*."

Addison laughed. "You got me this time, Bud. I didn't hold back at all. You won, fair and square. Man! I can't believe you beat me. Next time, we're gonna have to eat some food first. I need some fuel if I'm going to stay ahead of you. Let's drink some water and then head back to the camp site."

From the top of the hill, they could see almost all of the state park. It was such a clear day; they could easily see the lake and the river down below. The river bank was dotted in an array of colors from the people camping in tents. That kind of camping was a little too *rustic* for Addison's taste. The camper had air conditioning or heat, if it was needed, and no bugs. Or snakes.

"Ready to bike down to breakfast? What do you think Dad is making for us this time?" Addison asked Martin.

"I'm ready. I bet he's sticking with scrambled eggs and sausage. In fact, if he makes something else, I'm going to be blown away. I don't think he KNOWS how to make anything else." Martin turned his bike around and climbed back on.

"Ha ha ha. You're probably right. He is a bit of a one trick pony when it comes to cooking." She let Martin lead the way down the road, keeping an eye out for any vehicles that might have driven up this far. This was a dead-end road once you reached the parking lot by the little hut.

Riding back down to the camp site took them much less time than riding up. Martin loved to coast down the hill. He said that it almost felt like he was flying. It seemed like they got back extra fast today. Martin was excited to share the news of his victory with the rest of the family. They wheeled around the curves to their camp site, Martin shouting at Ryan as he pulled up next to the camper.

"Dad! Dad! I did it! I beat Mom up the hill today. She didn't stand a chance," he boasted.

"Hey now. It was a close race. You just barely edged me out." Addison beamed at her son. It was rare that he felt proud of an athletic endeavor, so she let him play it up some.

"I did what you said, Dad. I just kept telling myself that it

25

wouldn't last forever and pushed and pushed and suddenly, I was at the top. AND I was there first!" He jumped up and pumped his fist into the air again.

"Great job, Buddy! That's fantastic. I knew you could do it." Ryan gave Martin a high five. Addison wheeled her bike around to reattach it to the bike rack on the back of the camper. "Liv just went over to the restroom facilities to shower. Joe opted to go for a swim instead. They should both be back any minute. Who's ready for some breakfast?"

Martin ducked inside the camper in response, making his parents laugh. Soon they were all inside enjoying Ryan's signature sausage and eggs breakfast creation. Joe tried to claim the last sausage saying that Olivia made him run a mile further than he'd bargained for, so he deserved it more than the resident biking champion. Addison settled it by cutting the sausage link in half.

"It's only nine o'clock. What should we do with the rest of the morning? We could rent a couple paddle boats or use the kayaks. Go for a walk together? Play another game of horseshoes? I read in the newsletter that the park has some of those new "Aqua Zorbs" for rent. I thought we could try that out this afternoon. Maybe we should walk over and get our names on the list first." Ryan offered ideas up to family.

"What in the world is an Aqua Zorb?" Joe asked.

"You don't know? Ha ha! Well, my dear, sheltered, older brother, let me tell you. An Aqua Zorb is a water walking ball. It's an inflated ball that you can stand inside, well, try to stand inside, and walk on the water. You don't get wet because the ball keeps the water out. But it isn't easy to stay upright either. They look really fun! The balls are tethered to cables, so it's not like you can drift away to a waterfall or some other hazard, but it gives you enough play to have some fun." Liv informed Joe.

"Sounds like we have a winner. Maybe we should all put on our swimming gear and do some tubing this morning after we sign up to use the water balls." Addison suggested.

"Aqua Zorb, Mom. Aqua Zorb." Liv corrected.

After changing into their swimwear and locking up the camper, they followed the foot path over to the water house. The kids led the way, pretending to not care who was first in line while Ryan and Addison chatted from behind. They laughed as they watched their kids playfully carrying on ahead of them.

"This was a great idea, Ad. I'm really glad we're out here together," Ryan said.

"Thanks. Me too. We probably only have a few of these weekends left, if we're being honest with ourselves. Our kids get busier and busier. Joe is less than a year away from college and Liv will be out of high school before we know it too."

"Not to change the subject abruptly, but how realistic is this collaboration opportunity? 50-50? More?"

"I think it's probably better than 50-50. He gave me his card, so I'll get in touch with him next week. I don't think our research overlaps too much that we would be battling over authorship or anything on papers, but it overlaps enough that we could do some interesting studies together. Did I tell you that my new department chair was actually Strydent's graduate school advisor?"

"What? How funny. I guess you could talk it over with him too. See if he has any reservations about you teaming up with the guy."

"Technically, I would have to get his approval because we would be sharing some things that fall under the intellectual property umbrella within the university. I haven't ever heard of someone being turned down though. The nice thing about science is that most people are really open to sharing and working together."

They reached the water house and requested time slots for the Aqua Zorbs in the afternoon. The kids were already grabbing innertubes and discussing who could float down the river the fastest and why. Addison and Ryan each checked out tubes for themselves and caught up with their crew. The state park had a little shuttle "bus" that you could ride from the bend in the river where everyone stopped back to the water house. They called it a shuttle, but in reality, it was just a trailer bed that bumped along the dirt road. On really warm days, your tube would be totally dry by the time you got back. The river current slowed down as you neared the bend, allowing you a chance to get out of your tube and the water. Just in case though, they had two lifeguards helping people stop and exit safely.

It was early enough that the river wasn't too crowded yet. Tubing was such a popular activity, the state park actually roped off a portion of the river for tubing only during the warm months. It prevented someone who just wanted to swim in the river from getting injured by a wayward tuber. The river didn't freeze over in the winter, but the water temperature dropped enough that no one did any swimming or tubing from December to mid-February.

After several trips down the river and back, the Fischer family returned the rented innertubes and walked back to the camper to make lunch. Not everyone was a fan of the PBJ and chips lunch option, but it saved space in the cooler. Plus, it was fast and easy.

"PBJ again? Did you at least buy the baked chips? All of the other kinds are so greasy and nasty, or they turn your fingers orange. Gross." Liv complained.

"Oh, fair sandwich princess. Forgive your meager parents for their thrifty ways and nourish thyself with the food they offer." Joe teased her. She punched him in the arm and rolled her eyes.

"Very funny. Not everyone likes Cheetos, Joe. Most people outgrow liking Cheetos by high school, you know."

"Most people also don't complain when someone else brings lunch," he raised his eyebrows and shrugged.

"Enough, you two. Let me enjoy my sandwich and chips in peace." Ryan barked.

They finished lunch and after cleaning up the mini kitchen, everyone relaxed on their beds with a book or magazine until it was time to go try out the water walkers. Addison reminded everyone to drink some water while they were relaxing as they did not want to get dehydrated. She refilled everyone's water bottle before settling in with her latest crime thriller. Ryan always teased her for being such a crime drama junkie, but she didn't care. She found them entertaining. Luckily, no one needed to set a timer to remind them to head back to the water house. Ryan's time with the Navy had trained him to have a good internal clock. Sure enough, right on time, he sat up and announced it was time to get moving again.

They raced down the foot path back to the water house, excited to try out the new inflatable balls. The park let you sign up for thirty-minute time slots and actually had five Aqua Zorbs so they could all play at the same time. It was a comical half hour as they each tried to navigate their floating orb around the water. The park had sectioned off a portion of the lake to set up their Aqua Zorb station and keep kayaks or other watercraft from damaging the inflated balls. Not surprisingly, Ryan was the most adept at steering his Aqua Zorb and staying upright at the same time. Martin was continually crashing into the bottom of his, even without getting bumped by another family member. Olivia was the only one who succeeded in knocking Ryan down. She rolled in from the side as he was taking aim at Joe.

"I'm not sure if my legs hurt more from trying to stay on my feet or if my sides hurt more from laughing at all of you," Addison said as they walked back to the camper. "That was really fun. I can't remember when I've laughed that much."

"I can't remember when I've fallen so much. I think ice skating is easier and I've never even tried that!" Martin exclaimed as they all laughed. His knees were a little red from repeatedly falling.

Chapter 6

Emmitt paced the office in his downtown studio apartment. He needed to get the wording in his email to Addison—*Dr. Fischer* just right. He really needed this collaboration to work out if *Apothecom* was going to continue with the drug trials and funding his work. And he needed the phase 3 drug trial to get started if the Nobel people were going to keep moving him up their short list for the award. He grimaced. He was so close to reaching his goal. He just needed to keep things moving in the right direction.

As he passed by his desk, he picked up the little stress ball his secretary had given him for Christmas last year. He had thanked her, but thought it was a gift for wimps at the time. It was a fist-sized version of the globe: blue for the oceans and green for the continents. He found it was actually relaxing and helpful to squeeze it while he paced the room. He mulled over the idea of bringing up Laina Hibber as a potential postdoc to send to the Fischer lab in this initial email. He wanted to sound committed, but casual. Emmitt paced back and forth, squeezing the blue and green ball. Maybe it was too soon to mention his idea for Laina to join her lab. He could bring her up over the phone call, assuming she agreed to the phone call.

"Good grief!" He thought. *"Why does starting a collaboration feel like asking a girl out on a date?!"* He hadn't gone on a real date in years.

His first marriage had ended in divorce less than two years after it began. Patrice was constantly nagging him to be home more often, to spend less time at the lab, to spend less time talking about the lab when he was home. She was beautiful, but annoying. Luckily as a postdoc at the time, he didn't owe her any alimony, nor did her retail job paycheck result in her owing him any money. Emmitt's mom had kept tabs on Patrice for a little while, maybe hoping that they'd reunite? She quit when she learned that Patrice had married a banker and moved to northern California. *"Good riddance."* Emmitt thought.

He glanced at the laptop on his desk, the blinking cursor silently nagging him to stay on task. He squeezed the ball and resisted the urge to hurl it across the room. He should have just had his secretary send this, but she always seemed annoyed when he asked her to work on the weekends. He took a deep breath. He could do this. Maybe he should just take the band-aid approach. Follow Nike's advice. *"Just Do It, Emmitt!"* He thought. He sat down at the desk chair and began typing, hoping that his words would be convincing without coming across as overbearing.

Chapter 7

On Sunday morning, the Fischer family quickly cleaned up around their campsite after eating breakfast. Each of the kids had homework that was due the next day and they wanted to attend youth group that afternoon. They each had a quick bowl of cereal and a banana before packing everything up to leave the campgrounds.

"So, what do you think? Are you going to email that Strydent guy? Get a collaboration rolling?" Ryan asked Addison as they headed for the park's exit.

"You know, I think I am. We can discuss what kind of fit we have and then get it approved by our respective schools, you know for intellectual property stuff. Assuming Anthony can get his act together, the Strydent lab could be a prospective postdoc for him after he graduates."

"Oh Anthony! That's a tall order. Talk about an absentminded professor. That kid needs a personal assistant!" Ryan laughed.

"He had better hope that he can graduate soon then, or he won't be able to get a job that will cover the cost of said assistant. He *borrowed* cells from Becky last week, without asking, of course." She rolled her eyes. "Part of me is afraid he is going to leave a Bunsen burner on one day and burn the whole lab down!"

"Luckily, you've got Eleanor to keep an eye out most of the time."

Addison had hired Eleanor, who was in her fifties, when she first started at the university. Eleanor had recently gone back to school to get a masters degree in biology. She had previously worked as a veterinarian, but found research science fascinating and decided to make a switch. She was very knowledgeable and organized, and everyone thought of her as the mother hen of the lab.

"That isn't really in her job description, but yes, thank goodness for Eleanor. Did I tell you that her husband Gary had his DNA screened for common mutations last month?"

"He is really a neat guy—very supportive of Eleanor and her

work in the world of science. Did she share his results with you? Anything interesting?"

"She did and yes. Gary has had unexplained high blood pressure since college, I guess. You know, he exercises regularly and has a healthy diet, but it's always on the high side. He has had to take medication for it for years. Nothing he does brings it down. His doctors have said that it's probably genetic and out of his control. Turns out, they were right; it IS genetic. He has a mutation in a cardiac membrane protein. She couldn't remember which one off hand. I think she is bringing the printout in this week to see if we know anyone who researches his mutation. Though, as pro-active as Gary is, he probably already looked it up himself." She smiled.

Ryan glanced up in the rearview mirror. The three kids had fallen asleep. "Would you look at that?"

"What?" Addison whipped her head around, initially alarmed before she saw his meaning.

"I can't remember the last time they all fell asleep in a car ride. Guess we really wore them out yesterday! Hope they are resting up so they can carry all this stuff in when we get home." He winked.

A few minutes later, they were pulling off the interstate, taking the exit for their little suburb of Atlanta: Peachtree. They drove through the historic downtown towards their neighborhood on the west side of town. Ryan backed the camper into the alley to make it easier to take it back to their storage unit later.

"Okay, rise and shine, campers! It's time to clear out the ship!" Ryan barked at the kids, startling each of them awake. They emptied the camper in record time and soon everyone was back to their Sunday routine. Addison went into their home office to check her email and do some more reading about research on the Strydent lab. When she pulled open her university account, she saw that Emmitt had already contacted her.

Dr. Fischer-

I hope you don't mind, but I looked you up after our lunch on

Friday. I think we could really have a great collaboration between our labs. If you're interested, let me know a good time to call and discuss. I can make my schedule flexible on Monday.

Regards,

Emmitt

The email ended with his signature block, which included his office number and lab website within his university. She fished his business card out of her purse. He had written his cell on it too. Before responding, she opened up the lab website and scrolled through the list of his most recent papers. She selected one from the *Proceedings of the National Academy of Science (PNAS)* and skimmed through it. His lab mostly studied a small membrane protein called STABL, as she had read about in the café two days before. They had shown how the structure of STABL changes as a result of a relatively common mutation.

She clicked on another paper. In this one, they had created an animal line that carried the mutation in the STABL gene, demonstrating that the mice also had high blood pressure similar to humans with the same mutation. Addison wondered if the mutation that Gary's DNA screen had turned up would happen to be this same mutation. All of the background information she was reading sounded very familiar to what he had experienced as an adult, according to Eleanor anyway. Fortunately for the mice AND the humans, the high blood pressure was reversed in the animal model with the gene therapy that the Strydent lab had developed. The paper concluded by saying that it would be interesting to study if a gene therapy approach could remedy the high blood pressure issue, allowing people with the mutation to be weaned off of their long-term blood pressure medications.

Addison had only read about gene therapies; she had never studied them before. In theory, the correct copy of a gene could be incorporated into a patient's DNA. Several different vectors had been studied and subsequently used to carry the DNA into the cells of interest, where the *correct* copy of the gene would be replicated instead of the mutated one. It was a newer type of treatment but a very promising one.

Thinking of her own research, Addison wondered what connections she could have with the Strydent lab. They definitely used different techniques and methodology, so her work could support conclusions the Strydent lab had already made, but just in a different system. She wondered if STABL interacted at all with Anthony's little protein of interest, alpha9. Maybe STABL, alpha9, and the cardiac sodium channel had a mutual interaction or signaling pathway. Feeling herself getting excited about potential experiments and possibilities, she decided to respond to Emmitt's email.

Dr. Strydent—Emmitt,

We welcome the opportunity to collaborate. Give me a call on Monday at 11 and we can discuss how to proceed.

Best,

Addison Fischer, PhD

Her email included her office phone number for him to call. She quickly added it to her calendar with a reminder alarm so she wouldn't get caught up in something and forget. She wanted to continue reading through his research, but decided that she had done enough work for now and shut down her laptop.

It had been a great weekend, and the rest of the morning and afternoon flew by between laundry, homework, and getting the kids out the door for youth group. Thankfully, Joe could drive the three of them to youth group now, so Ryan didn't have to miss any of the Falcon's game. Addison had planned to do some more prep for her call with Emmitt and went back to the home office after they left.

"Come watch the game with me! I promise not to shout." Ryan called out to her.

"Don't make promises that you can't keep, Ry."

"Okay, I promise not to shout *too* much." He grinned as she walked down the hall with her laptop and notebook in hand. "That doesn't look like relaxing. *That* looks like work."

"I just want to make a few notes for my call with Emmitt

tomorrow. This could be a really good connection for my lab, so I'd like to start off on the right foot." She explained, settling into the couch with her feet tucked under her. She put the laptop on a TV tray and opened it up.

Now that their kids were older, they had finally replaced their rather worn-out furniture. They had a black leather couch and loveseat as well as two turquoise soft-leather easy chairs. The home had been built with hardwood floors, so they had a turquoise and coral accent rug to tie the pieces together. Their most recent addition to the family room had been a glass-topped coffee table with a black frame. Addison's best friend and neighbor, Melinda, had made all the curtains throughout the house. Addison wasn't really knowledgeable with interior decorating, so she'd just given Melinda a list of colors that she liked and let her run with it. Ryan had taken up woodworking since leaving the Navy and had made all of the rods and stained them with Melinda's guidance on the best shades.

Addison downloaded several more of the Strydent lab papers to read through. She made notes about areas that could conceivably work as collaborations. Knowing Emmitt, she figured his lab would be requesting first authorship on the papers that resulted from their work. She decided that it wasn't a battle she needed to fight at this point. They could form a connection and see where it led.

By halftime, she had amassed several pages of notes. Ryan had remained mostly calm as the Falcons led by 6. They heard the kids pull up in the driveway and realized that it was almost time to get dinner started. Martin led the group into the house, opened the door, immediately asking about food.

"We're making homemade pizzas, remember? You wanted to help?" Addison reminded him.

"Oh yeah! Let me get my hands washed and we can get started! Who wants anchovies?!" He laughed at the grossed-out looks on his siblings' faces.

Martin and Addison got the pizzas assembled and baking in the ovens while the older kids watched the start of the second half with Ryan. They left the game on and continued watching from the table while they ate their pizza together. Martin wasn't at all interested in the game as usual. He wanted to talk to Addison about some of the new computer programming he had been learning. Ryan was only half-listening to what he was saying but was drawn in when he heard the word *code*.

"Woah, did you just say *code*? I hope you're not getting ready to tell us about how you can hack into someone's website again." He turned to Addison with his eyebrows raised.

"No, Dad. I promise. I learned that lesson over the summer. I will not try to hack into anything ever again. I will only use my knowledge for good. My days on the dark side are over. Scout's honor." Martin raised four fingers to his head.

"Yeah, clearly, you're not a scout with that salute, but I believe you. I'm glad to hear that last summer's experience with the school district will be the end of your evil ways."

Martin had been obsessed with computers and coding languages since he could write his name. He had taken multiple enrichment type courses for fun that taught coding to kids and had taught himself twice as much. No one had realized how skilled he'd become with computers and programming until the school's internet servers were taken "hostage" last summer. The resulting investigation had led the cyber team from the state police to the Fischer house. While Martin had successfully hacked into the school district's servers, he hadn't hidden his tracks well at all. Luckily, he hadn't demanded ransom money or anything devious. He had just spammed their email accounts with terrible knock-knock jokes. Loss of electronic devices, internet usage, and community service scared him straight. The school ended up not pressing charges for his invasion; Addison and Ryan still made Martin ride his bike up to the various campuses to paint classrooms, clean out storage rooms, and scrape gum off of desks.

"Also, I think the district is fairly happy that I was able to help them close any backdoor hacks into their system. Without me, they never would have known how vulnerable they were. AND don't forget that I wrote that program for you to monitor all of our phones and internet usage. You're the most informed parents on the planet, thanks to me!" Martin grinned.

"Yeah, yeah, yeah. Let's not get ahead of ourselves, shall we?" Addison asked.

"I was reading about a new key that has been developed to track computer key strokes on computers or laptops—even tablets! It allows people to know every email you send, every document that you type, everything!" Martin's eyes were big.

"Those aren't new. I read about them in my books all the time." Liv rolled her eyes.

"Right, because everything in a crime novel is real and happens all the time." Martin returned the eye roll. "These keys are electronic or digital. As in, they don't have some sort of bug that they upload through physical access to your computer. It can be done remotely with the right sort of email attachment. All the anti-virus software companies are scrambling to make updates to block them."

"Guess I'll have to hold off on opening those emails from the Nigerian prince for a few more days. I've lived without his millions for this long." Ryan joked, turning his attention back to the game. It looked like the Falcons were going to hold it together and pull out a win after all.

"Well, they certainly tried to snatch defeat from the jaws of victory today, but I'll take the W." Ryan said.

"I'm telling you, Dad. This is the year. Superbowl fifty-eight, here we come!" Joe pumped a fist in the air.

"What was it that your mom said earlier, about not getting ahead of ourselves? It's September. We shall see."

Chapter 8

Addison pulled her car into the faculty level and steered over to her assigned spot in the garage. It was nice to be able to park so close to the building. She was especially thankful for this perk during the scorching heat of the summers. She was just locking her car when she heard her cell phone ringing. She fished it out of her bag, trying to balance her keys and her coffee as she looked to see who it was. *The lab?*

"Dr. Fischer speaking," she answered.

"Oh good. I caught you. It's Eleanor. Umm, are you close?" Eleanor sounded out of breath.

"What's wrong, Eleanor? I'm just walking out of the parking garage," Addison commented, picking up her pace with concern.

"Oh, well. It's…It's Anthony again, I think."

Addison sighed. "What now?" She cringed imagining what horror awaited her. Surely, she would have heard the fire alarms by now if that were the issue.

"Well, I think he was working over the weekend. He left his ice bucket out, which on its own isn't a big deal, but this time, there are several samples in it. They're just floating in room temperature water. They're ruined, right?"

She grimaced and groaned. *How could Anthony be so careless? AGAIN?!*

"Yes, they are ruined. Do me a favor? Just leave them out for now. I want to see what was lost and take inventory. I guess I'll be meeting with him again today."

She sighed. It wasn't a total loss, and the samples could be replaced. It was just continually frustrating to lose things to laziness and blatant carelessness. She rolled her eyes as she stepped onto the elevator in the main building. The doors were closing as a hand reached out to stop them. She cringed, remembering the stories about people getting hurt from old medical school elevator doors. Thankfully, the doors retracted for the daring soul. She looked forward, wondering who was in such a rush. It was Anthony. Of course, it was.

"Dr. Fischer. Uh, hi."

"Anthony. Unfortunate timing it seems. I just spoke with Eleanor. Rushing back for some reason?"

His shoulders slumped and part of her regretted the underlying sarcasm with which she'd laced her words.

"I'm sorry, Dr. Fischer. I-I-I..." He stammered.

"Let's go see what we can see, Anthony." She held the door for him and followed him down the hall.

The red ice bucket was sitting on Anthony's bench with five little tubes floating in it. Eleanor was across the room, sitting at her desk. She kept in fairly good shape by biking with her husband, Gary, and was about medium height for a woman. Eleanor had wavy brown hair with a little gray mixed in here and there. She kept her hair fairly short most of the time as it was rather thick and could get really hot in the Atlanta humidity.

Addison walked up to the bench and set her bag down. She removed a notebook and turned to an empty page.

"Let's see what we lost here, shall we? Can you read the labels to me?"

Anthony slowly pulled the little microcentrifuge tubes from the water and dried them off on his pants. He read each label out while Addison recorded them in her notebook. Thankfully, two of them were inexpensive pharmaceuticals that they regularly used in the lab and one was actually an empty tube that he just hadn't tossed when he finished with it. The others were DNA constructs, which would take a few days to replace. Unless Anthony could talk someone into sharing some of their reagents with him, he would not be doing any more experiments until the end of the week.

"Okay, so you lost one sample of the sodium channel and one of alpha9. I'm guessing that since you have an empty from another alpha9 sample that this was your last one, correct?" Addison asked.

"I'll have to double check my box, but yeah, you're probably right. No one else uses that right? We just have the master sample?"

"Yes, and I will get that for you because we need to be really careful not to lose all of it, or you'll really be behind. Anthony, didn't we just talk about not being so messy and irresponsible with supplies?"

"I'm sorry, Dr. Fischer. I really am. I was so excited about setting up my experiment and being ready to go for this morning that I just got distracted, I guess." He apologized again.

"I think we need to make a reminder poster. I know it seems silly and, well, juvenile, but we need something that says, "ANTHONY! STOP! DID YOU PUT ALL YOUR THINGS AWAY?!" She spread her hands apart and spoke the words slowly and deliberately.

Anthony grinned. "I guess you're right, as usual. I'll start on that after I set up the DNA constructs."

"Let me grab those for you really quick. Eleanor has some sharpies that you can use and the main office will have large paper." Addison said as she walked out of the lab.

She sighed as she reached her office. She wasn't sure if recommending Anthony to the Strydent lab as a future postdoc would reflect well on her or not. The kid was a hot mess sometimes, but he did good work. Speaking of, she was so intent on figuring out what needed replacing, she didn't ask if he had set up the experiment when he came in over the weekend. She grabbed the office phone to check back in with him. Eleanor answered.

"Hey Eleanor, is Anthony nearby?"

"He sure is. Anthony—it's Dr. Fischer!" She called out. Addison twiddled the old school phone cord in her fingers while she waited.

"Yes, Dr. Fish?"

"I realized when I got back to the office that I hadn't asked about your experiment. Were you able to get one set up for today?"

"Oh! Yes, I did! As soon as I get these cultures going—AND the poster set up—I'm going to start getting my cells ready for the experiment. Did you have a question about it or something?"

"Not really; I'm just excited to see how it goes. Keep me posted." She hung up the phone and pulled her laptop out of her bag. She needed to get ready for her phone call with Emmitt.

Chapter 9

Emmitt spent the weekend drawing up talking points and plans for his phone call with Addison. *"Dr. Fischer."* He grumbled to himself.

"Easy. We want her on our side, remember, Emmitt?" He admonished himself. *"Great, now I've resorted to talking to myself. Get it together!"*

He looked through his outlines and lists. He had a meeting planned with Laina to go over his proposal and her role as the potential postdoc. She had been with his lab for over six years now and was someone he trusted. As much as he was willing to trust anyone. Laina didn't quite know everything about his lab and his history, but she was motivated and willing to make things happen. Emmitt had learned early on that not everyone was capable of seeing the big picture like he was and had to frequently replace his lab technicians when they got too curious. He was hiring them for their loyalty as much as their intelligence.

Emmitt thought back to his first experience with a lab tech that had taught him to be more guarded in his approach to lab personnel. The man was young. He had expressed hopes of one day attending graduate school himself but wanted to get some lab experience first. See where his interests were and what kind of work he was going to enjoy the most. Mike was obviously smart. He could follow the logical concepts of Emmitt's projects easily. He got too curious though. He started questioning why Emmitt insisted that all of the experiments use the specific reagents designed by Emmitt within Emmitt's lab. He had suggested experiments that would have revealed that Emmitt's graduate studies had a major flaw. A flaw that only Emmitt was fully aware of still to this day. A flaw that could have brought the whole plan down in flames. Mike had to go. Emmitt had written a letter to the graduate school dean at a nearby school, suggesting that Mike be admitted with a full stipend. Mike was elated by the opportunity and Emmitt had convinced himself that he had Mike's best interests at heart.

The next lab tech didn't last as long as Mike. The woman was way too smart for her own good. She had worked in another lab previously and had it in her head that there were certain policies and standards that *every* lab needed to abide by. *"Pfft,"* thought Emmitt. *"No, we do NOT need to establish a baseline background standard to compare our results to before doing more in-depth experiments. It has already been done. I did it in grad school. Stop pushing me, WOMAN!"* He felt himself getting angry about it again just thinking about it. She was fairly unrelenting in her statements, almost demands. He was right on the edge of firing her when she gave him her two-week notice. He gave her a two-week vacation as a parting gift. Good riddance.

He ran his finger down the list, mentally checking things off as he looked through it. He knew Laina would be on board. He thought about the talking points that would convince Dr. Fischer. He felt like she was genuinely interested and it wouldn't take much to get her to agree to Laina joining the lab, at least temporarily. He glanced at the handwritten list again:

- *Laina needs to broaden her exposure to new techniques.*
- *Laina needs to show that she can succeed in other environments outside of the university in California.*
- *Laina needs experience leading a project without my close supervision.*

All of these were true, more or less. This experience would benefit Laina's career in the long run, but Emmitt found that as just a bonus. Laina was going to provide the stepping stone he needed to get his drug trial back on track and into the phase 3 studies. With HUMANS! He could almost imagine the accolades once he achieved his goals. Laina saw that some sacrifices had to be made in order to reach the heights and dreams that you desired. Emmitt knew she was willing to cut a few corners to get there too. He sent off a quick email to Laina, asking her to be on hand in case Dr. Fischer wanted to include her at the end of their phone meeting this morning.

Chapter 10

Addison looked through her notebook and leafed through the papers she had printed from the Strydent lab. She had printed out the university's standard agreement regarding collaborations with outside institutions and read through it again to familiarize herself. She felt pretty confident that Dr. Watt would approve the request, especially since the proposed collaborator had been one of his students. She felt rather ignorant or naïve that she hadn't realized that her own boss had mentored one of her former classmates, but that's what happens when you lose touch with your hometown after graduation.

Checking her watch, she pulled out her notepad where she'd jotted down questions that she wanted to ask Emmitt. Some things could wait for future phone calls, assuming they did decide to collaborate, but others were more relevant to establishing some boundaries within their prospective interactions. Her graduate school advisor had started a collaboration with one of his former colleagues without setting any ground rules and it had ended badly for everyone. Doing the experiments was one thing, but deciding who was the first author and whose lab got the most credit became a huge fight. Thankfully, it hadn't been her project that was caught in the mix, but she still remembered how hard it was on the postdoc who did have the project. His publication had been delayed significantly and other labs published similar results first, which sort of stole his thunder. She didn't wish that on anyone. Hopefully, she and Emmitt could see eye to eye from the get-go and it would be smooth sailing.

She checked her email one more time while she waited for Emmitt to call. It made her feel silly, having almost first-date-like anxiety as she tried to busy herself in anticipation of the phone ringing. She had already confirmed that *he* was the one calling in, not the other way around, so she just needed to be patient—

"Hello. This is Dr. Fischer speaking." She grabbed the phone on her first ring, still feeling a bit ridiculous.

"Addison—is it okay if I call you Addison?" Emmitt's voice

boomed through the office line.

"Yes, that's just fine, Emmitt. How was your trip home?"

"It was easy, I mean, the traffic out here is other-worldly, but I made it back in one piece. Did you have a nice weekend? Get that student of yours back on track?" He ran his fingers through his hair, trying not to sound over-interested.

"That, well," she paused. "That remains to be seen. So, how do we start this off? I haven't done a lot of collaborations outside of our department, so why don't you get the ball rolling here?"

"As you wish. As you know by now, my lab has established a strong structural correlation between our protein of interest, STABL, and the ion channel getting into the membrane correctly. We have done a few animal studies, but the pharma companies would like some experiments that show a functional effect on the cellular level before they are willing to start a drug trial in humans. That's where you come in."

"Okay, so you're needing some voltage experiments using the wild type and comparing it to the identified mutations? Are you thinking an entire paper here or just a side story within a bigger story?" Addison asked as she put the phone on speaker so she could take notes more easily.

"Oh, I think this can definitely be a paper all on its own. I actually have a postdoc in mind for the work. I think it's probably easier if I *send* her to you, so to speak, rather than trying to recreate your set up in our lab. Is that doable? We can figure out a way to share compensation if that's an issue."

"Oh, does she or he have experience with these types of experiments? I have an experienced postdoc, Juan, who could easily run all of these for us without the trouble of moving someone down here—"

"My postdoc needs some more exposure to other labs and techniques. She has great hands and picks up on things really quickly. I need to help her broaden her horizons."

"Well, sure, but Anthony and Juan are more than capable." She paused. "It just seems like an added expense for you to move her out here for a small project."

"I get what you're saying, but really, I think this is the right choice. She knows the rest of the project from top to bottom, so I think it is logical for her to continue with it."

"Okay, I understand. I know there are some administrative hoops we would need to jump through, but it shouldn't be too much of a challenge. As far as the potential paper goes though, I think we should both be up front with our thoughts and plans for that before we get too far down the road."

"I know a lot of people get hung up on authorship and credit, but honestly I would rather do what is easiest for everyone and make it as little of a headache as possible. Since the experiments are going to be done in your lab, why don't you take that last author spot? Laina—that's my postdoc, she can be first author, since she'll be doing the work." Emmitt offered.

"That seems very reasonable." She checked off a couple items on her list. "Would Laina be bringing all of her own reagents or what kind of arrangement do you foresee there?"

"Yes. This might sound kind of obsessive or controlling, but we always use our own reagents and materials in our collaborations. It just cuts down on any confusion regarding solutions or mutations. We will overnight those to you once we get a timeline established." Emmitt tried to control his breathing, hoping Addison wouldn't make any objections to this request.

"I don't have a problem with that. There are a couple of standard wash solutions and things that we use for our voltage experiments; I can send you the make-up of those after we hang up. Everyone in my lab gets their own space in the freezer and we can definitely make room for Laina's boxes too."

Emmitt cringed a bit. "Well, um, again, this probably makes me sound a little crazy, but past experiences have led me to employ some rather high standards in regards to my reagents. I also have a couple of patents on some of my stuff, so I have to be very careful. Hopefully, it's not too much to ask that Laina use her own freezer that will also have a coded entry for her use only."

"Oh. Um, I mean, I think that will probably be okay. I do have an approval form that we need to run by the department chair before we actually get Laina down here and in the lab. I think we can find a place for an extra freezer if it's not too large. What size are you talking about?" Addison grimaced. This seemed a little bizarre and paranoid.

"Oh, nothing big, smaller than a hotel mini-fridge for sure. I know it makes me sound paranoid and delusional, but our legal team here won't allow me a lot of wiggle room."

"I will make sure to include it on the approval form and let you know if there's any issue. I sent that over in an email. Did you get a chance to look at it yet?"

"I did. It looks like you fill it out and then I need to sign it and fax it back? Or can I e-sign?"

"We have exited the dark ages recently and do allow e-signatures on forms now. So much easier than the back-and-forth faxing! Did you have any other questions or concerns before we start filling it out?"

"For right now, I think my only other question is who will be working with Laina? Who will be teaching her how to patch clamp—is that the right phrase?"

"Ha ha. Yes, patch clamp is correct. I was going to get my senior grad student to do most of the helping or training, but I'll work with her initially to get her set up. Anthony is surprisingly good at teaching others how to patch clamp, so I really think she'll do well with him."

"He isn't your off-track student, by any chance, is he?" Emmitt questioned.

Addison drew in a breath. "Yes. That's Anthony, but like I said, he will do a good job training her even if he doesn't do a good job keeping himself in line."

"Okay, I guess I will trust your judgment there." Emmitt wondered if his voice sounded as uncertain as he felt, but he didn't want to be too pushy at this point. "Let's take a look at that form."

Addison pulled it up on her computer and read off some of the lines to Emmitt. They were able to work through it fairly quickly. Addison saved it and emailed it over to Emmitt to sign and return.

"After I get this back from you, I'll take it over to the main office for approval. I'm not sure what the typical turnaround is for these. I'm sure Dr. Watt's secretary can tell me. Unless you have anything else, we'll just plan on staying in touch until we hear from Dr. Watt."

"Sounds good to me. I'm glad we're trying to make this work. I look forward to hearing from you."

"Thank you, Emmitt. I'll keep you posted. Goodbye." Addison said as she ended the call.

That went fairly well. She looked through her notes and paused when she got to the part about the locked freezer. It did seem a bit over the top, but she had been around people that had similar policies in their labs. It wasn't totally unheard of, but it was a little unorthodox. She always wondered if people that kept their reagents under lock and key had something to hide. Emmitt seemed like a normal person and was not someone who was dishonest in high school, so maybe she was just being judgmental when it came to things like this. He also really wanted to get his postdoc to Georgia, but Addison had to agree that this was really his project. Her lab was just there to assist. She made a mental note to mention it to Ryan later; he always had a good perspective for situations like this.

Hopefully Dr. Watt wouldn't object to it either. This collaboration could be a real stepping stone for Addison's lab. Emmitt was very connected and well known within the ion channel world; even just one project could boost her visibility too. *Let's not get ahead of ourselves, shall we, Addison?* She chastised herself. She printed out the form and got up to take it to Dr. Watt's office. *One step at a time.*

Chapter 11

Emmitt spun his chair back and forth as he thought over his meeting with Addison. She seemed to take the locked freezer policy in stride. He really couldn't risk his samples getting out of his or Laina's hands. It could bring everything down. He wished this wasn't such a struggle and he could just do all of this himself, in his lab! Or that the stupid pharma company would just move forward without this work. At least he knew Addison and she seemed to find him trustworthy so far. They could breeze through this little project and be back on track. It was just a slight detour.

Emmitt heard the little ding that told him he had a new email. He clicked open his inbox and saw that Laina had responded. She wanted to meet to discuss this new project and relocation. Maybe he was trying too hard to read between the lines, but it sounded like she was annoyed or put off by the idea. He typed off a quick response agreeing to meet immediately. She must have been expecting it because someone knocked on his door almost as soon as he'd clicked send.

"Laina?"

"Um, no. It's Beverly. I was just bringing by your mail, Dr. Strydent," a meek voice called out from behind the door.

"Oh! Of course, bring it on in." He smiled at Beverly, the department administrative assistant in charge of communications.

Beverly was just backing out of his office when she was startled.

"Oh Dr. Hibber! I'm sorry, I didn't realize you were back there. Excuse me." Beverly apologized for bumping into Laina.

"No problem," Laina said dismissively as she closed the door in Beverly's face.

Emmitt frowned. He waited a moment for Beverly to work her way down the hall.

"You really need to be more polite, Laina. We need everyone looking favorably on us."

She rolled her eyes. "Whatever. She needs to watch where

she's going." Laina pushed her blonde hair out of her eyes, tucking it behind her ears. Most of her hair was tied back in a tight ponytail, but some of her bangs didn't quite reach. Plus, she knew it made her more attractive to have to brush her hair out of her face. Her dark brown eyes were looking pointedly at Emmitt.

"I'm serious. Please do your best to be at least cordial, even if you think people don't deserve your time. You're smart; you must realize that being rude won't get you far."

"More small-town etiquette lessons? Okay, fine. I'll work on it. Now why are you sending me to this small lab near Atlanta? It's hot as balls down there and sounds terrible." She pouted.

Emmitt groaned. "I have told you all along that we might have to get out of our comfort zones to get where we want to be. This is one of those times. We need these experiments to get *Apothecom* to start the next phase of trials. They won't test our drug in humans without it!"

"Ugh. I know. Fine. I can't believe I have to go live in *Hot*-lanta for this whole thing."

"Um, I don't think anyone calls it that anymore," Emmitt interjected.

"Ugh. Stop already. I will go and get the experiments done, but you promised me first author on this paper. You got that for me, right?" Laina whined.

"Yes, she was fine with that idea. I told her about the code-locked freezer too. She hesitated a little, but I think she can make it happen."

"Do I really have to work *with* someone? I mean, isn't that a risk?"

"Do you know how to patch clamp?"

"Patch what?"

"Exactly. The grad student you'll be working with sounds like a bit of a mess, but she said that he's good at teaching skills in the lab. Keep your eye on him. She mentioned at lunch the other day that he has rather poor lab etiquette."

"Not with the etiquette rules again, Emmitt!"

"I'm not talking small town here. She said that he doesn't clean up after himself and stuff."

"Well maybe I can teach him a thing or two..." Laina said while twirling her hair coyly.

"Please don't even joke about that. You're not going down there to make friends." Emmitt rebuked her.

"Oh God, Emmitt. Like I want to hook up with some kid from the south. Don't worry, I'll be the penultimate professional. I'm planning on requesting to work off hours, like nights, weekends so that I can be more *incognito*." She smirked at him.

Emmitt struggled to keep from rolling his eyes. He found it so irritating when Laina acted like some sort of... spoiled child instead of the intelligent, young woman that she was.

"Okay, sounds like we're on the same page with all of this then. I don't know when this is going to start. We have to wait for the department chair and university to approve the scope first."

"I thought he was your mentor and it would be a breeze."

"It still takes time, so we just have to wait until we get the green light before we can make any travel plans."

"Are you going to be okay here without me?" She teased.

"Enough, Laina." He grumbled at her as she turned and walked out of his office. If she wasn't such an asset to him, he'd find someone else to do the work. He hoped Addison got back to them soon. He could feel that the end was in sight; he just needed a few more things to go his way.

Chapter 12

Addison walked back slowly to her office. When she'd dropped off the document for the scope of work and request to collaborate, she had noticed the secretary's face kind of cloud over for a moment. The woman had tried to hide it, but Addison spotted a note of alarm in her face when she read the cover page. But ultimately, she had smiled and said that she would get it processed through the proper channels as quickly as possible. Addison didn't know her well, yet. She had come to the department with Dr. Watt. *Another thing to discuss with Ryan tonight*, she thought.

She passed by her lab and peeked in to see how things were going for the day. Everyone must know the sound of her walk in the hallways because it seemed like everyone was just getting up, putting on new gloves, or minimizing something on the computer screen as she walked in. Everyone, except Anthony, who was actually hard at work on his reminder poster, which was fluorescent pink.

"How's the poster coming, Anthony?"

"Good, Dr. Fish! I was just adding a couple bullet points and color to catch my eye," he said as he drew some bright yellow stars on the poster.

"It is definitely eye-catching! I hope it does the trick." She laughed.

"Oh, it will, Dr. Fish."

Addison caught Becky mid-eye roll out of the corner of her own eye and stifled a laugh into a cough.

"And how is your work coming along today, Becky?" She asked, walking over to the younger student.

"Great! I've got my cells set up for a big experiment on Thursday that I can then analyze results from on Friday. Barring, um, disaster, I should have some good data for lab meeting next week, one way or the other."

"Wonderful! Maybe the week after, we can talk about getting you started with some experiments in the cardiomyocytes."

"Really? Those are the ones we get from the mice, um hearts, right?" She hesitated a little.

"Yes, Eleanor is going to prepare some this week too for another experiment that Juan has planned. Maybe if you observe what she does and possibly Juan's experiment too, it will set your mind at ease?"

"Maybe so. I hadn't thought about how animals were used in research before joining your lab and it kind of makes me feel funny."

"I understand. We can talk about it some more later and see if there is an alternative approach." Addison offered.

"Thanks, Dr. Fischer. I appreciate that. I will, um, try to observe Eleanor's process this week too. Maybe that will help."

Addison smiled. She knew that using animals in research was not an easy thing for everyone to do. She and Eleanor tried to be very respectful of the animals her lab used. The problem was that no person was going to volunteer to be used in basic science research—and no one would let you do it anyway. Animals were the next best thing to help scientists learn how our bodies work. Addison knew that some people didn't think twice about using animals, while others were much more sensitive, like Becky.

Becky joined her lab last spring after completing her rotations that were required through the graduate program. She had curly blonde hair and pale blue eyes. She was petite, and her personality reflected her diminutive size. Addison really had to coax information out of her sometimes.

Addison checked in with Juan before returning to her office. He was in the middle of writing a manuscript that they hoped to send to at least a second-tier journal. Juan would be moving on from her lab soon. He wanted to go into teaching, rather than continue in research. She could respect that. He was newly married and knew his wife Sophie wanted to start a family soon. A teaching position at a college had fewer demanding hours than a research professorship. She had some colleagues at a nearby university where she was trying to coordinate interest for him. Juan was in his thirties and was a first-generation American in his family. His parents had immigrated from Ecuador as children and met in college in Florida. Juan was a couple inches shy of six feet tall with straight black hair and dark brown eyes. He was easy to get along with and a hard worker. Addison had gotten to meet his parents when they visited last fall. They were really proud of their oldest son and his accomplishments.

"How's the paper coming, sir?"

"It's getting there, Dr. Fish. I'm trying to tell the story in the most interesting way. That bibliography program has been really helpful!"

"Oh good. I'm glad it's useful for you. Do you think you'll have a rough draft together by, say, Friday?"

"Maaaaybe." Juan drew the word out. "I will certainly try my hardest."

"Let's plan on going through it together after lab meeting then."

"You got it, Dr. Fish."

Addison returned to her office to catch up on emails that had piled up over the weekend. She double-checked her phone first and noticed that she had missed some texts from Liv. *Please tell me you didn't forget your gym clothes again!* Addison thought as she pulled open the message app.

"I get to be in the homecoming court, Mom!"

"I got voted as the freshman attendant!"

"I need a new dress for the parade!"

"PS Joe is one of the homecoming king candidates. He probably doesn't care!"

"Hello?"

"MOM!?!"

Addison laughed to herself as she thumbed off a text assuring Liv that they'd find time to go dress shopping this weekend. Ryan would probably suggest wearing a dress from last year, but she would have to remind him that Liv had grown three inches since last year and that he really didn't want that. She was not looking forward to going to the mall this weekend though. She texted Ryan about Olivia's good news and then got back to her work emails.

She had a departmental meeting after lunch and needed to review the agenda again before it started. She printed it off and added it to her lunchtime reading pile. Before putting her computer in sleep mode for lunch, she opened her calendar to double-check the week.

"Shoot!" She cried out loud. "It's our turn to lead journal club on Friday. I haven't sent out an article yet."

Like many departments, hers had a weekly journal club where they took turns selecting recent scientific articles to discuss as a group. It was kind of like a book club, but without the wine and the entertaining novels. Addison needed to pick out an article for the group by noon tomorrow. She quickly added that to her to-do list. Her reading pile was growing fast. She sighed and headed for the break room to heat up her lunch.

Chapter 13

Emmitt spent the week detailing his plans for Laina's assumed trip to Atlanta. He planned to go with her so he could see the lab, make sure she was settled and adjusted, as well as get a feel for this Anthony character that would be training her. He had shopped around for a small freezer that came with a coded lock feature for Laina to use in Atlanta. He wanted the freezer there before he overnighted the reagents. He couldn't risk anyone getting too curious and using any of them before she was in the lab.

He had trained Laina to code her lab notebooks so that no one could flip through them and immediately understand the experimental set up or which reagents she was using. It was a trick he had learned from a postdoc in Dr. Watt's lab so many years ago. The man had completed his first postdoc with the National Institutes of Health (NIH) in D.C. where labs were really cutthroat. No one was above snooping in someone else's lab notebook to see what experiments were working and how. Many times, multiple students or postdocs were put on the same projects, and whoever solved it first got the credit. Everyone else was out of luck and sometimes, out of a job, or at least starting over with a new project. They even coded their solutions so that no one could steal a formula to copy their results. Emmitt hadn't gone that far, but he was considering it now that Laina would be in a different lab for some time. He wasn't sure how to justify that to Addison though. He thought he had already sensed some concern in her voice with just the locked freezer and adding in the ciphered solution labels might make her too suspicious. He'd bounce the idea off Laina later; she had a good feel for what would fit in best most of the time. A knock at his apartment door startled him from his thoughts. He looked at his phone app to see who was on the doorstep. Laina?

"Why are you here? And how do you know where I live?"

She rolled her eyes. "Easy. I have friends in the mail room and in payroll. I have lots of friends in lots of places, Emmitt." Laina said pointedly.

Emmitt was taken back by Laina's insinuation but kept his face neutral.

"What did you need, Laina?"

"I *need* to know about living arrangements down in *HOT*-lanta," she said, running her finger along the seam of his leather chair. She was wearing an incredibly short black dress with four-inch spike black heels.

"I told you that I was going to get that taken care of. We can't really make any inquiries until we have confirmation from the Fischer lab that the collaboration is a go." Emmitt had maintained a very guarded personal life as an adult. It wasn't from a lack of interest. He stayed in great shape and stuck to a strict diet. Many people were surprised to discover that he was closer to 50 than 40 years old. But he couldn't trust anyone that much to have a personal relationship with them. His life's work was too important. He couldn't say that he didn't find Laina tempting, especially in her current get up. She was a knockout and incredibly intelligent. He also knew that she was ruthless and, like him, looked out for number one first.

"Yoo-hoo! Emmitt! Penny for your thoughts. I have an Uber driver waiting in the lot. We could go out for a few drinks to celebrate the collaboration approval. Or…we could…stay in." Laina broke into his wandering mind. She was twisting a stray lock of hair around her index finger as she spoke to him.

"You shouldn't be here, Laina. I keep my personal life very separate from my lab life. If there's nothing else, you need to go."

"So that's how it is." She pouted out her lips. "Well, can't hurt a girl for trying. Your loss, Emmitt." Tossing her hair over her shoulder, she turned on her toe and let herself out.

Emmitt let out his breath, not realizing that he had been holding it. He found it troublesome that Laina had found his home address. It wasn't just that she'd found it, but that she had gone looking for it in the first place. He had to tread carefully with her. She knew virtually all the lab secrets now; she could ruin him. He didn't think she'd try anything before they made it big with *Apothecom* though.

He reminded himself to keep his eye on her. You could never be too guarded in his world.

Chapter 14

Addison pulled into the parking lot and scanned it for spots that weren't galaxies away from the mall entrance. *Why was the mall always so crowded every single weekend?* She glanced over at Liv who was a ball of excitement to get a new dress. Addison was glad that Liv still wanted her around to help pick out a dress. She knew it wouldn't be long before her friends' opinions ranked much higher than her mom's.

"Where should we start?

Do you think we can at least *look* at Nordstrom's? I've heard that they have really, really great dresses this year." Liv asked hopefully.

"Sure, sweetheart. We can look wherever you want." Internally, Addison hoped that it wouldn't take *too* many stores to find a dress. Shopping was really not her thing, but seeing Liv's excitement about the excursion made it more enjoyable.

It could be a long excursion. Ryan had requested "*not too short or too low cut*" on their way out the door. She was pretty sure even the neighbors saw Liv roll her eyes in response to that comment. Hopefully they could find a good compromise.

Three hours and at least thirty-four dresses later, they finally found a Kelly-green dress in a smaller dress shop next to Nordstrom's. It was sleeveless with a short, flared skirt, *but not too short*, Addison thought, laughing to herself. She was exhausted, but Liv was thrilled with her selection. Addison was just relieved when she heard Liv say that she already had the perfect shoes to go with it. The idea of repeating the experience except in search of shoes might push her over the limit. She called Ryan on the way home with the vehicle's Bluetooth feature.

"So, what do you think of the dress?"

"Were they running low on green fabric? Couldn't they have used a little more?"

"Geez, Dad. Don't be such a prude."

"I'm just kidding, Liv-bug. I think it's a great dress. You look very nice in it."

"Thank you, Daddy! I am SO SO SO excited to wear it next week!"

"Tell me again, why are there dances back-to-back weekends? Aren't you going to a school dance tonight too? Are they trying to give all the dads coronaries or what?"

"This weekend is the dance that STUCO is sponsoring and next week is homecoming. They're very different things. One is casual and just fun; the other is so much bigger. Everyone gets dressed up. Some people have *dates!*"

"Dates? Who said anything about dates?"

"Oh Daddy. You're hopeless."

Addison grinned, she knew Ryan loved to tease Olivia.

"We'll see you at home, Ryan. We already grabbed lunch at the food court."

"I would hope so. It's almost two o'clock. I was about to send out the search party!"

"Bye, Daddy. Love you."

"Love you both, too."

As she drove home, Addison thought back to her conversations with Ryan over the last week regarding her pending collaboration with Emmitt's lab. He thought the locked freezer request was a little strange too, but agreed that having patented materials was something neither of them was familiar with. It could be standard practice for all they knew. She rolled her shoulders to work out the tension. It had been a long week. In addition to all of the kids' activities, she'd managed to throw something together for journal club before the deadline, Anthony had actually gotten some lab work completed by the end of the week, and Juan had squeaked out a rough draft just in time for her to read it over the weekend. She wasn't sure if she'd eased Becky's mind about the animal research yet, but she was still at least considering it. Progress.

"Remind me, what time are you going over to Janice's to get ready for the dance?"

When they got home, Addison slumped down onto the couch,

hoping Ryan would feel up for driving Liv to Janice's house later, and picking up ice cream for Martin too. She needed some down time after being at the mall for what seemed like forever. Martin sat down next to her on the couch while they waited for Liv to show off her new dress.

"Everybody ready?" Liv called out from the hallway.

"Ready!" They all responded.

She twirled out into the room, as she always had since she was a young girl, to show them her new dress. Her green eyes were sparkling as she looked for approval from each of their faces. Martin clapped to show his support.

"Looks like a keeper, Liv. It passes my rules." Ryan told her.

"Good choice, Liv. I think you look nice, but don't upstage the royalty." Joe teased.

Liv's smile brightened further. "Thank you so much! I'm so excited to get to be the attendant. I think I almost squealed out loud in class yesterday when they made the announcement. I kept it cool though, don't worry, Joe." She winked at her big brother. She spun out of the room to change out of the dress. Ryan looked over to Addison to tell her that she'd done well with the shopping excursion too, and found her asleep on the couch. He chuckled. It had been a long week.

artin requested to have an ice cream and movie night while his siblings were at the high school dance. Ryan let Addison rest while he got the burgers ready for dinner, but she had woken up when she smelled them cooking on the grill. They were cleaning up the remains of dinner in the kitchen while Martin called out potential movie titles from the other room.

"So, did you think any more about Emmitt's request for the locked freezer?" Ryan asked.

"I mean, it definitely struck a chord with me, but I honestly think you're right. It is probably standard practice for people with patented reagents. I am going to keep my radar on for anything else that seems uncouth."

Ryan laughed. "Surely no one from your little town would be uncouth!"

"Shut it. I have to be objective about this. Yes, I knew him as a teenager and he seemed honest then, but I haven't seen in him in what, twenty or twenty-five years? Who knows how he has changed?"

"I'm just teasing, Ad. I think you're right to keep your eye out for anything. I know it's a big opportunity for you, but it's good to watch where you're headed with some measure of caution. When do you think you'll hear from the admins about your request to collaborate?"

"I'm not sure; I'm hoping this week. I've only done little interdepartmental collaborations prior to this that didn't need approval, so this is new territory for me."

"It seems like it would benefit your department and university too, right?"

"Yes, but they also have to be diligent that there are no problems or issues with anything proprietary. You know, things like that."

"That makes sense. Well, I hope it works out."

"What about Jurassic Park? Have you guys ever seen that

one?" Martin shouted.

"Only about fifty times." Ryan laughed. "But I'd love to watch it again, set it up, Buddy." He and Addison dried their hands and went to watch the movie with Martin.

"Do not scare him at the scary parts," Addison warned.

"You're such a fun-hater sometimes, Ad."

She rolled her eyes but smiled.

Chapter 16

By Monday morning, Addison was rested and ready for another week. The school dance had been fun for both her kids. She stopped by the mail room on her way to her office, part of her hoping that she would find an approval for collaboration notice in her box. Unfortunately, it was empty, minus her paystub. She tried to remember if any of her colleagues had recently collaborated with someone from a different school. Maybe they could give her an estimate on the typical turnaround for the request. As she was mentally going through all the PIs in their department, she almost bumped into someone. Dr. Shelley!

"Zenia! How are you this morning?"

"Hello, Addison. I'm doing well. And you?"

"Oh fine. Say, didn't you start a collaboration with someone from Penn awhile back?"

"Yes. It's going really well too. Why do you ask?"

"I ran into a former classmate of mine…anyway, long story short, we're hoping to start a collaboration too. I submitted the scope and request last Monday but haven't heard anything back yet. How long does it usually take? I'm kind of excited about the possibilities."

"Well, this was with our former department chair, but I think it was about a week. It isn't totally dependent on the department chair anyway; the university grants permission. I'm sure it will be any day now, Addison. Good luck to you."

"Thanks. You too. See you around." They had reached Dr. Shelley's office, which was a few doors up from Addison's.

Addison continued on to her own office and unlocked it with her free hand. She sat down and booted up her computer while she unloaded all of the papers she'd brought home over the weekend. She had managed to read Juan's rough draft and had made some corrections and suggestions in the margins. She organized her papers and got logged into her computer. Time to wade through the barrage of emails again.

She was clicking through what was obviously junk and

deleting it when she saw a message from a name she didn't recognize in the department. She mentally crossed her fingers that it was the admin who approved collaborations as she clicked onto the email. *Please, please, please*, she thought.

"Yes!" She silent-shouted to no one. The collaboration had been approved. Her excitement dropped when she realized that they hadn't filled anything out with Emmitt's university. Maybe she needed to tap the breaks again. She found their correspondence thread and sent him a quick email with the good news as well as asking him if there was any legalese they needed to wade through on his side. Unfortunately, it was 4:15 in the morning in Los Angeles, so she wouldn't hear from him for a few hours. *Time to get to work on other work, Ad,* she told herself. She fished Juan's paper out of her bag and set it aside to bring by his desk later. She would like for him to present his project again in their lab meeting this week, just to make sure they weren't missing anything before they sent the manuscript off to a journal. Luckily, the other two labs that they had a joint meeting with only had one student each at the moment, so her people could take a few more weeks in a row than normal. She finished catching up on the weekend's emails and grabbed Juan's paper with her to go to the lab.

Eleanor was already hard at work at her desk when Addison walked in. She rode the bus in from the suburbs at the crack of dawn so that she could avoid some of the traffic at the end of the day. Eleanor had worked with Addison's lab from the beginning and the two women had become good friends.

"Hey there, Eleanor. How's the morning going?"

"Oh, Dr. Fischer! I was just about to call you. I remembered that printout from Gary's DNA screening the other day. I have it right here for you. Did I tell you that one of the mutations they found is in our sodium channel?" She pulled a sheaf of papers from her bag. Eleanor always called Nav1.5 *our* sodium channel, like it was a family member or something.

"What? No! How interesting. I will look through the list and see if there is anything else of interest in it. I hope this can help get him some answers about his blood pressure. I know it's been a concern for both of you." Addison said as she took the papers from her.

"It really has. I appreciate your help. We're both pretty hopeful too. It seems like they are coming out with new treatments all the time."

"It really does. Any lab news before I check on the grunts?" She winked.

"Ha ha. Not really. Just reordering some of our standards."

Addison worked her way over to Becky next. She was outlining something in her lab notebook and didn't hear her approach. Addison tried to lightly clear her throat before she was too close so that she didn't make Becky jump, but all it did was startle her.

"Oh! Hi, Dr. Fischer. I didn't hear you coming. I'm just planning out an experiment for this week. Anthony said that I could shadow him while he does some patch clamp runs so I can see what I can learn."

"That sounds really great. I'll leave you to your plans."

Juan was just arriving and getting his things put away. She lifted up his paper as she walked over to his desk. He cleared a spot on the desk for the paper and moved some of his binders off the nearby chair for her to sit down.

"Did you want to go over it now? Or meet in your office later? I was planning on searching through the universities today to see where there are openings and what positions are out there."

"I am just bringing you my comments for now. We can discuss them in my office later if you'd like. I thought you might like to present this in lab meeting this week. You can get some feedback from the other two PIs. Plus, they might have some advice on which journal would be the best place to send it off to. I think it's a really great manuscript, Juan. I couldn't find a lot to suggest for improvement."

"Thanks, Addison. I appreciate that. Maybe we can discuss it as well as grant ideas this afternoon? I think I will be more marketable as an incoming professor if I come with a grant. I know that there are some small grants for undergraduate research work."

"You're right about that, Juan. I'd be happy to help give you some direction. I'll try to pull some things together by this afternoon too. Have you seen Anthony yet today?"

"Surprisingly, yes. He was already in the tissue culture room working with his cells when I walked by earlier. Guess you really lit a fire under him this time."

Addison bit back the *"It's about time"* retort that she wanted to say and said, "Let's hope so. I'll catch up with him later. I think he knows what his plans are for the foreseeable future." She tapped the corner of his desk and headed back to her office.

Flipping through the printout from Eleanor, she stopped short of her office door when she saw that the DNA screening had identified a mutation in the STABL protein that Emmitt studied. She quickly unlocked her door, almost slipping on a scrap of paper on the floor just inside the doorway. She sidestepped it and quickly logged into the computer to see if Gary's mutation was the same one that Emmitt was studying. Addison opened her browser and went to the NCBI database that she had bookmarked. She searched for Emmitt's papers and opened the first one to find the mutation site. *It was the same one!*

"How interesting," she mused. Maybe her lab would actually get to help Gary with his long-time struggle with high blood pressure. She wondered when Emmitt usually got to work. He seemed like a long hours, no fun kind of PI, so she hoped to hear from him sooner rather than later. This project just got even more exciting! Addison scanned the rest of the list for anything else that she was familiar with and noticed that Gary had a mutation in the sodium channel as well as one in the protein Anthony was studying, *alpha9*. One of them was more familiar to her than the other. She didn't want to get Eleanor's hopes up yet, but this definitely seemed promising for Gary. She would wait to tell Eleanor until she heard back from Emmitt and the project was fully underway.

Addison set the printout aside for now and pulled up a website that had grant applications for postdoctoral fellows. She opened a document to copy in links for the ones that she thought were relevant to Juan's interests and saved it for later. She wasn't sure if Juan and his wife would be willing to move or if they wanted to stay local with the job hunt. She mostly looked through the local universities and schools that advertised research opportunities for biology and science majors. Addison knew a few of the faculty at some of the nearby schools and thought she could use those connections to help Juan get his foot in the door. She added a few out of state opportunities to the list in case they were open to moving, then saved both documents to attach to an email for Juan.

She was about to close her email when she remembered that she had a committee meeting for another graduate student the following afternoon. The student had emailed some information about her project for the faculty to read through before the meeting. She searched through her inbox to find it and download the documents. More lunchtime reading! Before she could print them out, her office phone rang.

"Dr. Fischer speaking."

"Addison, it's Emmitt. Great news about the approval! And, no, we don't need any sort of paperwork on my side. I know that seems odd, but because I have patents, I get to make my own decisions regarding collaborations and such. So, it sounds like we've got clearance to continue, right?"

"We do. What's the next step?"

"I'd like to find some sort of housing or apartment for Laina that's not too far from the lab if possible. Can you steer me in the right direction for a search?"

"Definitely! I have one postdoc that's currently in university housing that's about a mile from the building, but we have great mass transit that comes with discounts for university employees." When Emmitt didn't respond, she tried to think of other options that she was familiar with.

"Of course, there's also some condos and townhouses just

down the street and some high-rise apartment buildings too. Those would be more expensive, though not necessarily out of the feasible price range for a postdoc."

"How about you send me a list of anything you think is relevant and I'll get Laina to look through it and pick something out."

"I'll get Eleanor—my lab assistant—to put something together for you this afternoon. I guess we'll just wait to hear that you've secured lodging for her for now?"

"Yes, I will be sending the small freezer to your lab later this week, so it's ready for her and the reagents when she gets there. Hopefully there is some availability, and we can get her down there quickly. Oh! By the way, do you know if they have short term leases at any of these places? 6- or 9-month type deals? I don't foresee this being a long project and didn't want her to have to break a lease and lose money if possible."

"I'll ask Eleanor to include any lease restraint information in her email as well. Thanks, Emmitt."

"Looking forward to working with you, Addison."

She ended the call and phoned the lab to ask Eleanor about putting the housing list together. Fortunately, Eleanor knew that the university already had that information in one place on its website. She said she'd look it up and forward it to Addison for Emmitt's postdoc. Addison was starting to get excited; everything was really going smoothly so far. She checked her watch. The grant and job search had taken longer than she thought. It was about time for lunch. She put her computer in sleep mode and started to leave her office when she noticed the slip of paper on the floor from earlier. She picked it up to throw it away but stopped when she realized there was some writing on it.

"Watch the Strydent lab closely. Especially Dr. Strydent. You've been warned."

The note was scrawled in black ink. Addison thought it was rather odd and couldn't imagine who would have left such a note or why. She tried to remember if she had seen anyone outside her office when she got to it earlier. She had been reading the printout from Eleanor and hadn't paid attention at all. *How strange. Besides Dr. Watt, who here even knows who Emmitt is?* She asked herself. She tucked the note into her laptop bag to show to Ryan later and tried to push it from her mind as she went to go heat up her lunch for the day.

Chapter 17

Emmitt summoned Laina to his office after receiving the email that Addison had sent with Eleanor's help. He knew that Laina would want to be in the more upscale housing options. He couldn't blame her; university housing was always run down and outdated. However, he didn't want her to attract a lot of attention, and he worried that getting her a nicer place would do that.

"You rang?" Laina said as she entered his office.

"I got the housing information for *AT*-lanta from Dr. Fischer today."

"Why do you insist on calling her Dr. Fischer? Why not Addison? I mean, you knew her when she was *just* Addison."

"I think she's kind of sensitive about it. I got that jibe--," he stopped. "You know what? It doesn't matter. Call her Dr. Fischer unless told otherwise." He was getting tired of Laina's forwardness lately.

"Geez. A little touchy today?" She rolled her eyes. "Now, what are my options?"

"I pulled it up on the laptop there. They have a variety of housing options, from university apartments to high-rise condos downtown. Why don't we look through it and see if we can find something to agree on?"

"I've never had help from my PI picking out an apartment before. Are you so *intimate* with all your worker bees?" She asked coyly.

"Laina." He looked at her with what he hoped showed sternness.

"Good grief, Emmitt. You know we're up to our eyeballs in this together. Can't you just relax and enjoy it?"

"Relax? Laina! I have explained to you—" he paused and took a breath to calm down. "I have explained to you how important this is to me, to this lab, to our livelihood. I need you to stop with all of this nonsense. Do we have an understanding or not?"

"Fine. This could be so much more enjoyable for the both of

us, but whatever." She sat down in the chair and started clicking on the housing links.

"What's my budget then? I'm guessing it's cheaper to live there than it is to live out here."

"Your stipend is not going to change just because you will be in Atlanta for a few months, maybe a year."

"A year?! Dear God, I hope not. Okay, it looks like I can afford *any* of these options with my current paycheck. However, I can't afford any of them *AND* pay for my apartment here. So how does that work? I really don't want to lose the place I have here."

"Would you be willing to sublet?"

"Well, it's against the lease that I signed, but I'm willing to overlook that. Who is going to sublet it?"

"We're getting a new graduate student—"

She cut him off. "Absolutely not. I don't want some lab gremlin that I've never met rummaging through my things."

"If you would let me finish. We're getting a new graduate student who needs short term housing while her house is finished. She's getting married next summer and will move in with her husband then."

"I'm moving my bed. I don't care what you say; that's a deal breaker. My bed, my mattress come with ME."

"That's fine, Laina. I understand. She just started at the beginning of the semester and is doing one of those rotations through our lab. Whatever you want to move to Atlanta with you is fine. She will have some of her own stuff too, of course. We'll make it work. Now I would like you to consider not renting the most expensive place on this list. We're trying to remain under the radar for now, you know?"

"If compromise is the name of the game, then I accept. I will fill out an application right now and see how soon I can move in." She pulled up one of the midrange places, still downtown, but not the high-rise option, and opened the application page.

"What about computer access in this other lab? I'm going to need some kind of log in and badge, right?"

"I'll email the lab assistant, Eleanor is her name, and ask how we go about arranging that for temporary access. I'm sure she can point you in the right direction."

Laina submitted the application and closed the browser. A message popped up that said her application had been received and that she would receive a confirmation email shortly. Almost instantly, her phone pinged with a notification.

"There it is, application received. It says I should hear back from them today, possibly tomorrow at the latest. If I'm bringing my bed, I guess we need to rent a moving truck then or some kind of moving company. It's not going to fit in my Kia."

"Let's get a move in date first."

"Fine. I'll be in the lab if you need anything. We need to make a list of the reagents I'm bringing and how much of each one. I'll start on that first."

"I'm going to set up a video call with Dr. Fischer for some time this week so that we can go over the project together and she can at least see who you are before you show up down there."

"You're not coming with me?!" She pouted.

"Of course, I'm coming, Laina. I will help you get settled and see the lay of the land, so to speak."

"Okay good. See you later, Emmitt." She got up and left the office.

Emmitt sighed. Laina was getting more and more unpredictable. He needed her help and he couldn't get these experiments done without her knowing what was happening. Still, it felt like she was goading him. He liked it better when she just did what he said when he said it. He would have to watch her more closely, which would be difficult with her going to Atlanta. He needed to find something that kept her loyal to him, to this project. Emmitt wondered who might have a little dirt on her. It was starting to feel like she was holding all of the cards.

He sat down to email Eleanor to ask about Laina getting a badge and access to the university's network. He also needed to email Addison to get the video call set up for later in the week. He mentally checked a few things off of his master plan. Things were starting to come together now. He just needed to keep Laina in line.

Chapter 18

Addison was delighted to hear that Laina had already found a housing option and could move in as early as next week. This was coming together even faster than she thought it would. She needed to create a space for her in the lab too. Of course, there were plenty of free desks. They just needed to clear out some old lab notebooks and things before anyone could actually use one of them. The video call with Emmitt and Laina seemed to have gone well. Laina sounded like a hard worker who was dedicated to the project. She hoped she would be easy to work with and get along well with the other members of the lab. *AND* put up with Anthony, though he was getting better. She crossed her fingers that this would hold true.

She and Eleanor had been very busy filling out lots of paperwork to get Laina set up in the lab. She would be arriving on Wednesday or Thursday, and they had a meeting set up with Emmitt for Friday. Emmitt said that they would try to attend the group lab meeting Friday morning if they could get Laina's apartment set up by then. They would be touring the lap space most likely on Thursday afternoon, but that was assuming that they made it to Atlanta as planned. Addison felt like she needed to get an assistant just to help her keep all the details straight. It was almost the weekend and she was ready to get away for a day or two. The homecoming parade was this afternoon and she had promised Liv that she would take off early so that she could watch. According to Joe, he couldn't care less who watched the parade.

Addison grabbed her notebook to flip through her notes from the lab meeting earlier today. Both Juan and Anthony had presented, though Anthony had just given a brief update. He had successfully executed experiments two weeks in a row without losing any reagents. This felt like progress. He just might get these experiments finished and graduate one day.

They had gotten some good feedback on Juan's paper too. Thankfully, everyone felt the overall *story* of the paper was complete; he didn't need to do any more experiments. One of the other PIs had suggested portraying the results in a different manner for one of the figures and Addison agreed with him. It made a bigger impact when you showed the results as a rate of change rather than just a change. Juan was already making the adjustment to the document. They planned to submit it early next week. She glanced at her watch and realized she needed to get on her way if she was going to make the afternoon parade for Liv. She grabbed the phone to call Eleanor and remind her.

"I'm just about to head out for the homecoming parade. Thanks again for locking up for me tonight."

"No problem! Be sure to congratulate your girl for me. I know she is just thrilled to be a part of this."

"She really is. Thank you, Eleanor. Have a nice weekend."

"You too. See you Monday."

They ended the call as Addison was getting her laptop back into her shoulder bag and grabbing all the papers she hoped to peruse over the weekend. She double-checked that she had her phone and her keys and then shut down the desktop computer. She grabbed her badge that she kept on the coiled bracelet so that she could swipe her way out of the building and into the parking garage. She texted Liv that she was on her way out the door and would see her at the parade, ready to take some photos and videos. Addison let her know where she planned to watch from, so that Liv could be looking when the float passed by.

Addison easily found a parking spot about a block from the corner she'd mentioned to Liv and walked to get in place for some photos. The sidewalks were already pretty full with other people from their town. Everyone supported the football team and looked forward to the homecoming parade each year. It wasn't long before the firetruck was passing by with its lights blinking, signaling the start of the parade. Several of the classes that were celebrating their decade reunions had the first few floats.

Addison tried to look past them to see if she could see Liv's green dress down the street. The freshmen class float was decorated and then some. Flowers, streamers, balloons, and blue pom-poms covered the float. Liv and the freshmen boy attendant were seated in the middle, waving at the crowds on both sides of the street. She wasn't sure if she'd ever seen Liv smile bigger. Addison waved and snapped photos with her phone. She took a little video too because she knew Liv would want to see it. Addison waved at some familiar faces on the sophomore and junior floats as she waited for the King and Queen candidates' float to get into view. The three boys were seated on the back of the pickup bed with their legs dangling over the edge while the girls were in chairs on the float that the pickup was pulling. Joe waved at Addison when he passed by.

The rest of the parade ended a few minutes later. Addison walked back to her car and called Ryan on the way to tell him what he'd missed.

"I'm sorry I couldn't be there. How did it go?"

"You could see her from several blocks away. Her green dress really stood out. She was so thrilled to be part of the parade, Ryan. I'm glad I was able to watch and take photos."

"And Joe?"

"Joe was Joe. He smiled and waved as instructed. Ha ha."

Ryan chuckled. "I'll see you at home around 5:30."

"What?! Did you forget why they had a parade?"

"Oh right. I will see you at the pre-game at 5:30. Another night of burgers it is. Love you, Ad."

"Love you too, Ryan. Drive safe."

Addison swung by the house to get their stadium seat cushions and pick up Martin too. He had his homework spread out on the kitchen table but was engrossed in his video game when she got there. He had at least gotten all of their football game gear together before starting up his console.

"Hey, Buddy. How was your day?"

"It was great, Mom. I just passed two more levels in my game!" He told her without taking his eyes off the screen.

"I meant your school day, champ."

"What? Oh. Yeah, it was good."

"I see you have some homework out here. Is it due Monday or sooner?"

"Monday."

"I'm going to change my clothes and then we'll head over to the game to save our seats, okay?"

"This early?"

"It's homecoming, Martin. It's going to be extra crowded."

"Ugh. I wonder what time Joel and Derek will get there."

"We can save them some seats too, if you'd like."

"You know, I'm in middle school now. I'm probably old enough to sit with my friends, by myself."

Addison smiled. "How about we ask Joel and Derek's parents what they think before we make that decision for them?"

"Fine."

"Okay, five minutes and we're outta here, Dude." She pulled her phone back out and thumbed off a quick text to the other two moms to get their thoughts on this independent seating idea. Martin had already gotten their football blankets, just in case the temperature dropped more than they expected. This was Joe's sixth football season, so Martin was well-versed in what went to the game every week. Addison changed into her MOM t-shirt, hoodie and jeans. The weather was finally cooling off in the evenings, so they wouldn't feel like they were getting baked on the bleachers tonight. She got back-to-back texts from Joel and Derek's moms right as she was tying her sneakers. They were both okay with the three boys sitting together as long as they stayed together and let their parents know if they were going to the concession stand or whatever.

"Okay. I'm ready. You ready?"

"Let me just save this really quick." Martin pushed a few buttons, then plugged his controller back in so it would charge. "Okay, I'm ready."

"Let's go, Eagles!" Addison clapped. They grabbed their bags and seat cushions and headed out to the garage.

Chapter 19

Emmitt had talked Laina into putting her bed into storage rather than driving it across the country. She was going to be renting a furnished studio apartment, which was cheaper than paying to get her precious bed moved. The new grad student would be moving in a week or so after Emmitt got back. She had been living with her grandparents for the first part of the semester and was ready for her own space.

Much to Laina's objections, Emmitt was flying to Atlanta rather than riding in the car with her. After her behavior the last few weeks, he had no desire to put up with her antics for four full days across America. She was thoroughly irritated about it, but he put his foot down and refused to listen to her complaints on the matter. The plan was for her to leave on Sunday and drive about 500 to 600 miles a day. He found hotel reservations for her in Tucson, Odessa, and Shreveport along the way. She should arrive easily by Wednesday evening with only eight or so hours of driving a day. Emmitt suggested that she find a friend to take along with her if she didn't want to do it by herself, but that "friend" would not be her boss. She was not amused at him referring to the drive as a "fun" road trip. He shrugged. They were all making sacrifices here.

Emmitt and Laina had discussed the approach he wanted her to take with the lab members as well as the project *ad nauseum*. He wanted her to learn the technique by first mastering what the host lab had already done. He knew that she was getting irritated with his constant reminders, but he didn't care. This was the moment that could send everything toppling.

It wasn't that Laina didn't agree with the approach. She was just tired of hearing about it. They decided that she would take the first few weeks to familiarize herself with the lab and learn the patch clamp technique. She could request access to the lab on nights and weekends to practice after everyone felt comfortable enough with her being there on her own. Once she was alone, she could figure out the settings that gave her similar baseline values to the Fischer lab. Then she could add in all of their modified components to complete the real experiments. Laina felt confident that she could complete all of it in under six months. Emmitt had told her not to rush it, but secretly, he was thrilled that they could be negotiating with *Apothecom* by the summer. He resisted the urge to call Laina one more time before she left in the morning. He was setting his phone back down when it started ringing. It was Laina.

"Laina?"

"Yes. I was just mentally going through everything that needed to be taken care of before I leave. I realized that I never asked where the new student would be working. Is she taking over my space or what?"

"No. I have another desk and bench space for her to use."

"What are you going to do with all of my notebooks while I'm gone? I can't really fit them in my car, nor do I want to keep them at the apartment here."

"I've already moved them into my office. I moved your computer in here too, just in case someone used it because it was free and stumbled onto something that you didn't realize could be found."

"Okay. I have gone through everything here. There is no trace of any lab things, any notes-to-self, or anything like that for the newbie to stumble upon."

"You shouldn't have had anything at your home in the first place."

"God, Emmitt. Enough already. I know how important this is. It's important to me too. I apologized, I said that I wouldn't bring lab materials home anymore. There is literally nothing else that I can do." She growled at him.

"We just need to be aware of our...our risks."

"You have made that very clear."

"Anything else?"

"No, that was it. I'll call you when I make it to the hotel tomorrow." She hung up.

Emmitt sighed. He hadn't realized until they started preparing for Laina to leave that she had been taking her lab notebooks home and planning experiments from there. He had discovered her misstep while trying to find something he could hold against her, but this wasn't it. If he threatened to report her for this minor proprietary offense, she'd laugh at him. Still, how could she have been so careless? The notebooks were intellectual property—part of his grants and the lab at the university. They were not supposed to leave the lab. Plus, what if someone had broken into her apartment and stolen one? Not that lab notebooks seemed like hot items to steal, but he couldn't be too careful. His research could not get into the wrong hands, which were really any hands but his and, unfortunately, Laina's. He sighed again. It was going to be a long six months.

Chapter 20

Addison was smiling to herself as she walked down the hallway to her office. It had been a great weekend. Joe hadn't been crowned homecoming king, but his buddy had been, which was just fine by Joe. What mattered to him was that their team had won the game and remained undefeated for the season thus far, not to mention that his girlfriend Taylor was relieved that Joe didn't have to pose in cutesy photos with the homecoming queen after the ceremony or at the dance. She and Martin had gotten to do their morning ride up the hillside too. She decided that her days of being the first one up the hill were numbered: Martin had beaten her to the top three weeks in a row now.

"Someone's in a good mood."

Addison almost jumped. She had been so lost in her thoughts from the weekend that she hadn't realized that Dr. Shelley was coming down the hall towards her.

"Oh, hi, Zenia. How are you?"

"Not as happy as you. I take it you heard back about your collaboration request?"

"What? Oh, yes. We got the approval. Thank you for asking. I was just lost in my thoughts from the weekend."

"Oh right, I think I heard that your son was a homecoming king candidate, right? Did he win?"

"No, but the football team won, which is what he cared about more anyway." She quickly added when Zenia seemed confused.

"Congratulations to the team then, *and* congratulations to you on getting the collaboration approved! I told you it would be any day."

"You were right. I actually got the approval later that same day. I'm excited to get the project rolling. It will be a short one, but hopefully we can build off of it and really make some progress in the field by working together."

"That's great, Addison. I'm on my way to the lab myself. We're getting some new equipment in this week and need to do some rearranging."

"Let me know if you need any help. We're just down the way."

"Thanks, I will."

Addison reached her office and unlocked it. She set her coffee on her desk and got her bag unpacked for the day. She needed to run her lunch over to the break room and get her mail still. Rather than get bogged down in her emails, she grabbed her lunch to take over to the break room. Her mailbox had a handful of fliers for upcoming conferences within the university. She wondered when they were going to stick with a digital format for these. Of course, people could ignore an email just as easily as they could ignore a flier.

She had heard from Emmitt that Laina was on her way to Atlanta and had made it to the first hotel in Tucson, Arizona last night. She would be driving to Odessa, Texas, today. Addison had asked if anyone was traveling with Laina. It seemed like quite a long way to drive by yourself in four days' time. Emmitt wasn't sure. He said that he had encouraged her to bring a friend who could fly home after a few days, but that Laina hadn't mentioned if she followed through on his suggestion or not. Emmitt's flight would arrive Wednesday afternoon. He was renting a car, so she didn't need to worry about having someone pick him up from the airport.

Addison scrolled through her unread emails and opened the ones that seemed important, deleting the ones that were junk. She was very meticulous with both her work and her personal email accounts. She found it was easier not to miss important emails, from the department at work or the kids' school administrators and teachers, if she didn't let her inbox sit with hundreds of unread emails. She never understood how people functioned that way but knew it was the norm for many. Her next stop would be the lab to make sure that Eleanor didn't need any help setting up Laina's space and lab bench.

Chapter 21

Laina was glad she had ignored Emmitt's suggestion to bring a friend on her trip across the country. She could listen to whatever music she wanted, choose a podcast or a book, stop whenever she wanted, or keep driving instead of constantly stopping for bathroom breaks. This was the best way to travel. All the control was hers. She also had the hotel room entirely to herself and all the meal decisions were hers alone.

The hotel in Tucson had been really nice. She had room service brought in—Emmitt was footing the bill, so who cared what she ordered and how much it cost? The room had a big, jetted bath tub too. She had used some of the complimentary bath salts and bubbles and soaked out all the stiffness from driving eight hours. Driving had been pretty easy so far though. The further you got away from LA, the fewer cars you saw. She had never realized how much of the southwest United States was made up of desert, endless miles of desert.

She had gotten her car serviced on Friday. She didn't want any surprises slowing her down on this trip. Emmitt had stressed repeatedly how important it was that she make it to Atlanta on time, though Dr. Fischer seemed more flexible about it. She knew Emmitt was a control freak, so she felt like it was a good idea to keep him happy rather than listening to him harp at her about it. She wished he would relax about it already.

Laina had been working with Emmitt for seven years. It was a longer than normal postdoc, but they had really worked well together. She had applied for a postdoc in his lab after making a list of all the PIs that had published more than five papers in the top-tier journals in the last two years. Emmitt's lab had more than everyone else by far. Her excellent academic record as well as her noteworthy success in graduate school, had earned her an interview with the university's rising star. She had read up on all of his past work and came to the meeting with an idea for a new project. Laina knew that her assertiveness and intelligence would help her get the position and she was right. Emmitt had hired her on the spot. It had taken almost two years with his lab for her to realize that everything wasn't exactly as it seemed. A lot of people chalked it up to Emmitt's demanding personality, but she had noticed some irregularities that made her start to question some things.

She realized that he wouldn't come clean just because she questioned him about his lab policies. She went behind his back to try to gather some evidence, but Emmitt was thoroughly in control and she never had a chance to test his reagents outside of his lab. At first Emmitt had denied that anything *funny* was going on and threatened to fire her for trying to get one of his reagents out of the lab, but she was relentless. She continued to question why he was so particular about reagents, why all their cell lines came from their own animal models rather than using more traditional cell lines. Eventually, Emmitt realized that she wasn't going to turn him over to the ethics police. She wanted in on his fame and rise to fortune. It took some time, but she gained his trust and now she knew the full extent of his deceit. Of course, at this point, she was complicit in covering up the lie that he had been telling for the last decade and change; she had even helped him improve his methodologies. Everything had been smooth sailing until *Apothecom* demanded the extra study before they would approve the human trials. She knew that was what really led Emmitt to tell her the whole backstory. Laina felt confident that they could get the data they needed to sway *Apothecom* their way. She knew that occasionally, postdocs were recognized along with their PIs when they received scientific awards. She was determined to show her worth to Emmitt by completing this project in a timely manner.

Chapter 22

Addison tossed and turned all Tuesday night. She really wanted everything to run smoothly on Wednesday and Thursday. Emmitt was supposed to arrive Wednesday afternoon. He was going to pick up Laina's apartment key since she might be arriving after the management office closed. He was going to help her get everything unloaded and into the apartment, so they probably wouldn't see either of them until Thursday. Addison wanted to make sure that everything was ready when they came to tour the lab on Thursday afternoon. She didn't want Emmitt or Laina to view them as second rate. She had worked hard for her lab and was proud of the people who worked in it, even if she did have fears that Anthony might burn it all to the ground with his carelessness.

At 5:00, she finally gave up and got out of bed. She grabbed some workout clothes and went into her home office. She tried to complete her yoga routine three times each week, but didn't always get it in. Today seemed like a great day to sweat some of her nerves out and be ready for what the day would bring. It was a short workout, but it got her heart rate up and helped her calm down about Emmitt and Laina's impending arrival.

She filled up her water bottle and got the coffee maker started. Soon, everyone else would be up too. Martin's bus picked him up at 7:20, so he waited until the last possible minute to get out of bed and jump in the shower. Liv got up earlier than all three of them so that she could shower, dry her hair, and do her makeup before Joe drove the two of them to the high school. Joe was a minimalist in the mornings too. The more sleep he could get, the better. Addison was glad they had two hot water heaters or someone was going to suffer through a cold shower every morning. She drank her water and grabbed a shower before anyone else was out of bed.

"You got up early today. It seemed like you were having trouble sleeping." Ryan said to her when she came out to grab some breakfast and help hurry the kids along in their morning rituals.

"I just really want everything to go well today and tomorrow *and Friday*." She laughed at herself.

"It's going to be fine, Ad. You have a great lab. They would be crazy to think otherwise."

"Thanks, Ryan. It just feels really big. Emmitt is fairly high profile. I don't want to be someone that drags him down."

"Stop. The only person that could do that is Emmitt himself, not you or your lab. It's going to be fine. Relax."

"Yeah, Mom. You're definitely the smartest scientist I know." Martin grinned at her.

"Thanks, Dude. Now get out to the bus stop before you get left behind. No one is driving you to school!" She gave him a hug and reminded him to grab the lunch he'd made for himself. She heard the blow dryer and knew Liv was hard at work to look her best for the day. The high school bell rang at 8:05. Addison was typically already at the lab by then and Ryan made sure they got out the door on time.

Martin scurried out the front door to catch the bus, while Addison put her own lunch together.

"Okay, I'm off to the lab. I'll see everyone tonight. Cross your fingers that the rest of this week goes as smoothly as possible."

"It's gonna be great, Ad. I'll see you later." Ryan gave her a hug and a kiss goodbye.

Her commute to the lab wasn't too bad, especially since they had invested in a toll pass and she could drive in the fast lane most of the way there. It usually took her about twenty minutes from door to door. She put on her favorite 80s music station and tried to relax. Ryan was right, she did have a lab that she was proud of and she had no reason to worry that they wouldn't live up to Emmitt's high standards.

Chapter 23

Eleanor was supervising Juan, Anthony, and Becky's clean-up efforts around the extra lab bench and desk that would be Laina's. Unfortunately, the desk was nearest Anthony's and Eleanor knew that Addison hoped he wouldn't be a menace with his sloppiness. Becky was organizing the old lab notebooks over on a spare bookshelf they had gotten from the department's storage room. Somehow, Anthony had taken on the job of cleaning off the bench top, but he seemed to be doing a thorough job of it. Juan was setting up the computer that Laina would be using while she was with them. They had heard that she might be bringing a laptop too, but wanted to have this for her in the lab just in case that didn't happen.

"Anthony, after you've wiped down the countertops, can you find her some tube racks and pipettes?"

"Sure thing, Eleanor. I'll get her a canister of microfuge tubes too and some pens."

"Becky, did we find an empty binder for her to use?"

"Yes, it's on my desk. I need to get some dividers for it from the office still and some paper too."

"Wonderful. Dr. Fischer is going to be so relieved to see how much we've accomplished already this morning. Great job! Now, how is that computer coming, Juan?"

"I'm just restarting it after getting all the previous user's files into a spare drive. It should be ready for her once she receives her login information from the department."

"Oh! I have a file for her from them. I bet it's in there. They usually set up a temporary password and then it prompts you to make a new one the first time you log in. The same thing goes with the email system. I think I hear Dr. Fischer coming now." She turned and looked toward the doorway.

Addison stepped in and her jaw dropped. "You guys! Wow! How early did you get here today? Everything looks so good. Thank you."

"Uh, Dr. Fish? Should we tape the absorbent, sterile pads down to her lab bench or do you think she has a preference with how that's done?"

"I think that would be great for you to do for her in advance, Anthony. Thank you for thinking of it. Wow, Becky! You got all of the old lab notebooks organized. I know that took some doing. Y'all are the best. Thank you! Does everyone have a few minutes to go over some last-minute details? I know we probably won't see anyone until tomorrow, but I wanted to be ready just in case." Everyone nodded in agreement.

"Okay, they are going to walk through the lab and make sure we have everything that Laina will need." She paused when she heard Anthony take a breath like he was about to speak.

"Pipette tips. I forgot to get her a couple boxes of each size. Sorry for interrupting, Dr. Fish."

"Quite all right, Anthony. Good job staying on top of everything. Okay, so assuming there aren't any extra tools or devices, we will also show them the rest of the department space— just the layout so that Laina has a feel for where she is going each day. I will meet them downstairs at one o'clock and bring them straight here to introduce everyone. Dr. Strydent also has an appointment with Dr. Watt. He is a former grad student—small world, huh? I think that is scheduled for later in the afternoon. Juan, if you could help Laina get logged into the computer after we do the little tour, that would be great. I don't think they will be here too long; Laina wants to get her apartment set up before she really starts working."

"I can do that. It sounds like we have everything ready for them to get here. Just let us know how we can make this transition easier for you, Dr. Fish. We know you've been worried about it."

"Thank you, Juan. I appreciate that. I will definitely let you know if something comes up. Unless anyone has any questions— lab-related or project-related, I'm going to get ready for that committee meeting that's at ten o'clock."

"I have one question. Will Laina be working with cell lines or cardiomyocytes or…?" Becky trailed off.

"Good question. She will be doing both. Dr. Strydent is overnighting some of their cell lines and other reagents to be placed in that freezer that arrived yesterday."

"The one with the keypad lock?" Anthony smirked.

"Yes, that's the one. Their lab has a lot of patents and needs extra precaution when it comes to their reagents. I know it seems a little paranoid. Anyway, Laina will keep all of her reagents in that freezer. They also have a couple of animal lines that they have developed. The mice pups will also be overnighted when Laina is ready to do experiments in cardiac cells."

"Sounds ambitious, but their whole lab seems ambitious to me." Becky smiled.

"Anyone else have questions? No? Okay. I'll be in my office if anyone needs anything, except, of course, when I'm at the committee meeting. It should only last an hour or so."

Addison left the lab and walked back to her office. She had already taken her lunch to the break room, so she sat down at her desk and logged into the computer. She had a new email from Emmitt. Laina was still on schedule to arrive in the late afternoon or early evening. He was at the airport and his flight was on time. He had a direct flight and would have internet access if she needed to send him anything. Otherwise, he planned to see her tomorrow. She sent off a quick response that they were all looking forward to meeting Laina and having the two of them tour their lab. Part of her almost expected him to pop in unannounced today, which was why she wanted everything ready by this afternoon. She knew he was anxious to get started and wouldn't put it past him to show up early.

She was really touched that her lab had arrived early to get everything finished. She assumed Eleanor was behind that plan. It was such a relief to see all the clutter cleared away and the space looking ready for its next user. She wondered what Eleanor had bribed Anthony with to get him to help clean someone else's space. She laughed to herself. She probably made him some more cookies!

Addison closed her email and pulled up the documents she had saved for the committee meeting. At any given time, she served on anywhere from five to ten graduate student committees. She was more frequently on the post-candidacy advisory committees than the pre-candidacy ones. Students had to complete a candidacy exam once they had put some time into their projects and found the direction they were headed in their research. Following the exam, they formed a second committee that was more tailored to their research. This committee would advise the student on techniques or approaches to experiments and ultimately give them permission to start writing their dissertation. Once a student passed their candidacy exam, they were officially considered a PhD candidate rather than just a grad student. Everyone still called them grad students though. Her meeting today was with a pre-candidacy student. Everyone was hopeful that she would be ready to take her candidacy exam soon. Addison looked over the documents the student had emailed everyone. She seemed to know her project well and understand where it was headed. It should be an easy meeting.

Addison realized that Becky was probably overdue for forming a committee. She grabbed a sticky note and wrote herself a reminder to chat with her about it next week after Laina had arrived and things were more settled. Knowing Becky, she probably already had a list of who she wanted on her committee and a time frame of when they could have her first meeting.

Chapter 24

Emmitt boarded his flight. He had purchased a first-class ticket because he felt too claustrophobic in coach. He put his carry-on bag in the overhead bin and settled into his seat with his messenger bag. He planned to do a little work while he was in the air for almost four hours. He lost three hours traveling from California to the east coast, so even though his flight landed at 3:30, it would feel like lunchtime. He had promised Laina that he would pick up her apartment key first before finding something to eat. The plane filled quickly for once and soon the flight attendants were going over all of the safety information. As usual, there was a huge line of planes in the queue to take off. Emmitt pulled a paper out of his bag and grabbed his favorite pen to mark anything of interest. He had printed out a couple of papers to read until they reached the altitude that allowed him to use personal electronics. He wanted to familiarize himself with Addison's work a little bit more before they met with her tomorrow. He also wanted to revisit Dr. Watt's work. He had followed his mentor's work fairly closely over the years since he'd graduated from the lab, but he didn't want to seem out of touch when they got together tomorrow. Watt was taking Emmitt and Laina to dinner, partly to welcome Laina to Georgia and partly to catch up with his former student.

Eventually, the plane took off and Emmitt was granted use of his laptop. He pulled down his tray table and navigated the internet purchase quickly. He had several unread emails. One was Addison responding to the email he had sent from the airport and another was Laina checking in before she left Shreveport that morning. Laina was not impressed with either Odessa or Shreveport. One was a "*middle of nowhere desert*" and the other was a "*horrible swamp town*". So much for broadening this California girl's horizons. Apparently, he hadn't been completely dishonest with that statement after all. Emmitt congratulated himself on helping her see more of the country. She would thank him later. He scrolled through the rest of the emails and decided the rest could wait until later. He wanted to get up to date with Dr. Watt's lab.

Emmitt went to the university's webpage and found the listings for the faculty. Dr. Watt was the chair of the Integrative Biology and Pharmacology Department. This most likely allowed them to hire any professor with any specificity in the biology field. He had a rather large lab, which was not surprising for a department chair. His lab included a handful of research professors that probably did a lot of the grad student and postdoc training so that he could focus on some of the more administrative areas of his job. Watt's lab had four postdoctoral fellows and six graduate students. It looked like he was still studying various membrane proteins using crystallography.

Watt had won several awards in research since Emmitt had been a student, though he had won a few during Emmitt's time too. Emmitt noticed a link to view photos from the welcoming reception the department had for Watt when he was brought on as the chair back in the spring. He decided to click through them as well. He had scrolled through five or six photos when he thought he saw another familiar face. He tried to zoom in, but the resolution was too poor. He went through the remainder of the photos, but didn't see the person again. For some reason, it gave him an uneasy feeling. He made a mental note to figure out who this person was. He didn't want to raise suspicion, but uncertainties were what brought down empires. He went back to looking through Watt's list of recently published papers. It would be fun to catch up with his mentor and talk science together.

After reading through three of the papers, Emmitt checked his watch. He was irritated to see that there was still an hour left in the flight. Everything was taking forever lately. He clicked back over to the faculty list and found Addison's name. He had visited this site many times and was already familiar with the people in her lab, but wanted to read another paper or two before he toured the lab tomorrow. He pulled out a notebook from his bag and a pen so he could jot down any notes or thoughts.

He wondered how long it would take Laina to learn the patch

clamp technique. She was very confident that she could master it easily, but Emmitt had heard that it could be challenging. It was probably like many things, some people caught on fast and others struggled. Laina always seemed to fall on the lucky side of challenges, so maybe he shouldn't worry about it at all. He read through the two papers he'd selected and took a few notes for later. He was just closing the second one when he felt the plane start to dip down. *Finally! We're starting to descend,* he thought. He shut down the laptop and put it back into his bag with the notebook and pen.

Atlanta's airport and car rental facility could not have been further apart. Emmitt knew this from his trip last month, but still found it irritating. The office at the apartment complex closed at five o'clock and Laina would be pissed at him if he didn't get her key today. He tried to mentally will the plane to get to the gate faster.

Chapter 25

Laina was tired of driving. It seemed like she had been in the car for weeks and she would never get to Atlanta. Maybe she should have listened to Emmitt and invited a friend to ride along with her. She groaned. Inviting a friend was not without risks though. They would want to know why she was going to Atlanta and have literally days to pepper her with questions about what she would be doing and how long she would be gone. She wasn't sure she could give vague and ambiguous answers the whole way. Plus, she wasn't sure she had a good enough friend to ask anyway. She spent most of her time in the lab or sleeping or going to her daily Pilates class. Who needed friends anyway?

She saw a sign up ahead and hoped it would say that Atlanta was less than fifty miles away. *Why hadn't someone invented a teleporter yet?* She sighed when she saw the sign: *51 miles. Of course, it had to be just over what she had wished for. Ugh.* Emmitt really owed her one for making her drive this whole way. She was determined to find a way to get him to drive her car back to LA in six months. This cross country driving sucked.

Thankfully, her car had Bluetooth, so when she got desperate, she could call someone. She checked the time and mentally adjusted it for the new time zone. Emmitt should have landed by now and hopefully had secured her apartment key. She thought about calling him to check in. He had been really on edge lately. Obviously, things were starting to heat up with this project, but she had hoped that his continued trust in her and her abilities would amount to more significance. He had shut that idea down, but she knew he was tempted. She'd try again in a few weeks. Invite him down for Thanksgiving or something festive like that. She was playing out the idea in her mind when her phone rang through on Bluetooth. It was Emmitt. Speak of the devil.

"Well, hello, Emmitt. Please tell me you have my apartment key."

"I just unlocked your new front door, Laina. The apartment

looks really nice. I'm not sure if you realized this when you made the arrangements, but it is across the street from the building that the Fischer lab is in."

"It's not *university* housing, is it? I specifically made sure not to look at any of those options. Gross."

"No, it's not university housing. No student could afford this place. All of their housing is about a mile away. They take the bus."

"Phew. And yes, I knew it was close to the campus, but the campus is huge. This could be an added advantage. I will always know when someone is there and when I can work alone."

"Very true. I don't know what floor the lab is on, but it's quite possible that your apartment faces the lab. I guess we'll find out tomorrow."

"I don't believe for a second that you aren't going to go over there today. It's only 4:30. I know you're tempted."

"I actually already called to see if I could stop by since I got here early. Dr. Fischer said that it would be fine if I wanted to drop by, so I'm headed over there next. I just wanted to check on your apartment first. You're on the sixth floor. Call me when you get in and I'll come back over with the key."

"Don't keep me waiting, Emmitt. I am so ready to get out of this car and never drive it again."

"Oh, I got your parking pass for the garage too. I guess you should call me sooner so that I can help buzz you into that too."

"Great. I'll see you in half an hour. Be ready for me to call." She hung up. She was really getting close now. She was getting Chinese food delivered and relaxing the rest of the evening. Maybe she would schedule a massage for tomorrow morning if she could find one. She was so stiff from being cooped up in this car for four days.

Chapter 26

Addison ended the call with Emmitt and dialed over to the lab. Just as she had suspected, Emmitt was *in the neighborhood* and wondered if he could stop by a day early. She was doubly thankful that her lab had shown up early to get the space ready. She didn't want him to second guess his decision to collaborate with their group.

"Hey, Eleanor. I'm sure you're about to take off. I just wanted to let you know that Emmitt is headed this way. He got in early and wants to stop by."

"I can stick around if you need me to, Dr. Fischer."

"Don't be ridiculous. Is anyone else still working?"

"Anthony is cleaning up after his experiment, but everyone else is gone."

"Perfect. If you could just let him know that I'll be by with Dr. Strydent in a few minutes, that would be great. I'll see you tomorrow, Eleanor!"

"Will do. Thanks, Dr. Fischer."

Addison had given up trying to get Eleanor to call her something other than Dr. Fischer at work. She was always very proper and business-like at the lab and would not use her first name or Dr. Fish like some of the other lab members. Addison grabbed her keys and double checked that her badge was still on her wrist. Emmitt said that he would be out front any minute now, so she hoped the elevator didn't take forever.

Fortunately, the elevator was just opening as Addison walked up. Dr. Shelley was already waiting for it. *Perfect timing,* Addison thought.

"Hello again, Zenia. How was your day?"

"Oh, about the same as usual. You look like you're in a hurry. Where are you headed at the end of the day?"

"My new collaborator *just happened* to be in the area and asked if he could drop by the lab." She said with air quotes.

"One of those, huh? Well, at least you know he'll be working hard to get the project finished if he's already chomping at the bit to get it started." She laughed.

Zenia got off at the second floor to take the cat walk to the parking garage. Addison tapped her foot as she waited for the doors to close and the car to take her down another level. The elevator opened up and Addison spotted Emmitt waiting outside the glass double doors. She waved him over and opened the door to let him in.

"Hello, Emmitt. How was the flight?"

"It was pretty easy. I had a direct flight, so the only challenge is navigating the time change. Thankfully they gave us some snacks on the plane. I'll probably eat an early dinner though. Snacks can only carry you for so long."

Addison pressed the up button on the elevator and was relieved that it was still there from her trip down. They stepped onto the elevator and she hit the 8 to go back up to the lab.

"Have you spoken with Laina? How is the driving going?"

"She is almost here, I think. I told her that I was just popping over to say hi and that I would be back down to buzz her into her parking garage by the time she arrived."

"Wait, back down? Did you walk here from her apartment?"

"Yes, it's actually right across the street. She wanted something a little nicer than the, uh, university housing options."

"Oh! Wow. Well, that will certainly be convenient for her." Addison tried to hide her surprise and judgment. The apartments across the street were rather expensive for a postdoc, in her opinion. Of course, maybe compared to prices in California, they seemed cheap.

"I think it will work out nicely. After you," he said, holding the elevator open for her.

"Thank you. Right this way. We're the last three doors at the end of the hall." She pointed to the right.

"How nice that you get some space with windows! Lots of labs that I have visited are all in the interior of the building." He looked out the window and saw that Laina's apartment did indeed face the lab. *How fortunate.*

"Well, this is it. There's not a lot going on right now. Everyone came early today to finish setting up for Laina, so Anthony is the only one still here."

"I noticed that the doors have keyless entry rather than being unlocked with a key. That's pretty modern."

"Yeah, the university put all of that in. They said they needed to know who was in the building and where, so we all have these fobs to get in and out of the lab. We keep it open during the day when everyone's here, though, so I'm not sure how effective the system is." She walked into the second room where Anthony was finishing cleaning up his bench.

"Anthony, this is Dr. Strydent. He just stopped by to say hi. We'll be meeting with him and Dr. Hibber tomorrow."

"Dr. Strydent. It's great to meet you."

"Please, call me Emmitt. *Laina* and I are looking forward to this opportunity. Did you have a good day in the lab today?"

"Oh, yes. Definitely. I'm really starting to make some progress with my project. I just need to buckle down and get a few last experiments completed. Dr. Fish—uh, Dr. Fischer has asked me to help train, uh, Laina with patch clamp. It's a fun technique." He stammered a bit, unsure which names to use.

"Relax, Anthony. We're much more casual with names. Hell, even Addison lets me use her first name now."

Anthony blushed. "Yes, sir, uh, Emmitt."

Emmitt laughed. "Well, we won't keep you from your day. Nice to meet you, Anthony. Good luck with your project."

Addison walked past Emmitt and Anthony to the bench they had cleared for Laina. "This will be Laina's space here. Her desk is just next to the bench. We also have a postdoc room for them to take a break in if they need it. Juan can show that to her tomorrow."

"It looks great, Addison. I think this project is really going to be a good thing for both our labs." His phone started to ring with a little island music. Emmitt's face got a little red as he quickly pulled it from his pocket.

"This is Laina. She must be close. Can I show myself out, or do I need an escort?" He asked while accepting the call.

Addison waved goodbye to Anthony and led Emmitt from the lab back to the elevators. The official policy was that visitors were supposed to be led from the building, so she decided not to push her luck and rode down the elevator with him while he talked to Laina.

Emmitt moved the phone away from his ear for a second. "We will see you tomorrow, Addison. Thanks for the quick tour." She nodded in agreement as the elevator doors closed. The spontaneous tour had gone pretty well from her perspective. She waited for the elevator to return her to the eighth floor and texted Ryan, *"Emmitt just stopped by. Surprise, surprise."* She pocketed her phone and went back to see if Anthony had finished cleaning up yet.

He was just putting his ice bucket back into the cabinet when she walked in.

"Hey, Dr. Fish. How'd I do?"

"Ha ha. You were great, Anthony. Thank you for taking a moment to chat with—Emmitt." She paused before saying his name. She normally didn't care at all about names, but Emmitt had rubbed her the wrong way when they ran into each other at the keynote address last month. She wished it didn't bother her so much.

"Well, I'm all finished up here. My experiment went really well, by the way. You'll get to see and hear all about it in lab meeting on Friday."

"I'm glad to hear that. I knew that you could get through this if you put your mind to it. I'll lock up. See you tomorrow, Anthony."

"Thanks, Dr. Fish. See you then." He grabbed his backpack and left.

Addison double checked that everything was turned off and shut down. Anthony did seem to have turned over a new leaf, but a little caution didn't hurt. She was pleased to see that everything was as it should be, so she shut off the lights and pulled the doors closed. She went back to her office and gathered up her things so that she could head home too. Hopefully, tomorrow would go just as smoothly as today.

Chapter 27

Laina pulled up at the entrance to the parking garage of her new apartment complex. She scanned the sidewalks for Emmitt and was about to dial him again when she saw him waving by the card reader. She waited for him to hop into the car, then pulled forward.

"Here's your new parking pass, Laina."

"Thanks. Hopefully I won't have to do too much driving around here. I mean, it's not LA traffic, but it's still there. I'm so tired of being in this car!" She grabbed the card from him and swiped it at the reader. The arm didn't move.

"Ugh! What is wrong with this thing? Are you sure they activated it?" She said with irritation.

"Maybe try it a little slower. I think you did it too fast." Emmitt suggested.

Laina glared at him and made a show of how slowly she could run the pass over the card reader. She was almost dismayed that his suggestion worked, but the desire to get out of the car was much stronger.

"Okay, at least it works. Are there assigned spaces or can I just park wherever?"

"There aren't assigned spaces, but there is a catwalk to each floor of the building, so you will probably want to park on the sixth floor."

"Number 6 it is." She said as she wound around the garage and up the levels. There were plenty of available spaces on the 6th floor, so she parked nearest the entrance to the catwalk.

"I have three suitcases, one wardrobe bag, and a handful of boxes that need to be carried inside." She told Emmitt.

"Why don't you get the roller bags and I'll see what all I can handle in one trip. We can always come back for more."

"I'm only making one trip. I'm exhausted, Emmitt. I've been inside the car for four days. You wouldn't ride here with me, at least help me out by carrying my bags and stuff." She dragged two of the roller bags from the trunk and started wheeling them towards the catwalk.

Emmitt groaned inwardly. Laina was really getting to be high maintenance. He pulled out the third roller bag and grabbed the wardrobe bag too. Laina was already at the cat walk entrance.

"I think you want to lock this in between trips." He called out to her.

"Here." She tossed her keys back at him and then realized that she couldn't enter the cat walk without some sort of pass.

Emmitt picked up the keys and locked her car. He had the card to get into the cat walk in his front pocket, so he pulled that out before walking over to Laina.

"This is your building pass. It's separate from the parking pass. The office lady recommended that you not leave the building pass in your car if you drive it to work or wherever because it's not very heat tolerant. The parking pass should be fine though."

Laina took the pass and got the doors open. She hurriedly walked down the hallway then realized she didn't know which unit was hers. She turned around and waited for Emmitt.

"Where am I going?"

"Unit 631. It's the third one on your left." He caught up to her and got her apartment key out of his pocket.

"This is just a regular old key. It works in the knob and the deadbolt."

Laina stood the suitcases up and unlocked her new apartment. It smelled clean and fresh, which was reassuring to her after being cooped up in her car forever.

"Thank you for helping me carry things in. I'm sorry if I'm rude by not helping, but I really am tired. I think I might see if I can book a massage somewhere for tomorrow." She sat down on the couch and sighed.

"Laina, in case you forgot, I'm your boss. Not the other way around. I'm not your servant and I'm not carrying all your damn stuff inside. He handed her the car keys.

Laina's mouth dropped and her eyes widened in anger. Who did he think he was, trying to put her in her place this way? Emmitt was normally very in control and rarely lost his temper, but she could see that it was about to boil over this time. She glared at him but bit her tongue. She watched as he stomped out of the apartment and wanted to cry thinking about all the trips she needed to make to get her things inside. At the last second, he stopped and turned back to her.

"Don't forget, I'm meeting you downstairs by the entrance tomorrow at 12:50."

Laina pouted. "You aren't going to help me unpack either?"

"No. You're an adult. Act like one." He turned and walked out the door.

Chapter 28

Addison was up early again on Thursday. Ryan had wished her well and said that he'd make sure the kids were on their way out the door on time. She wanted to get through any email and departmental duties well before Emmitt and Laina arrived at one. Thankfully, she didn't have any meetings the rest of the week. They did still have lab meeting and journal club on Friday, but since she went to those every week, they didn't feel like extra work. She remembered that she hadn't read the journal club article yet and made a mental note to do it before lunch.

She had to balance her coffee, lunch, and phone to get her key out to her office door. She managed to get the door open without dropping anything, but the process made her remember the note she'd tucked away to show Ryan. She had completely forgotten about it and couldn't remember where she'd stuck it. Hopefully it wasn't destroyed in the wash. She should have taken a picture of it and texted it to him right then. *Think. Where did you stick that note, Addison?* Then she remembered - the laptop bag. She rummaged around in all of its pockets before she found the scrap of paper, wishing she had remembered to mention it to Ryan ten days ago. She couldn't imagine who would have had a beef with Emmitt that also knew her. The only person that she knew who knew both of them was Dr. Watt. He had obviously approved the collaboration, so he must not have any issues with Emmitt being associated with one of his faculty members. She put the note in her jeans pocket and thumbed a text to Ryan. *Remind me to tell you about a random note that someone left in my office.* He responded with the big eye emoji.

Addison got settled for the day and started going through her emails again. The university really needed a better spam filter. It took some doing, but soon she was back to zero unread messages. She checked her watch and realized that Eleanor was usually at work by now, so she picked up the phone to call her.

"Hey Eleanor. Just wanted to check in and make sure

everything is ready for our tour and guests this afternoon. I mean, it looked great yesterday. Thank you again for making that happen."

"We're happy to help. We all know this is a big opportunity for you and for our lab. Everything is just as it was yesterday. Clean and ready to show off." She laughed.

"Wonderful. I assume everyone will be here in the next half hour or so. I'll stop by around ten to check in."

"Sounds good. We'll see you then."

Addison looked up the journal club article and downloaded it to print and read. She still liked to have paper copies so that she could write on them and highlight anything of interest. It was only seven pages, so she should be able to read through it quickly. She just had to will her mind to focus. She was ready for it to be time for the tour and meeting Laina, as well as introducing her to the lab.

Chapter 29

Laina had searched through Yelp reviews for a good massage place near the apartment building. Thankfully, there were several nearby hotels that also had spas with good ratings and reviews. She was able to book an appointment at 9:30 a.m. Thursday morning. She slept in until 8:30, realized she had no food, so she skipped showering and got some coffee and a bagel from the hotel lobby. She was irritated that she hadn't thought about needing groceries until she was hungry. Maybe the stores in Atlanta offered grocery pick up or delivery. She could ask the masseuse or the lab people. Someone would know. She really did not want to have to drive anywhere for at least a day or two. She still had to make a list though.

The 60-minute massage was worth every penny. She wondered if she could find a way to squeeze a monthly massage into her budget because she felt so much better when she walked out of the spa. The masseuse said that stores did deliver groceries, but she wasn't sure which store was the closest. Laina put off unpacking for another thirty minutes while she found the closest store with delivery and placed a grocery order. Since it was her first time using the service, she only had to wait 24 hours for a delivery time. It looked like the normal wait time was two to three days. For only $5, she could make that work. Thankfully, she had decided to bring her own Keurig to Atlanta because the apartment did not have a coffee pot, nor did it have any coffee for her to use. *How can you call it a* furnished *apartment if there isn't a coffee maker?!* She wondered to herself. She added a big package of pods to her grocery list and then submitted the order. It would be delivered tomorrow at eight, which was before the lab meeting thing that everyone wanted her to go to.

Laina had an hour and a half before she had to meet Emmitt out front, so she decided she might as well start unpacking. What a dreadful job. She couldn't wait until she and Emmitt made it big and she could just pay people to do whatever she didn't want to do.

Chapter 30

After reading through some of the recent first tier journals that he subscribed to, Emmitt spent the morning checking in with the other members of his lab in LA. He knew it was a little early, but he was also familiar with their daily routines and when they typically arrived to the lab. He didn't want everyone taking time off just because he wasn't there, so he called to check in whenever he went out of town. He knew that they were aware of that after being with him for a few years. He didn't think that he was an overly demanding boss or advisor, but he was clear about how he wanted things to work. Normally, Laina was still there when he went out of town. He occasionally had her travel to conferences and give talks about their projects in his place, but usually, it was him who was on the road and she who was left in charge. It was a bit of a risk to not have either one present, especially if someone got curious or suspicious about how the lab was run with its own reagents and cell lines rather than purchasing things from vendors like most labs. Emmitt wondered where he would be if he had just come clean about the mistake back in graduate school. *Not on my way to getting funded by a big pharmaceutical company!* He thought. If only he hadn't gotten curious and used the lab's new DNA sequencer to look at the channel. He wouldn't have learned that it had a mutation. He was lucky that no one had studied his little protein before, so no one knew what to expect of it. He got to introduce STABL to the world and tell its story. Requesting retraction back then would have derailed his career early on. He would never have made it as big as he had now.

He called each of his other postdoctoral fellows first. He knew neither of them had what it took to make it as a PI and that both hoped to get a research position either as faculty at a small school or under a project manager with a pharmaceutical company. Neither one could come up with the thought-provoking, technical questions that helped push a project forward. They were happy to be told what to do and when and how.

He called his lab manager next. Her name was Cindy. She didn't really know a lot about science, but she was very organized and made sure reagents arrived on time as needed. Cindy was coordinating the shipment of the mice pups as well as the cell lines and other reagents that Laina would be using while in Atlanta. Emmitt had left her a detailed list about what was to be sent and when it needed to arrive.

"Hi, Cindy. It's Emmitt. Just checking in. Is everything set for the various shipments we discussed?"

"Hi, Emmitt. Good to hear from you. Yes. I overnighted the cell lines and the DNA constructs yesterday afternoon, so they should arrive sometime today. They are all on dry ice and packaged appropriately. I can forward you the tracking numbers if you need them."

"That's not necessary. Thank you for arranging everything. I let Addison know that they would be coming today or tomorrow, so her lab should be expecting the delivery. Maybe it will arrive while we're there!"

"Wouldn't that be nice? I know you have been a little nervous about getting the reagents there safely. Hopefully, it won't be an issue at all."

"I think it will be just fine. People overnight reagents all the time without any issue. I think that's all I needed, so I'll let you get back to it. Feel free to call me at any point if you have any questions. I fly back tomorrow afternoon."

"Sounds great. I guess I will see you Monday, then."

"See you Monday, Cindy. Thanks again." He ended the call and tried to decide if any of the grad students would be at the lab yet. He could have asked Cindy, but he liked to pretend that they didn't all know that he called all of them while he was away. He decided to give them a break for now and call later. He wondered how Laina was doing. He needed to figure out what to do for lunch so that he would be ready to meet her later. The hotel had a restaurant on the second floor, and he figured that would be just as easy as anywhere else. He pocketed his phone and walked over to the elevator bay to ride it down to the restaurant.

Chapter 31

"Okay, everyone. I'm going to head downstairs and get Dr. Strydent and Dr. Hibber. Does anyone have any final questions before I go?"

"No, Dr. Fish. We're ready. We'll be here when you get back up." Juan told her.

She pressed the call button for the elevator and tried not to feel anxious while she waited for the car to arrive. She had been stressing out about this meeting and tour for over a week. She took a deep breath to try to relax. She was prepared and couldn't do anything else to make it better. The elevator finally opened. She stepped on and lifted her chin. She was confident in herself and her lab.

Emmitt and Laina were walking up to the building when Addison stepped outside. She smiled and waved them over to the entrance. Laina didn't look as tired as Addison had expected.

"Welcome. It is so great to have you both here."

"Dr. Fischer, this is Laina. Laina, Dr. Fischer." Emmitt said, introducing the two women.

"Please, call me Addison. It's nice to meet you, Laina. If you follow me, I will take you up to the lab."

"It is great to meet you, too, Addison. Thank you for giving us a tour this afternoon. I'm really excited to see the lab space and meet everyone too." Laina smiled.

Laina had pulled her long blonde hair back into a low ponytail and was wearing black slacks, low pumps, a white button-up shirt, and a blazer. Emmitt was surprised that her clothes looked so fresh after traveling across the country in a wardrobe bag for three days. Emmitt was wearing a suit as usual. He had brought his favorite black suit that had a pale blue pinstripe and matched his blue tie perfectly. Addison held the elevator doors open for them as they stepped into the car.

"The lab is on the eighth floor, as is my office and the rest of the department. Occasionally, we have to use some equipment on other floors, but for the most part, everything we do takes place on eight." Addison told them.

"That's very convenient. How many labs are in your department?" Laina asked.

"I think we just hired our fifteenth PI in August. Dr. Watt has a plan to expand to twenty over the next five or six years."

"That's ambitious! Emmitt has always had great things to say about Watt, though."

"He is very driven," said Emmitt.

They stepped off of the elevator and followed Addison towards the lab space.

"Our labs are the last three doors on the right. Everyone is waiting to meet you just inside the second door."

They stepped inside the room and found Becky, Anthony, Juan, and Eleanor sitting at their desks. They all immediately stood up when they heard them enter. Eleanor rushed over to greet each of them.

"Good afternoon! We are so excited to have you here today. I'm sorry that I missed you yesterday, Dr. Strydent. I heard that you stopped by right after I left for the day." Eleanor said, reaching her hand out to shake theirs.

"Please, call me Emmitt. Everyone does."

Eleanor just smiled and Addison had to stifle a laugh, knowing that Eleanor would never call him Emmitt.

"Dr. Hibber, we are thrilled to have you working with us too. I hope the drive wasn't too terrible for you."

"It's Laina, and I survived." She smiled at Eleanor and shook her hand.

The rest of the lab members walked over and introduced themselves too. Emmitt paused when it was Anthony's turn and turned to Laina. "This is Anthony. He's the one who's going to teach you how to patch."

Anthony looked a little awkward for once and stuttered out his introduction. Addison wondered if he was surprised by Laina's good looks. Addison had seen photos of her on the Strydent lab webpage but hadn't realized that Anthony had never looked through the site on his own. She tried to hide her amusement. Hopefully, he could get over his awkwardness quickly and help Laina learn the technique.

"Well, nice to finally meet you, Anthony. Sounds like we are going to get to know each other really well over the next few months." Laina said to him. Addison noticed Anthony had blushed just slightly and wondered if Laina had winked when she spoke. She had a bit of a flirtatious air about her. Addison glanced at Eleanor to see if she had noticed. Eleanor's face told her all she needed to know: that was a yes.

Addison broke the tension by clearing her throat. "Laina, your benchtop will be over here, next to the one Anthony uses. Becky and Juan share the other side. Your desk is at the end of the row there. Juan set up a desktop computer for you. We knew you were bringing a laptop, but figured you would want something that was connected to the departmental servers too." She walked over to the desk and Laina followed.

"That's perfect. I will probably only bring the laptop in from time to time. Thank you for thinking ahead. Do I need to set up a login today or has that already been taken care of?"

"The folder on the desk has all of the network access information. You will start with a temporary password and then be prompted to reset it once you log in the first time." Eleanor told her.

"Great. I guess that can probably wait until tomorrow."

"Certainly. Tomorrow we can get your login set up as well as get you an ID badge to enter the building. They will issue that along with the fob to get into the labs. Now, the room behind us has all of the patch clamp equipment in it and the room that we already passed is our tissue culture bay and freezers. Which would you like to see first?" Addison asked.

"Tissue culture bays are a dime a dozen. Let's go see where the magic happens." Emmitt responded.

They filed out of the lab room and went into the patch clamp room. Addison let Juan and Anthony do most of the talking about the experimental space. She knew that they were familiar enough with it.

"This is where we pull the glass pipettes, which is actually pretty fun. Some of the neighboring labs will occasionally borrow time on the apparatus, but it's a quick use item, so there's never a line or anything." Anthony told them.

"How many patch pipettes do you need for one day of experiments?" Emmitt asked.

"Well, that depends on if it's a good day or a not so good day. If you're patching cells well and getting a good seal, you only need one per cell that you patch. You can't reuse the pipette from cell to cell because components of the cell membrane will stay attached to the glass and could alter your readings. On a really good day, I can probably get data from four or five cells. Other days, I might go through several pipettes trying to get a baseline going because I lower the pipette too far and break it, or the pipette was too jagged and ruptures the cell or it's too humid…it can be finicky some days. Other days, you find a rhythm and get lots of data."

"Over here is where we run the experiments," Juan spoke up. "We place our solutions up on the shelf above and have tubing that runs down to the dish with the cells that we are studying below. Then, we use the microscope to lower the patch pipette down to the surface of the cell. All of this is connected to the computer, which gives us a read out of our measurements. We can switch solutions by using this apparatus."

Emmitt and Laina stepped closer to look at the experimental setup. Neither had ever tried this type of technique and found it really interesting to see all the gadgets that went into the process.

"While our crystallography work is very different from what you're doing here, it still involves a lot of math once you have a crystal to measure and study. Fortunately, they have developed a lot of useful software over the years to help you sift through all the data that you can get from analyzing a crystal. Do you use specific software with your process here?" Emmitt asked.

"We do for some parts, but for others we are able to do some fairly simple calculations on our own, or in a spreadsheet," Juan answered.

"Any other questions?" Addison asked.

"Is there any chance that we can watch an experiment in action today, or does it take too long to set something like that up?" Emmitt asked the group.

"Actually, I have an experiment set up for today. I was going to start it after we finished the tour, but I can get going on that now. It will take me twenty minutes or so to get everything going."

"Why don't we go look at the freezer and make sure that's set up while Anthony gets ready?" Addison suggested. As the rest of the group turned to head toward the door, she turned around and mouthed *thank you* to Anthony. She had not expected them to ask to watch an experiment.

"Sounds good to me," Laina said and stepped out of the room.

Juan stayed behind to help Anthony gather supplies while the rest of the group went back to the main lab room. Addison had plugged in the smaller freezer by Laina's bench so that it could start cooling off before anything arrived. They hadn't engaged the coded lock, yet.

"We got your samples this morning and put them in the freezer straight away," Eleanor said from her desk. "I can show you the packing slip if you need to make sure that everything made it. A couple of the items were listed as cell lines, so I put those in our liquid nitrogen freezer—that's how we store all of our cells."

"We didn't set up the lock mechanism yet. We assumed you and Laina would want to take care of that." Addison explained. The whole freezer thing made her a little nervous because she knew it was important to them. She hoped everything was how they expected.

"Thank you for thinking ahead about the cells, Eleanor. I had forgotten that they would need to be in the nitrogen tank instead of this freezer." Emmitt opened up the freezer and removed the square cardboard box with a piece of bright yellow tape that Eleanor had labeled *Strydent lab—Dr. Hibber samples*. The box held six microcentrifuge tubes with various labels and three other vials as well. "Everything looks great. Thank you for taking care of this for us."

Addison turned to Emmitt. "I know your cell lines are patented too. Is it going to be okay that they are in our nitrogen tank? It doesn't have a lock, but it is kept locked in our lab when no one is here."

"I will double check with my legal team, but I think it should be okay." He responded. In truth, no one required him to use a locked freezer for any of these reagents. He just didn't want anyone else to have access to them without his knowledge. The cell lines were less of an issue since everyone else in the lab wouldn't have any reason to borrow those as they had their own system already.

"Great. We'll just stick with how it is until you say otherwise then." Addison said. "What time are you supposed to meet with Dr. Watt?"

"Not until 2:30. I wasn't sure how long it would take to tour your lab, so I gave us plenty of time. He said we could come by earlier if we finish up before then."

Addison checked her watch. It had been about twenty minutes since they left Anthony and Juan to set up the experiment. "Let's go see if Anthony is ready for us."

While they were walking to the room next door, Addison realized that Becky had been hanging back and not getting involved in the discussion much. She knew she was young, but wished she would show a little assertiveness. She couldn't really put her on the spot right now. Becky seemed to be fairly shy and Addison knew that wouldn't really help her join the conversation.

Juan was adjusting some of the tubing in the solutions when they walked back in. Anthony was at the microscope tinkering with the dials. The computer screen had an empty graph displayed. Juan looked up and waved them over.

"Anthony is just getting a cell patched now. You will see the signal show up on the graph once he gets it." Juan pointed at the screen.

Addison was mentally crossing her fingers that Anthony would have some success. Part of her was glad that she hadn't considered that they would need to put their technique on display. She would have lost even more sleep if she'd known that! She kept her eyes on the screen as Anthony fine-tuned the dials while looking through the microscope. She released her breath silently when she saw the blue line appear on the graph. Anthony had a big grin on his face.

"Got it! Awesome. Okay, so this is just the baseline measurement for this cell. It's what we typically see. If you see any big fluctuations in the voltage reading before you have added a new solution to the mix, then your cell is probably about to die. It's a rather delicate procedure, but you can get a lot of information from it if you're careful." He stepped over to the solution apparatus and turned the dial to the right.

"I'm adding our control response drug now. We start each experiment with it to make sure the cell is healthy and responding in the normal way." The line on the graph went up briefly and then back down.

"So that change in voltage shows us that the channels opened and then closed, returning to baseline." He told them.

He walked them through the rest of his experiment for that cell, explaining what he was looking for and how he expected the cell to respond as he did it. Addison couldn't have been prouder. He hoped that this was giving Emmitt more confidence in their group.

"This is incredible! You make it look so easy." Laina told Anthony, whose neck turned red. Addison hoped Emmitt wasn't noticing Anthony's reaction to Laina's praise.

"Umm, Dr. Fischer?" Becky spoke up. Addison looked her way with curiosity. "I'm sorry to interrupt, but I really need to go treat my cells for tomorrow, or I'm going to have to scrap my experiment."

"Oh, of course, Becky. Go right ahead." That must have been what was keeping her extra quiet. She checked her watch again.

"It's about 2:20 now, so if you don't have any more questions for us, I can walk you over to Dr. Watt's office."

"I'm all set. Laina?"

"I'm ready. Thank you for taking time to show us your equipment and even put on a little show here. I'm really excited to get started on our project." She smiled at Anthony and nodded towards Juan and Addison.

Chapter 32

"She seems a little flirty." Juan observed after Addison had left with their guests.

"You think so?" Anthony asked.

"Oh, come *on*. She winked at you and everything. Watch yourself, man."

"I can handle myself. I'm a professional."

"I'm not sure you can handle her. Don't say I didn't warn you."

"It will be fine. She's only gonna be here half a year anyway. Nothing to worry about."

"I better not see you being her little whipping boy then. You can teach her how to patch, but you don't need to be her servant."

"Hey, man. Relax, I'm telling you, it will be fine."

Juan rolled his eyes and left the room, almost running into Addison on his way out.

"Anthony! Wow! You really saved us there. Thank you so much for stepping up to do your experiment for our visitors. I had no idea that they would want to see a display of what we can do. I'm sorry that they put you on the spot."

"Hey, no problem, Dr. Fish. I'm glad I had one set up and ready to go today. Plus, I even got some data that I can use for my project."

"Wonderful. I can't tell you how much I appreciate your assertiveness and leadership today." She paused. "Um, is everything okay with Juan? He seemed upset on his way out of here."

"Oh, he's fine. We were just discussing the goals of our newest lab member. It's not a big deal."

Addison crooked her head at Anthony, but didn't say anything. She didn't really want discord in the lab, but she also didn't want to press him on it after he had risen to the lab's needs earlier. She decided to let it drop for now.

"Okay, well, I'm going to check in with Becky before heading back to my office. Let me know if you need anything."

"Will do, Dr. Fish."

Addison walked over to Becky's desk, where she was writing in her notebook.

"Hi, Dr. Fischer. I'm just getting my next experiment mapped out. I'm hoping to run it tomorrow. Will Emmitt and Laina be here most of the morning?"

"I'm not sure. I know that they are coming to our lab meeting and Laina will need to work with the front office staff to get her badge and fob set up. Emmitt flies out later tomorrow afternoon, so he probably won't stay past lunch." Addison wondered if Becky was uncomfortable with them being around.

"Oh okay, but we don't need to really *host* Laina tomorrow, right?"

"No, I think Eleanor can help her with anything that the office staff can't."

"Okay, great. Sounds like I will be able to do my experiment tomorrow."

"Is everything okay, Becky? You seemed a little extra shy while Emmitt and Laina were with us today."

"Everything is fine. It just takes me a little while to interact with new people, you know? I'll try to communicate more tomorrow." Becky smiled.

"Okay. I'll leave you to it, then."

Chapter 33

Emmitt and Laina waited in the office for Dr. Watt to come to get them. It looked like his lab space was behind all of the offices, but also had a side entrance from the hallways. Emmitt glanced at some of the certificates and photos on the wall. One of the photos was of the whole lab and he immediately noticed the familiar face from the website. He just couldn't place where he had met the person before.

"You look deep in thought," Laina observed.

"I'm just checking out the photos and accolades on the wall. Seeing if I recognize anyone."

"And do you?"

"Do I what?"

Laina rolled her eyes. "Recognize anyone?"

"Maybe. I'm not sure who it is though."

"This conversation is fascinating." She rolled her eyes again and started to pull out her phone. "What did you think of the Fischer lab?"

Emmitt tore his gaze from the photo. "I was surprisingly impressed with Anthony. Addison had said that he was kind of a hot mess, but he definitely knows what he's doing with that equipment. It was neat to watch."

"*Neat.* What are you, five?" Laina said derogatorily.

Before Emmitt could answer, Dr. Watt entered the front office. They both stood up to greet him.

"Emmitt! It's great to see you. Thank you for stopping by."

"Ben, it's great to see you too. This is my top postdoc, Laina Hibber." Emmitt said, introducing Laina.

"Nice to meet you, sir," Laina said politely.

"The pleasure is all mine, my dear. I have been following your work since you graduated from my lab, Emmitt. You are really making strides in the membrane world. I'm sorry that I missed your talk last month. Too many responsibilities to get away for something fun. I've cleared my schedule for this afternoon though. Let's go to my office."

They followed Dr. Watt to his office, which was beautifully decorated. It had mahogany arm chairs with turquoise cushions and plush, pale turquoise carpet. His large mahogany desk faced the door, but behind it you could see the Atlanta skyline easily. Two of the walls were filled with ceiling to floor filing cabinets. His desk had photos of young children, which Emmitt assumed were his grandchildren.

"Please, have a seat." He motioned to the two cushioned chairs. "So, you're going to be collaborating with the Fischer lab from what I hear. I have only met Addison in passing—haven't gotten to sit down with her yet, but her colleagues speak highly of her."

"I actually went to high school with her, if you can believe that. We didn't stay in touch, but I ran into her at that symposium last month and turns out, we're working in the same field."

"What a small world it is. I take it Dr. Hibber is going to be with us in Atlanta for the time being?"

Laina spoke up before Emmitt could answer. *She needs to relearn her place here.* He thought.

"I'm hoping that it will only be about six months, but yes, I will be here." Laina smiled at him. "And you can call me Laina."

"Well, we are happy to have you, Laina. Maybe you will fall in love with Atlanta like I have and do a second postdoc here. You know, Emmitt was one of the best graduate students that I ever trained. He had a mind for science from the beginning and was driven to find answers to all his questions." Dr. Watt laughed.

"He's definitely very focused on his work. I have learned a lot from him."

Emmitt cleared his throat. "Thank you, both. How are things going with your lab these days?"

"I don't get in the lab as much as I would like to anymore. I have a couple research professors that basically run the lab for me. I still meet with our grad students once or twice a semester, but being the department chair has a lot of other demands that take up most of my time. It's very different than being a full professor. I don't serve on any advisory committees, but I do give the occasional lecture for med students and grad students."

"We appreciate your taking time to meet with us today," Laina said.

"I wouldn't have it any other way. Are the two of you free for dinner? I would love to treat you to my favorite steak house."

Laina remained stoic, but cringed inwardly. She was a vegetarian and had been since high school. She had no desire to go to a steak house or watch other people eat red, juicy steaks.

"That's very kind of you, but I will have to take a rain check. I just arrived in town yesterday and have a lot of unpacking to do still. Thank you for the offer."

"I'd love to catch up over dinner. I'm staying down the street at the big hotel with the Greco-Roman architecture. What time would you like to meet?"

"I can pick you up from your lobby at 7. My secretary made us a reservation already."

"Sounds great. I know you cleared your schedule, but we should really let you go. Thank you again for meeting with us this afternoon. It is great to see you again." They each shook hands with Dr. Watt and walked back out to the main office.

"Sheila can take you down to the lobby. I'll see you in a few hours, Emmitt."

An older woman with long dark hair stood up at the mention of her name. She smiled and opened the office door for them. They already knew the way to the main elevators but knew that they had to have an escort still.

"Right this way," Sheila said, guiding them down the hallway. She rode the elevator down with them and watched as they exited the building before calling the elevator back to the ground floor.

"I think that went really well. What are your thoughts?"

"I'm anxious to get started so I can get back to California."

"I understand that, but what do you think of the facility and the people?"

"They all seemed nice. I'm not sure if the small, blonde one trusts me though. She was pretty quiet and stand-offish."

"Maybe she's just shy."

"I'm going to keep my eye on her. You never know with the quiet ones."

"Are you okay for dinner? I know you haven't been to the grocery store yet."

"There is nothing that I want from a steak house. Gross. And for your information, I ordered my groceries to be delivered and they will be here at 8 a.m. tomorrow."

"I know you're a vegetarian, Laina."

"I'll see you tomorrow, Emmitt. Lab meeting. 9:30 a.m." She turned and walked towards the entrance of her apartment building. Emmitt wondered if she was going to be angry about him not helping her unpack forever. He rolled his eyes and wished he didn't need her help.

Chapter 34

A ddison got home a little later than usual on Friday evening. Joe's football game was out of town and while she hated to miss it, she was ready to just sit down and relax. Even though things couldn't have gone more smoothly, it had still been a stressful two days. She grabbed her phone and dialed Ryan. The game was about to start and she wanted to touch base with him before it was too loud to hear.

"Hey, honey. How was your day?"

"It was long, but good. Anthony gave a great presentation of his work thus far for lab meeting and seemed to have won over both Laina and Emmitt. Becky even asked a couple of questions and wasn't just a wallflower in front of the two of them, so that's promising."

"Did everything go okay with Laina getting a badge and a fob and everything?"

"It did. Eleanor walked her through it and made sure she had all the right forms before they went to the different offices. It was easy."

"How were things with Juan and Anthony today? You said that things seemed tense between them yesterday."

"I'm not sure. Juan and I worked on submitting his paper most of the afternoon, so I didn't really see the two of them together today. Hopefully, it's all blown over now. How are the kids?"

"We haven't seen Joe yet. They should run onto the field any minute now. The cheerleaders are getting everything set up on the visitor side as we speak. Liv is sitting with her cross-country friends and I've got Martin next to me. His buddies didn't come this time, so I thought it was better that we stick together with all the old people."

Addison laughed. She could hear Martin groaning next to Ryan. "Okay, well, I will let you go. Cheer extra loud for me. I'm going to watch it online. Love you."

"Love you too." They ended the call and Addison wondered what she could have delivered for dinner. The Asian place up the street had recently started delivering. She liked their pot stickers and pad Thai bowl. Plus, while it wasn't really fast food, they did put it together quickly, so she wouldn't have to wait very long. She pulled up their app on her phone and placed an order for delivery. Then she grabbed a bottle of white wine from their fridge and poured herself a glass. She filled a water glass too and then turned on the TV while she waited for her food to arrive. She could stream the game over the internet and cast it onto the TV, which Martin had shown her how to do yesterday evening. She had written all the steps down because she was sure she wouldn't remember otherwise. She texted Martin an image of the TV with the game getting ready to start to show off her new skill. He gave her a thumbs up in response.

Addison kicked off her heels and waited for the game to start. Joe had mentioned that there might be some college scouts at this game, so she hoped he wasn't nervous about playing in front of them. She and Ryan had encouraged him to do his best and not think about the scouts, especially when he didn't know for sure that they would be present. She yawned. Luckily, Liv's cross-country meet was at home tomorrow and not until 10 a.m. She could sleep in a little bit before going biking with Martin and heading over to the golf course where they held the meet. Her team was getting to host the district meet this year, so it was their second home meet of the season. Next week was the regional meet and her coach thought that their team stood a good chance of qualifying for the state meet the following weekend. Addison yawned again. Hopefully she could get more sleep now that the collaboration was officially starting and virtually underway.

Chapter 35

By Monday morning, Addison was ready to be back at the office again. The weekend, while fun, had not been very restful between all of Saturday's activities and then Sunday's church activities. She had fallen asleep during the Falcon's Sunday Night Football game against the Saints, which Joe and Ryan were appalled by. *"Oh well,"* she thought, *"it's not like my watching or not watching has any effect on the game. Not my fault they lost!"*

After getting everything unloaded in her office and checking the mailroom, Addison swung by the lab to see who had arrived already. She knew Eleanor would already be there and probably Becky too. Juan had mentioned that he was going to be coming in a little later now that his paper had been submitted. She never knew with Anthony and didn't know what to expect from Laina now that she had her own badge and fob. Eleanor was at her desk sorting invoices.

"Hi, Eleanor. How was your weekend?" Addison asked, wondering why Eleanor hadn't even looked up when she entered the lab.

"Oh, it was fine. Quiet." Eleanor said simply.

"Okay. Anything else I need to know?" Addison felt like she was getting in Eleanor's way or distracting her, so she decided to forego their usual Monday morning chat where they recapped their weekend excursions.

"Oh, I think she is going to get it fixed, but Laina's fob wouldn't let her in the building this morning. Thankfully, she had her badge too, so another person let her in. She is over at the admin office seeing if they forgot to activate it or what."

"That's weird. Hopefully, it's an easy fix and not too frustrating for her. I'll be in my office if you need me."

She turned to walk out of the lab and was almost run over by Laina herself.

"Well, that was an adventure, but I think it's fixed now. They couldn't figure out why it wouldn't work. It worked fine with their system, so we took the elevator down and tried it on the door and at first, it still wouldn't activate the lock. We came back up and he reset it and reactivated it. Then we tried it again downstairs and it seems to be working again. I guess this fob was made for this high-maintenance girl." She smiled at Eleanor and Addison.

"Goodness. You would think they'd just give you a new one." Addison said.

"He said that they were currently out of new fobs. Apparently, a lot of people have been losing theirs lately, so they placed an order for new ones. Of course, those are on backorder too. Hopefully this one will be okay for now. Is Anthony back yet?"

"I think he's in the common lab still setting up some DNA cultures. I can walk you over there on my way back to my office." Addison offered.

Laina nodded and followed Addison down the hall to the space they shared with three other labs, mostly for their biochemistry assays and growing cultures. Anthony was bent over a Petri dish and had three others stacked to the side. Addison said goodbye to Laina and went back to her office.

"Oh, hey, Laina. I didn't hear you come in."

"Probably because you've still got the Bunsen burner flaring full blast." She said as she reached around him to turn off the gas.

"Oh, whoops. I was so focused on getting my sample spread out on this plate, I didn't think about it. Thanks for shutting that off. Dr. Fish is always afraid that I'm going to burn down the lab or something."

"Well, the Bunsen burner would be an easy way to do it."

"Nobody's perfect," Anthony grumbled.

"A little testy today, huh?" Laina teased.

"Nah, just honest." He smiled.

"What are you trying to grow?"

"I'm just getting some more of my two DNA samples to use in upcoming experiments as well as a couple that Becky uses too. I, uh, borrowed some from Becky a while back and need to replace those."

"That's very kind of you." She looked at his ice bucket with the microfuge tubes in it. "Two of these tubes aren't even labeled. How do you know what they are?"

"Labeling takes *forever*. I have my own system. Two lines for the channel, the alpha symbol for alpha9, you get the idea." He pointed to the little symbols. "I write down the concentration in my lab notebook and aliquot them into multiple tubes of the same color to use. I get a new color when I run out and make note of that."

"Yeah, that seems a lot easier than just writing a date and concentration on the tube in the first place, not to mention the actual name." She rolled her eyes. "Looks like Becky labeled her tubes without issue."

"Let me just stick these in the incubator and clean up. Then we can get started."

Laina watched while Anthony cleaned up the space, including disconnecting the Bunsen burner from the gas line. He removed his gloves and scrubbed his hands clean at the sink.

"Have you done tissue culture work before?" He asked while he dried his hands.

"Not actively since grad school several years ago."

"Well, stop me if I'm telling you something you already know. The most important thing is that you clean your hands well and then don't touch your face at all while you're under the hood. You would be surprised how fast bacterial contamination can spread."

"That I remember. Remind me why the solutions are in this water bath?"

"The cells need to stay at about 37°C, so we warm all the solutions to that temperature too."

Anthony walked her through sterilizing the surface with 70% ethanol and showed her which incubator they kept their cells in. Emmitt wanted Laina to use their cell line for the project, but they weren't going to thaw those until Laina had gotten comfortable with patch clamping.

"Does anyone in the lab work on the weekends?"

"Umm, occasionally Eleanor or Dr. Fish will come in to feed

the myocytes when we have those in the lab. Otherwise, everything is fairly self-sufficient. Sometimes, I'll come in on a Sunday to set up cells for an experiment, but usually I stick to Monday through Friday."

Anthony showed her how to tell if the cells were ready to be separated into more dishes, which was called splitting the cells. He demonstrated how to rinse a dish of cells with saline, and finally how to add back the media that provided sustenance for the cells.

"Will your cell line require special media? Or will you be able to use what we use? By the way, everyone has their own bottle of media and saline. That way if you only leave a little bit of solution in a bottle, you're only hurting yourself."

"Good to know. I will double-check with Emmitt, but I'm pretty sure that we just use the standard solutions."

Anthony plated some cells in a few dishes and explained what sort of cell density you would want to have in the dish for patch clamping. He set up eight dishes for them to use later in the week in their practice experiment. Addison had encouraged him to set up his cells as he would for a normal experiment while he was teaching Laina. He could still get some data for himself while helping her learn the technique.

"Tomorrow, we're going to do a transfection. Are you familiar with that?"

"Is that when you use the lipid solution to help get a DNA plasmid into your cells? I did them in grad school, but we haven't needed to do them since we made our own cell line."

"That's pretty much the gist of it. I have a few different combinations of interactions that I'm wanting to test this week. Hopefully, we can get some more readings like last Thursday. If there is anything you'd like to test from your samples, just let me know. I'm going to set aside this extra dish of cells for you to use for practicing and learning. You won't have any ready to experiment with until next week, though."

"Sounds good. I don't think I'm ready to start testing any of our reagents yet. We only shipped over a limited quantity and I don't want to stress Emmitt out by running through it too quickly."

"Okay, well, the next thing I'm going to do is finish analyzing my results from last week. You're welcome to look over my shoulder, if you'd like to learn about that too."

"Wonderful. I'm going to go check my email while you clean up here and then I'll see you at your desk in the lab?"

"It's a—" he coughed, "plan." He blushed a bit as he almost said, *it's a date!* Laina winked at him before exiting the tissue culture bay. He was glad that Juan wasn't around to witness it. He would have just gloated about being right again.

He wiped down the tissue culture hood with alcohol again and put all of his solutions away. He secretly congratulated himself for really sticking to his new directive of being a better lab-mate. He hadn't left anything out or lost any samples to his own delinquencies in over three weeks now. Maybe he had turned over a new leaf!

Laina was at her desk when he got back into the main lab room, but she heard him enter and closed down her browser window. She rolled her chair over to his desk while he booted up the computer.

"What's really nice about our department is that we have a local network that we can use for file sharing, so what I save on the computer over there, I can still access over here, or any other computer that I go into. If I save it in the general "Fischer lab" folder, then anyone in our lab can access it, but if I save it in my own folder—" he paused while he hovered the mouse over a folder labeled *awydrow*, "then only I can access it."

"Yeah, we have that too. I think the admin office was able to get me linked to this lab as well. I'm not sure if I have a folder yet or not." She said, looking over his shoulder at the screen.

"Oh, you have to create that yourself. If I created it for you, you wouldn't be able to open it. The only person who can access any of the files is Dr. Fish, but if you password protect your folder, she can't get into it without help from the IT department. Anyway, let me just pull up my files from Thursday." He clicked on his folder and dozens of other subfolders filled the screen.

"I label my experiments by date. So far, I've never done more than one experiment on the same day, so it works for me. Juan uses a more complicated labeling system."

Laina nodded, "Well, I've seen how you label your microfuge tubes, so I'm not surprised to see that you use the simplest option to label your data files as well."

"Some people are always critics. *Anyway*, here is my folder from Thursday." He opened the file and six other files appeared. "Each time you record an experiment, it makes a new folder and labels it with the subfolder's title, in my case the day's date, and a number, starting with 001. You can change the file names later if you want, but this is how they are organized to begin."

Anthony clicked open the first folder and showed Laina how they imported the data into a spreadsheet. Then he explained the calculations they ran to analyze the data from the experiment. He repeated these steps with each of the recordings from the previous Thursday and then created a graph to show Laina what he'd discovered.

"I have to repeat each condition with multiple cells on multiple days for any of the results to be statistically significant. It's different from some of the biochemical assays in that you only need a total of three experiments for comparison. So, while you can get a lot of data really fast, you also have to repeat it more for it to be valid. I also have to show proof that we were expressing the various components by doing a Western blot. Thankfully, you only do that once. Wait, are you familiar with Western blots?"

"Yes, I assume you have your own antibodies to recognize each of your proteins, like the channel, your alpha9 protein, etcetera?" Laina asked.

"Yes, we have them tagged so that we can check for different proteins on the same gel. I'm going to make a gel and run it this afternoon if you need a refresher. I'm guessing you don't do a lot of Western blots when you're working in the crystallography field."

"We do them on occasion. Once we know that we've isolated

our protein and purified it, we don't need to do them again, though. I'll take you up on that offer. Thanks for all of your patience with me. I hope my learning curve isn't too steep."

"Happy to help. I want to have my own lab one day, so this is a great experience for my future too. I'll catch up with you after lunch then."

"Speaking of lunch, does everyone usually bring their own lunch? Do you eat together?" Laina asked.

"Eleanor usually eats with some of the other lab techs in the department, and Becky eats by herself in the student lounge. Juan and I will sometimes eat together. You're welcome to join us; we usually eat right around noon."

"I am used to buying my lunch every day, which it sounds like you two do not, so where should I pick something up?"

"Most people like the sandwich shop downstairs. It's next door to our building. You can't miss it."

"Great. Thank you again."

Laina checked her watch and saw that she had about thirty minutes before they were going to break for lunch. She decided to get her own folder set up in the system before she did anything else. Then it would be ready when she started doing her own experiments. She logged back into the desktop and got started. Emmitt had asked her to call and check in at lunch. She decided she could do that quickly on her way down to grab a sandwich. Fifteen minutes later, she was on her way downstairs to find the sandwich place.

Chapter 36

Juan cleared his throat after he was sure that Laina was gone, causing Anthony to look his way.

"What's up, man?" Anthony asked.

"How are things going with your new trainee?"

"Fine, why?"

"I heard you invite her to join us for lunch."

"She's new. What would you have done?"

"Show her the postdoc lounge and let her figure it out."

"Well, I prefer to be more hospitable when we have new people with us."

"Do you now…" Juan rolled his eyes at Anthony's comment. "I seem to remember it taking you about two years to eat lunch with me."

"Why are you so bitter lately? First, you accused me of flirting and now you're grumpy about me including you for lunch? I could have left you out, you know?"

"I'm not bitter. I just, I'm reserving judgment on our new labmate until she's been here a little while. Something about them seems off to me."

"Off in what way?"

"There's just something, I don't know, fake about their personalities. Maybe I'm just being sensitive."

"Yeah, you are. Try to lighten up, man."

They heard someone approaching the lab from down the hall, so they stopped speaking. Juan went back to staring at this computer screen, as did Anthony. When no one entered the lab, Juan rolled his chair away from his desk so that he could see Anthony better.

"It just seems like she is trying to underplay her intelligence and I don't know why she would do that."

Anthony rolled his eyes. "We've only known her, like, two days, man. Let's give her the benefit of the doubt here."

"Okay, but I'm still keeping my eye on her."

Chapter 37

Laina pulled out her phone while she waited for the sandwich guy to fill her order. Emmitt would have been in the office for a couple hours now. She was starting to get used to the three-hour time difference. It probably helped that she drove across the three zones over four days, though she would never admit it to Emmitt. He picked up after the first ring.

"Laina! I've been expecting your call all morning. How are things?"

"Everything is fine. I got a crash course in tissue culture procedures from Anthony this morning and learned how to analyze the data, which will be especially helpful once I start doing my own work here."

"How soon do you think that will be?"

"God, Emmitt. This is only my first *real* day here. It's going to take some time. Two or three weeks, minimum." She could almost hear him crane his neck backward and look at the ceiling.

"Ugh. I know. I KNOW. I'm very anxious for you to get going on it."

"My *instructor* is very nice and helpful. He basically showed me how to access all the lab files today."

"What?! Don't they have some sort of password protection on their files?"

"Calm yourself. Yes, but I know *how* one accesses their own files and so it won't be hard for me to get to other files either."

"Don't do anything stupid, Laina."

"I'm not, Emmitt. I'm telling you that I know how to replicate their files."

"I realize that, but you're not dealing with idiots here. I think they might notice if you stole their work."

"I'm not going to steal it; I'm going to *borrow* it and work it into my own experiments. It will be smooth. Don't worry."

"Why should I not worry about this? We are trying to stay off the radar. This seems very...*on* radar." He tried to keep his voice down, but didn't like what he was hearing.

"We don't know that I'll be able to replicate their baseline data with our cell line or their normal responses to the well-studied drugs. I might need to sub something in or subtract something off. *Finagle* it. You know." She looked around the café to see if anyone was paying attention to her. It was almost empty except for an older man seated with his back to her. "I should let you go. Call me when you get home and we can talk more." She ended the call. The sandwich guy had signaled that her order was ready. Time to get to know her co-workers better.

Chapter 38

L aina busied herself in her apartment, finally unpacking the last of her things while she waited for Emmitt to call. Lunch with the boys had gone smoothly, though Juan didn't say a lot. Anthony seemed eager to teach her how to patch clamp, which was good. It meant she could get out of here sooner rather than later. She wondered how much it cost to ship a car across the country. She really didn't want to drive all the way back. She cleaned up her kitchen from the box meal she'd cooked for herself earlier and was just sitting down on the futon to watch TV when her phone buzzed.

"It's pretty late in the day."

"Hello to you too. How was lunch?"

"It was fine. I'm getting to know some of the lab members better."

"Good. Now, explain to me about this file copying business that you were talking about earlier. I understand your reasoning, but I don't like the idea of hacking into a collaborator's files."

"I'm part of *their* lab right now, Emmitt. They're technically my files too."

"I think you know that's not entirely true."

"Whatever. It's fine. Anyway, as you know, I had to learn a little computer programming in college in order to graduate. I actually really enjoyed it and have continued to teach myself other things here and there over the years. There's this new thing where you can plant a little hidden file on someone's computer, and it gives you access to all of their files. You can look through as much or as little as you like. See their calendar, read their emails, all of it, but they never know because it's like a copy of their hard drive that goes on your drive. Kind of like planting a listening device, but for computer data."

"It sounds illegal."

"Of course, it's illegal, Emmitt."

"I'm not sure we need to stoop to spying yet."

"They'll never know. I won't even access it unless I need to. It will just be there, like a safety net, if I run into trouble."

"I'll think about it."

"Well don't think too hard because I already installed it this afternoon." With that statement, she ended the call and put her phone on silent. She knew Emmitt was pissed, but she didn't care. He'd come around to seeing things her way. It's not like he could fire her. How would that look to everyone at this point?

Chapter 39

"You look deep in thought."

Addison looked away from the TV program she hadn't really been watching to see Ryan walk into the family room. "Yes, sorry. I was just thinking about Eleanor. She wasn't herself this week. I never had a chance to talk to her and see if everything is okay with Gary or what was wrong."

"What do you mean when you say that she wasn't herself?"

"She was quieter, less talkative. She seemed hesitant about something whenever I was in the lab. It was as though she wanted to ask me something or tell me something, but kept holding back. I hope everything is okay. I can't imagine running the lab without Eleanor."

"You could call her."

"I know, but it feels like I would be blurring the personal/professional lines somehow there. I mean, yes, Eleanor is my friend, but she's also my employee. I don't want her to think she *has* to tell me whatever it is. Maybe I'll be able to catch up with her next week."

"Are you ready for the football game tonight?"

"Oh my goodness! What time is it? I've completely lost track of time worrying about Eleanor."

"It's only just after five o'clock. I was actually surprised to find you home this early."

"Everyone was jetting out early for one thing or another today. I decided to follow the crowd." She grinned sheepishly.

"Senior night on the football field, are you ready for this?" He asked again.

"Will I be a complete embarrassment to all of our kids if I cry?"

He smiled and stuck out a hand to pull her off of the couch. "I wouldn't expect anything less. I've got our *Football MOM and DAD* buttons ready. The boosters dropped them off earlier today at the warehouse. I think Joe will really appreciate seeing us wear them."

She laughed as she stood up. "Did they make them for the

cross-country team too?"

"Yes, and we can wear *those* at the regional meet tomorrow. I'm sure they will make Liv run faster every time she sees us." He grinned. "The kids are already at the field. Melinda picked them up earlier. Liv's cross-cross country team is doing shifts in the concession stand tonight. They each only have to work a half hour, so it won't wear anyone out for their big meet."

"Oh, right. I had forgotten about the concession stand duty. I guess Martin is palling around with Joel and Derek then?"

"That was the impression I got. I gave him ten dollars in case he wanted to get something from the stand."

"Ten dollars! You know he's going to keep the change from whatever he buys."

"I do, but I figure that he gets carted around to a lot of his siblings' activities and when it's his turn, they'll be off at college. So, it's a bit of reciprocity for the young man."

"I think he calls it hazard pay."

"Potato, puh-tah-toe." Ryan laughed. He handed her the *Football MOM* button with Joe's football picture to pin onto her coat.

Chapter 40

Emmitt stewed in his apartment all weekend. He was furious with Laina. Her little tracker key could jeopardize everything. Having access to their files *was* something that he had spoken about with Laina. Hacking into their system had never been discussed. He had only wanted her to have access to the files so she knew what her experiments should look like. If someone found her bug and traced it back to her? He squeezed his little stress ball. He would be finished. Laina would spill all his secrets to save her own neck.

She had stopped answering her phone too. He didn't want to text her because those could be evidence against him later, should it come to that. He had hit redial every five minutes for an hour before accepting that she must have either put her phone on silent or turned it off. He had known that entrusting his project to someone else had its risks, but Laina had seemed like a safe bet. She saw the end goal and wanted it just as much as he did. She was an incredible scientist. His lab had done nothing but prosper since she had joined.

Now she was in Atlanta and was trying to have full control of the reins. He had always worked hard to maintain control of his environment. Planned for every possible contingency. He had gone back and forth about letting Laina into his world. He saw her potential and her intelligence. Ultimately, *Apothecom* forced his hand when they needed the other experiments. He couldn't collaborate with someone local, that would have meant sharing reagents with someone out of his control. Pulling in Addison's lab had felt like a stroke of genius at the time. She trusted him because he had been reliable and trustworthy in their pasts.

Emmitt walked into his kitchen. He rarely drank alcohol; he didn't want to lose his edge or lose control. Here it was, Sunday night, and it felt like things were on the verge of spinning out of control for good. It was time for a few fingers of Scotch.

Chapter 41

Laina got up early on Monday to try and beat everyone to the lab. She needed to open the little tracking device on each of the lab computers in order to activate it. She figured it would seem suspicious if she was found using someone else's computer when they weren't around. Luckily, her fob worked and let her into the building on the first try.

Laina wondered how early Eleanor got to the lab each day. She had gotten a feel for the daily routines that Anthony, Juan, and Becky kept. None of them arrived before 7, but Eleanor had already been there each day when Laina arrived. Laina had considered staying late but thought that they might wonder why when she wasn't really doing her own experiments yet. If she arrived early, she could always take care of her business and then lay low in the postdoc lounge until a more reasonable hour.

She rode the elevator up to the eighth floor and immediately looked down the hallway to see if the lab was open yet. The lights in the halls were still out. *"They must not come on until six,"* she thought. She raised her fist in celebration when she saw that all of the labs in the hall were closed and dark. Quickening her pace, she hurried to the main lab and swiped her fob at the lock. Nothing happened.

"Damnit!" She hissed. "Why did they have to issue me this shitty fob?" She slowed down and gradually moved the device across the lock mechanism. She heard a click and pushed the door handle down. "Success!"

Moving from Eleanor's computer around the room to Anthony's, she quickly activated the tracker key on each desktop computer. Because of her familiarity with computers, she also knew that it would save her username on the login screen since she had accessed the machine last. Before moving on to the next computer, she entered the username of its typical user to hide that she had accessed it.

When she was finished, she debated risking exiting the lab and running into Eleanor on her way out or just playing it cool at her own desk. She checked her watch. It was almost six o'clock. She was guessing that Eleanor usually arrived around six, because she was usually packed up at four to go home. Before Laina could decide, she heard footsteps in the hallway headed her way. She moved quickly to her desk and logged in just as Eleanor entered the room.

"Laina! Aren't you here early today?"

"My internal clock is all out of whack after moving three time zones east. I fell asleep watching TV last night and when I woke up at five o'clock this morning, it seemed silly to get in bed to try and sleep longer. So, here I am. I've been catching up on my reading." She hoped Eleanor would buy her story.

"I can imagine that it's an adjustment. I wouldn't know; I've lived in the Atlanta area my entire life."

"Oh wow! You know, I guess I have lived in SoCal my entire life until now."

"You and I are what my dad always called *homebodies*. We like to stay close to home." Eleanor smiled.

Laina faked a smile that she hoped passed as genuine. In truth, she was an orphan. Her parents had died when she was very young, so she had been raised by her great aunt Mae. By Laina's calculations, Mae had been close to eighty years old when she took on her younger sister's grandchild. By the time Laina was in middle school, Mae had been showing signs of dementia. Laina was more than happy to help her hide it because she knew that meant she wouldn't become a ward of the state. She had worked hard and taken classes every summer so that she could graduate early. She knew if she was in college before Mae was declared cognitively diminished, no one could make her move into a foster home.

Before moving into the college dorms, Laina had arranged for Mae to be moved into a memory care facility. The guidance counselor at her high school had helped to make sure Laina stayed out of the foster care system by writing a letter supporting her independence and emancipation as a minor. Laina had just started her second semester of college when Mae had a stroke and died at the age of 96. Laina turned eighteen a month later and gained control of the trust fund her parents had left her. Laina immediately quit the job she worked at the mall to help pay her living expenses. She had earned a full ride academic scholarship, but it didn't cover her lodging. She welcomed the financial independence and hadn't had to worry about expenses ever again. She was free to pursue her dreams of becoming famous, world-famous. And Emmitt was going to drive her there with the success of this project.

"Yes, I suppose the familiarity is a comfort." She replied to Eleanor.

"Well, I'll leave you to your reading. I'm going to open up the other labs and get my lunch put away."

Laina waved goodbye and decided she should probably pull up a paper to read since she'd claimed that's what she'd been doing. In reality, she was brainstorming ways that she could get her tracker onto Dr. Fischer's computer. She didn't have access to her office, so that meant she needed to send it in an email. As of now, she didn't have a reason to email her with an attachment. Emmitt had plenty of reasons to do it, but after his little temper tantrum, she knew he wouldn't do it. She would just have to wait until she completed an experiment and could email the results. Anthony had said that she could try a few practice runs this week and see if she could get a patch on a cell. If it went well, then she, Emmitt and Addison would discuss thawing the cells and starting experiments with those. Until then, she was going to be transfecting their version of the channel and STABL into the Fischer's cells and testing how the channel responded to various stimuli. The trick would be keeping Anthony from watching too closely. She didn't know how their channel would respond to the standard tests. If it was significantly different, she knew he would recognize it right away. Hopefully, she could prove herself this week and not need a babysitter next week.

Chapter 42

Addison almost felt like skipping down the catwalk after she parked her car in the building's garage. She was still grinning ear to ear after reading the text Joe had sent to her and Ryan that morning. His coach had stopped him in the hallway before school started and handed him an envelope. Joe had texted his parents:

Full ride offer to the Colorado School of Mines for football!

The Colorado School of Mines was a dream come true for Joe. He had always hoped to play football in college. Plus, it was a great academic school too. The only drawback was that Colorado was so far away from Georgia.

Addison stepped off the elevator and saw Zenia coming down the hallway. She waved good morning. Zenia stopped and waited for Addison to catch up to her.

"You look especially cheerful this morning!"

Addison beamed. "Joe just found out that he's being offered a scholarship to play football in college. He's been hoping for this for years."

"Wonderful news! Please congratulate him for me. You must be very proud."

"I am. Ryan is thrilled too. Joe's coach gave him the letter this morning."

"You will have to do something fun to celebrate," Zenia said as they reached her office.

"Yes! We will." Addison nodded her goodbye to Zenia and unlocked her own office. She set all her bags down on her desk and pulled out her phone to call Melinda.

"Addison? Did Martin miss the bus? I can give him a ride. Joel just got on, so we should still be on time."

"Oh no, nothing like that. Joe just found out that the Colorado School of Mines offered him a full ride scholarship to play football!"

"Oh, yay! That's awesome! Good for Joe."

"I'm so happy for him. Even if Colorado is forever away, but it's an engineering school, which is where his interests lie. I can always join a frequent flyer program."

"Wait. Isn't that the school that stole my fight song?" Melinda was a Georgia Tech grad.

Addison laughed. "I don't know if I'd say *stole...*"

"It's the same song!"

"True, but it's a Division II school. It's not like they would ever play against each other."

"Fine. Well, I'm happy for him. Ryan must be over the moon."

"I'm not sure which one of them is more excited."

Melinda laughed. "Is he decided on Mines then? Or is he going to see if other schools are interested?"

"I'm not sure. He did apply to Tech, as you know, but he doesn't think he could play football there. This scholarship could tip the scales in Mines' favor."

"Understandable. I wish Tanya would just fill out an application and submit it already. She has partially filled out five or six now, but hasn't submitted any. Driving me nuts!"

"Hopefully, she can get them finished up soon. Well, good luck! I've gotta get back to it."

"Congrats again, Ad. That is really exciting news. Maybe it'll light a fire under my girl." She laughed and they ended the call.

Addison grabbed her lunch and pulled her office door closed behind her. She would grab her mail and then go check in with the lab. As she walked down the hall, she reminded herself to check to see if they had any news regarding Juan's paper. Occasionally, journals would request revisions after the manuscript went through peer review, but she hoped that they wouldn't have to mess with that.

Her mailbox was empty, so she stowed her lunch in the fridge and headed over to the lab. Laina was going to try to patch a few cells this week. Addison thought Laina seemed fairly proactive and driven. She knew why Emmitt had chosen to send her for this project. She was a hard and diligent worker.

Addison had been looking forward to sharing Joe's exciting

news with Eleanor, but she didn't even glance her way when Addison walked in. Normally, Eleanor asked about all of the kids and Liv had good news too—her cross-country team had qualified for the state meet! Addison frowned as she passed Eleanor's desk, wondering what had changed to make her so quiet.

Laina was sitting at her desk, looking at her computer screen when Addison walked over. She had a paper pulled up on the screen that Addison recognized as Juan's first paper with the lab three years ago.

"Catching up on some light reading?" She joked.

"Always. What's up?"

"Nothing much, just wanted to make sure you feel ready to tackle patch clamping this week. I'm sure Emmitt is anxiously awaiting to hear how it goes."

"Oh yes. Always." She smiled. "I actually just finished getting my cells set up in tissue culture. Anthony suggested that I not transfect anything this week. That way I can get a feel for the technique without using any extra materials."

"Sounds like a great idea. Good to take it one step at a time."

"Yes, if it goes smoothly on Wednesday, then I'm going to try some of our constructs next week."

"Speaking of those, do you need to amplify your DNA at all, or did Emmitt ship you enough?"

"I do need to amplify it. It's been a while since I've done it, but I'm sure it's like riding a bike."

You're welcome to use our kit, if you'd like."

"Well, Emmitt prefers old school on that. He emailed me a file with the steps. I was just getting ready to open it."

"I will leave you to it. Good luck."

Addison stopped briefly to chat with Becky on the other side of the lab. She was hoping to hear how her experiment had gone last week. Becky had settled on a project at the beginning of the semester after trying out several options during the summer.

"How did your experiment turn out last week? Anything exciting?"

"I think it went pretty well. I wanted to see if I could maybe tease out the binding site by using all of the segments of the channel that we have in the lab. Several of them overlap, so I figured I could narrow the area down some if I tried all of them."

"Right. That was a good starting point. What did you find?"

"It feels sort of inconclusive. I tried both halves, you know, and it only bound to the left side. But then, it bound to several of the smaller segments from the left half. None of the segments overlap." She showed Addison the map she'd drawn. Several areas were highlighted.

"Ah, well this might be one place where looking at the structure of the channel will aid you. Our department chair actually published that a couple decades ago."

"Really? Wow! So, is that going to require a trip over to the archives or is there a digital version?"

"It's been modernized, yes. Just search Benjamin Watt and sodium channel 1.5 in PubMed."

Becky opened up her browser and typed in the search criteria that Addison suggested. She found the paper of interest and opened it. It was a *Science* paper from 1995.

"Okay, so here's the structure of the channel. Looking at that and comparing it to what you know about the binding areas, what does that tell you?" Addison asked her.

Becky looked at her notes and back at the screen. She would make note of an amino acid position on the screen and put a little star by it on her paper map. She did this for multiple locations on her map of the channel.

"Oh! So, my protein binds across the left side here, most likely." She pointed to the screen, moving her finger across some coiled ribbons that were called alpha helices in the structure community.

"Exactly. It might be challenging to show scientific proof in our lab of the binding site on the channel."

Becky frowned. "So did I waste my time?"

"Not at all. This is very informative. Just because we can't pinpoint the site on the channel doesn't mean that we—"

"Can't find it on the smaller protein! Of course!" Becky finished for her. "Any chance you've already made the constructs of this protein?"

"No such luck. Why don't you see if you can tease out some segments that you think would work well? We can go through them this afternoon if you'd like."

Becky nodded and turned to a fresh page in her notebook. No one else was in the lab at the moment, so Addison went back to her office to check her email. She quickly deleted all the junk and then slowly scrolled through the others looking for one from the journal. She clapped when she saw it.

Accepted for print. Signature documents attached.

Addison grabbed her office phone to call Juan, then remembered that he wasn't in yet. She dialed Eleanor's extension instead.

"Hey Eleanor! Have Juan give me a call or have him stop by my office when he gets in, please."

"You got it."

"Thanks, bye." She hung up. This was really exciting news for Juan. He'd have three good papers to round out his postdoc with her. He should be able to easily get a position at one of the local universities with these on his *Curriculum Vitae* (CV). She wondered if he had started checking any of the universities' hiring pages yet. She knew most schools didn't start listing positions until later in the semester and on into January. She clicked over to the postdoc webpage for their university. Sometimes schools would announce forums for aspiring instructors on their page. She went to the networking opportunities tab to see the recent postings. She was about to open one when her computer popped up a reminder from her calendar:

ADDISON: REMINDER! PHYSIOLOGY LECTURE NEXT WEEK. BE PREPARED!

"Shoot! Glad I made that reminder." She said to herself. She pulled out the textbook and the bound notes that were required reading for the students taking the course. It was a med school class on basic physiology. Her lecture would cover high blood pressure physiology and recommended medications. The students always wanted to know if her questions would come from the notes or the book. She tried to do some of both because there was good information in both places. She put the two items aside on her desk to remind herself to go through her lecture from last year and update it as necessary.

She reset the reminder to go off again the following morning at nine and then went back to the list of networking opportunities. She knew that Juan was probably not ignoring this but wanted to help him in any way she could. She opened the first few to see how "local" they were. Several of the four-year universities were holding a joint conference on marketing yourself for the undergraduate classroom. She copied the link and sent it to Juan, suggesting that he register. She had just hit send when her office phone rang. It was the lab.

"This is Addison."

"Eleanor told me that you asked for me to give you a ring."

"Juan! Your paper was accepted!" She almost shouted the good news into the receiver.

"No revisions?"

"No revisions. It's all set. Congratulations, sir."

"This is fantastic! I can't wait to tell Sophie."

"By the way, you probably already saw this, but there is a local conference for people wanting to go into teaching—"

"Yes! I signed up last week. I snagged one of the mock interview spots too."

"Oh, great! Well, just ignore my email then. I haven't checked to see if any universities have posted job interviews yet, but definitely keep tabs on that."

"I have been. Thanks, Dr. Fish."

"I know that it's rather unlikely that an assistant professor position will post for the second semester, but don't feel like we're kicking you out of here just because your project is complete. We can always use you here as long as you need it."

"I really appreciate that. I'm not ruling out teaching as an adjunct at a community college yet. I feel like there are lots of options."

"Of course. You just let me know how I can help."

"Thank you. Ummm—Becky mentioned that she was going to be teasing out constructs for breaking up alpha9 into segments. I would be happy to help guide her through that if you'd like."

"That would be amazing, actually. I have a set of lectures to work on for next week, so that would really save me some time."

"I'll get to it. Thanks again." He hung up.

That evening, the Fischers went out to the new steak house to celebrate Joe's offer.

"Congratulations, Joe!" Martin said after the hostess had seated them.

"Thanks, Dude! I think I've been smiling all day."

"I can't believe my big brother is going to be a college quarterback. I'm happy for you, Joe."

"Thanks, Liv," he said, giving her a hug.

"We're so proud of you," Addison said.

"I think I told everyone at work at least three times!" Ryan laughed.

Joe blushed. "Thanks, everyone. I haven't accepted their offer yet. Coach said that I might get other offers still. I have until Thanksgiving Break to decide. I would be surprised if I got any better offers than this, though."

"Will your games be on TV?" Martin asked.

Joe chuckled. "Probably not. We're only D2."

Addison exchanged a look with Ryan when Joe used the word *we* as though he was already considering himself an Oredigger. Before she could say anything, the waitress arrived to take their drink orders and tell them the daily specials. After she left, they checked out the menus using the QR code at the table. Ever since the COVID-19 pandemic, few restaurants used paper menus.

"How are things with Eleanor? Did you find out what was

bothering her?" Ryan asked.

"I didn't and she was still quiet, almost stand-offish today. I hope she would tell me if she had a concern with something at the lab."

"Well, hopefully it's nothing."

It was a school night, so Addison was glad that the restaurant moved their meal along quickly. She could tell that Joe was embarrassed when the whole restaurant joined in a congratulatory song as the waitress brought out their dessert. He smiled and thanked everyone while Liv laughed at his awkwardness. She also knew that he hated being the center of attention. They thankfully got home before nine and Addison immediately instructed Martin to start getting ready for bed. Liv had her own bathroom and headed that way to go through her nightly routine too.

"I'm sorry that Taylor couldn't join us tonight, Joe."

"Me too, Mom. She said that she has a big project due this Friday and is behind on it. I think she is kind of overwhelmed by the idea of Colorado. She's only lived here, so the idea of going to school anywhere else is kind of scary."

"That's understandable. What do you think about it? You've only lived here too."

"I mean, it's all really new still. I haven't really had time *to think* about it. It will work out."

"If you ever need to talk about it, we're always here for you. Like you said, it's still fresh and no decisions have been made. Growing up is hard." Ryan patted Joe on his shoulder.

"Thanks, Dad. I'll see you both in the morning." He gave Addison a hug and then turned towards the hallway and his room, phone in hand.

"Don't stay up too late, okay?" Addison called after him. She knew he was going to call Taylor and talk about the offer. They had been dating since their freshmen year of high school. She wondered how their relationship would withstand a test like this. Ryan squeezed her shoulder.

"I can see your wheels turning, Mama Bear. We have to let him navigate this one and just listen when he needs us."

"I know. You're a smart man, Ryan Fischer. Growing up is hard."

Chapter 43

After five days of radio silence, Laina gave in and called Emmitt on Wednesday night. She waited until she knew that he'd be home so that he would have a real conversation with her. He was extra guarded at the office.

"It's about damn time, Laina." Emmitt barked when he answered her call.

"Oh, thanks, Emmitt. I've missed you too. How are things out west these days?" She poured on the sweetness to really get under his skin.

"Cut the crap. You are not to leave me out of the loop like this. We had an agreement."

"No, you gave instructions and assumed that they'd be followed."

"Damnit, Laina! I'm your *boss*. I give instructions—"

"Are you finished? I can call back tomorrow instead."

"Get on with it."

"This is a partnership. We both *know* things. We're both in this. So, you are going to have to give me some freedom of artistic license here." She waited for him to respond. She could practically hear him stomping around his apartment.

"We need to discuss how we approach the non-science portion of this *adventure* before springing a plan into action."

"Fine, Emmitt. I'll do my best. Now, I got to try the technique myself today under Anthony's guidance. He says that I'm a natural. I got a patch on several cells this afternoon. I'm going to watch his experiment again tomorrow to pick up any pointers, but next week, I get to fly solo."

"Great job, Laina! Who knows? Maybe you will wrap this up in half the time we expected." Emmitt had calmed considerably.

"Okay, pay attention. I'm going to send two emails tomorrow. One will be just to you with my data file. The other will be to you and Addison with what looks like the same file, but it will have my tracker key attached. When she opens it—"

"Laina—"

"Excuse me. I am not finished, *Partner*. When she opens it, the tracker will embed itself into her computer and be activated. She won't notice; it's invisible to all the anti-virus software."

"What if she *does* notice?"

"She won't. I'm telling you. It's virtually invisible."

"Okay, so what's your plan to keep next week's experiment on the DL?"

"*DL*? Emmitt, please. Don't try to be cool. I'm going to go in early. Do the bulk of the experiment *before* anyone else is there to see anything."

"What about lab meeting? Won't you have to give an update or something?"

"I will just say that I haven't fully mastered the process yet and that I'm not ready to present."

"What will you say if they ask why you are working alone?"

"Emmitt, we've already talked about this. Remember? I'm going to say that I'm trying to stay out of Anthony's way so that he can get his project finished. Write his dissertation and a paper, you know. It sounds completely innocent *and* responsible. We went over all of this before I left. Why are we rehashing this again?"

"I guess you've got it under control. Honestly, do *not* freeze me out of this. We are at a very crucial junction."

"I know, Emmitt. It's important to me too, to my career and yours. Now don't forget. Do *not* open that file that I'm sending to Addison tomorrow. It will put my tracker on your device too."

"I got it, I got it. Keep in touch. You got that?"

"Bye, Emmitt." She ended the call. Emmitt might think he was still running the show, but this was her gig now. That tracker was going to be attached to both files. She could keep tabs on his communications with *Apothecom* this way. She would no longer have to wait for an update from him. She should have done this to him years ago.

Chapter 44

The next day, after Addison had looked through the data that Laina sent, she responded to both Emmitt and Laina to see if they wanted to teleconference regarding the next experiments. She knew that Laina was capable of running this project herself but didn't want to exclude any experimental conditions that Emmitt was hoping to review. She was impressed with how quickly Laina was picking up the technique. Emmitt had mentioned that Laina was *all California-girl* at heart, but maybe she would want to continue this collaboration as a postdoctoral fellow with her lab. It was a good networking opportunity and could help springboard her into an assistant professorship afterward.

Addison called over to the lab next. She wanted to get a feel from Anthony about how he thought Laina was doing with patch clamping. The data looked good, but she didn't know how much Anthony had just coached versus actually handled with the experiment.

"Hi, Eleanor! Have you seen Anthony yet?"

"Yes, he just sat down at his desk. I'll transfer the call."

"Thank you." Addison waited for Anthony to pick up.

"Hey, Dr. Fish. What's up?"

"Good morning, Anthony. Could you swing by my office before you get started on your experiment today?"

"Uh, sure. I'll be right over." He hung up.

Addison opened her door and cleared off one of the extra chairs for him to sit in. She had been working on her lecture and had spread things out. She would be lecturing at 8:00 a.m., Monday through Thursday next week.

"Hey, Dr. Fish." Anthony knocked a knuckle on her door. He looked a little nervous.

"Hi. Have a seat. I just wanted to get your feedback on how things are going with Laina." She said as she closed the door.

"Oh, okay. I was worried that I had left something out again." He smiled.

"Oh, no, nothing like that. I'm sorry if I worried you."

"She is definitely a fast learner. She paid close attention to what I was doing and picked it up like a natural. You would have never guessed that this was her first time trying it."

"Do you think she's ready to run her own experiment next week?"

"Oh definitely. She made herself a checklist to go through for setup, so it seems like she has everything covered."

"Okay great. I know you have your own experiment planned for today, so I don't want to keep you from it. Thanks for coming by."

Anthony stood up. "Okay, Dr. Fish. I'll see ya around."

Addison went back to organizing her lectures for the physiology class. She didn't have to make too many updates to the lectures she gave last year. The course coordinator had requested that she turn in her presentation file by the end of the day today. She was about to put her computer in sleep mode when her email program dinged with an incoming message. She pulled it up.

Hey Addison and Laina,

I think if Laina can just send us her experimental protocol, then we can do any tweaking to it if necessary. Let's hold off on a teleconference until after she works with our cells.

Best,

Emmitt

Addison was about to respond that she could go over that with Laina before Monday when Laina's own response came through first. She had attached her plan for the experiment as well as the conditions she planned to try. She said that she wanted to run the experiment virtually the same way for at least the next two weeks to show that she could reproduce the results. Then she would look into thawing the cell line and running experiments with those.

Addison was impressed with Laina's foresight to get reproducible data. Too often, young scientists believe the first experiment tells the whole story and then try to shape their scientific narrative around results that they cannot replicate. Laina had also included all of the control parameters that Anthony had shown her. Addison couldn't think of anything that would improve upon Laina's experimental design, so she typed a quick *"Looks good to me."* She put the finishing touches on her lectures for next week and sent them over to the course coordinator. Tomorrow, Liv's cross-country team was being honored with a sendoff to the state meet, so Addison would be getting to work a little later than normal. She sent off a reminder email that lab meeting would be a half hour later and thanked the group for accommodating her schedule.

Chapter 45

On Monday morning, Laina arrived at the lab before everyone except Eleanor so that she could get her cells ready without anyone looking over her shoulder. She had noticed that she could get everything finished in the tissue culture hood before anyone else wanted to use it if she arrived by 6:30 a.m. Now that she had been in the lab for a few weeks, she knew where things were kept and had gotten familiar with her surroundings.

She came in a little bit later on Tuesday because she didn't expect her transfection to take long. She unlocked her freezer and removed the necessary DNA constructs that she had amplified the week before. They could thaw in the ice bucket while she got all of her tubes labeled for the transfection. She was just about finished labeling all of the little tubes when the lab phone rang. Eleanor signaled that the call was for her.

"Laina Hibber speaking."

"Hi, Dr. Hibber. This is Frank over at the admin office. We got the new fobs in yesterday and I had a note that you needed a replacement."

"Fantastic! I can come by later this morning to pick it up, if that's okay."

"Well, you can choose to wait if you want to, but it might be gone by then. We have a pretty long list of people needing replacements, so I would recommend getting over here quickly. We actually already handed over half of them out yesterday evening. The lab said that you had left for the day when we called for you."

Laina ground her teeth. "Oh, I understand. I'll be right over." She hung up and looked at her samples. No one else would be here for at least fifteen minutes, if not half an hour. Surely, she could make it down to the second floor, get the fob, and be back without locking these up and starting the thawing process over again. She grabbed her badge and told Eleanor she would be right back.

Rather than wait for the elevator, she raced down the stairs to the admin office. The elevators were so slow that she figured she could hit the call button, sign for her new fob, and be back in front of the elevator bay before the car showed up. She pressed the button and then turned to enter the office. Frank was waiting at the desk with the fob in his hand.

"If you'll just sign right here and then turn over your old fob. We're going to try to reprogram it again, but I think it's probably a lost cause."

Laina took the pen from him and scrawled her name on the line he had highlighted. She pulled the broken fob from her pocket and set it up on the counter for Frank to take back. He waited for her to finish signing and dating the form, but didn't set the new fob down when she finished.

"I don't know why they keep trying to salvage these things. They aren't really a big expense. It seems like they could save everyone time and effort by just tossing the dysfunctional ones from the get-go." Frank continued. Laina didn't want to make small talk. She just wanted to get back to the lab and her samples. She smiled at Frank and hoped he would stop talking and hand over the fob.

"Yeah, who knows? Thanks for letting me know about the new ones. I'll let you get back to work." She put her hand out for the fob.

"Do you want to go test it at the main entrance? You never know which ones are faulty when we get in a new batch."

"I will have to test it later. I was kind of in the middle of something when you called."

Frank's shoulders sagged a bit as he released the fob. "Oh, of course. I'll see you around." She nodded and rushed out of the office knowing the elevator had probably come and gone at this point. She didn't really want to go up six flights of stairs, so she hit the call button again. Surprisingly, the elevator opened less than half a minute later. When she walked past the tissue culture room, she groaned. Anthony was already in there!

"Anthony is here early today." She commented to Eleanor on

her way back into the main lab.

"He is. I thought maybe the two of you were having a contest to see who could get here earlier or something."

Laina faked a smile and walked over to her bench. Her samples were still in the ice and she just had one tube left to label. Hopefully, Anthony would be fast. Emmitt had told her that he was sloppy and irresponsible, but this seemed to be contrary to that information. She turned on her computer and logged in while she waited for him to finish in the hood. She could go through some of her emails until it was her turn. The department had added her to the postdoc group and while she appreciated the gesture, they sent a ton of emails. *Had they not heard of social media?* She wondered.

After fifteen minutes, Anthony had finally finished up his transfections. She grabbed her ice bucket and rushed past him to get her own experiment set up. She hoped that he noticed her irritated look as she zipped past him. She knew that was being childish; it's not like she had reserved the hood or anything. *Plus,* she reminded herself, *she needed to stay on his good side during this little adventure.* She sprayed the hood with ethanol and wiped it down as Anthony had shown her. Then she got all her samples distributed into each of her labeled tubes. She had planned on coming in early to do her work, but if Anthony was going to do that, then she would switch to afternoons and evenings. She needed to work out a schedule with him one way or the other. Laina put her cells back into the incubator when she was finished and cleaned up the hood. When she walked into the main lab, Anthony was at his desk. She stopped with her ice bucket.

"I don't want to step on your toes or get in the way of your experiments. Do you plan on working earlier in the day usually? I live across the street, so it's easier for me to be flexible as I don't have a commute."

"You live across the street?!" Anthony was shocked.

"I do. The rent here is incredibly low compared to California. I really should have the lab over for drinks or something. Then we can all get to know each other better." She put her hand on her hip.

"That sounds great. I mean, for the lab and everything."

"So, morning or afternoon? Which would you prefer?"

He raised his eyebrows. "I guess I hadn't thought about having to share the space. I mean, whatever is cool with me."

Laina did a mental eyeroll. *Couldn't he just make a decision?*

"This is your space. I won't be here forever. House rules." She smiled at him.

"Okay, I would prefer the morning, if that's really okay with you. I can always stay a little bit late if you need help setting up or getting things going." He said eagerly. Laina could tell he was disappointed that they wouldn't continue to work side by side.

"Thank you. That's very thoughtful of you." She placed a hand on his shoulder. "I'll be sure to let you know if I need anything."

Laina walked over to her desk and unlocked her freezer. She carefully placed all of her samples back in their places and closed it. She listened to make sure she heard it lock before getting up to empty her ice bucket. Everyone here seemed honest, but she didn't want to take any risks.

Becky and Juan were over at their shared lab bench sketching out an assay that he was going to help Becky do. Laina had overheard them planning out construct ideas last week and knew Becky was hoping to have successfully designed some new segments to test in her binding assays. It was tedious biochemistry work that Laina had always hated. Thankfully, Emmitt had a skilled lab assistant that could easily make any construct they needed for their experiments, so Laina never had to deal with it. The man had no aspirations of his own and was content to work his eight hours a day doing as he was told. Emmitt had told her that one of his early lab assistants had been really nosey and frustrating. He wanted to be involved in the research process and tried to take initiative by understanding the work. He dug into the background and started asking too many questions for Emmitt's comfort, so he found a way for him to move on without it seeming like he was displeased with the guy. Laina emptied the ice bucket into the sink and decided to take a moment to call Emmitt with an update regarding her schedule from the postdoc lounge. She hoped that it would be empty since it was mid-morning and most postdocs only used the room at lunchtime.

Chapter 46

Juan noticed Laina leave the lab and got up to speak with Anthony while she was out of earshot. "Did I hear her say that she lives across the street? In the apartment building? How does she afford that?"

"She said that it's a lot cheaper than in California." Anthony shrugged. "She wants to have us all over for drinks at some point."

"I don't think Sophie is going to go for that, but I can see that you are excited about the idea," Juan said.

"It's not like that. She's new here. I'm sure she just wants to make a few friends." Anthony told him.

"Yes, I'm sure that's *all* she wants." He made a kiss-face with his lips and walked back to the lab bench where Becky was deep in thought. Anthony frowned as Juan walked away. It seemed like Juan was jealous of his time with Laina, though that didn't really make sense. He wondered why Juan didn't find her trustworthy and was always seeing the worst in their new colleague. If he was being honest though, he had noticed that Laina wasn't only good at what she did, she *looked* pretty good too. He blushed at the thought and pushed it from his mind. He needed to get his update ready for lab meeting on Friday. Luckily, he could just add to or slightly modify his previous week's presentation as he wasn't gaining a lot of new data each week. He wondered when Dr. Fish would let him off the hook of updating every week. To be fair, he had been significantly more productive since she had instituted this new policy, but he hoped to earn a week off from it sooner rather than later. Maybe Laina would need to take a turn soon.

Chapter 47

B y Thursday, Addison was ready to be finished with her lectures. Even though she was only lecturing for ninety minutes each morning, she felt disconnected from the lab by being in the classroom instead. She was thankful that the medical school only requested that she lecture twice a year in their classes. She knew it was important information for the students to learn, but it wasn't her favorite part of her job. She stuck around while the students packed up their notebooks and backpacks in case any of them had any further questions for her. Occasionally, one of them would request an office meeting to go over the information in more detail, but usually they just wanted to know what would be on the test. By 10:45, the last student had finally packed up and exited the lecture hall, freeing Addison to do the same. She grabbed her things and went straight to her office. She had learned from Eleanor that Anthony and Laina had decided that the best way to share the lab space was for him to use it in the mornings and her to run experiments in the afternoons and evenings. She figured that Emmitt would prefer this too, in case Laina ever wanted to bounce ideas off of him mid-experiment. The time change wouldn't be an issue in the later part of the day.

After dropping her laptop off in her office, she walked over to the lab where she planned to find Anthony. He had been getting some good results the last few weeks and was getting close to finishing up his project. He just needed to repeat it a few more times. Then they could meet with his committee and get permission to start writing his dissertation. She didn't want to disturb him by knocking, so she waited in the doorway until he stood up to change a solution. She knew if he bumped the table, it could show up in the data and make him have to start over with that run. He looked up after a minute and waved her into the lab.

"Dr. Fish! Did you need me for something?"

"I just wanted to pop in and see how it's going. I know you're getting close to getting all your reps completed and thought I would observe after lecturing all week."

Anthony cringed. "I wish I had something good to show you. I'm not sure what the issue is. The baseline current started off higher than normal and whenever I add *mexipres*, the cell bursts within a few seconds. I think I must have mixed the dosage incorrectly."

Addison stepped over to look at the screen. Anthony had three graphs on the screen from his first attempts so far that day, with a fourth one currently recording. The data did look quite a bit different.

"Are you sure it's the dosage of the drug? You don't start with that in the solution, right? Something else would be throwing that out of whack. Are your cells old?" Their cell line could only be split into new dishes about twenty times before its properties started to change and the cells became less healthy.

"No, I have only split them four or five times so far. You're right; it can't be just the drug that has an issue. Something else is wrong too. Maybe I put too much salt in the control solution. I'll re-mix it and start again."

Addison left him and walked over to the main lab to check in with everyone else. Eleanor was on the phone with what seemed to be one of their distributors and Laina was working at her desk. Juan was helping Becky with a gel on their shared bench.

"How are the constructs coming?"

"I think I have a few that worked. Juan was just explaining to me how to gauge size with the DNA size marker that I used." Becky pointed at the gel and held up a card that had short, dark lines with a number to the left indicating how many kilobases corresponded to those positions in the marker. It was kind of like a ruler for DNA. "We were just about to take it over to the UV box to get a photo."

"Let me know what you find. I know you've been anxious to start growing some protein for your binding assay."

"I'll keep you in the loop," Becky said.

Their lab shared a UV box with the department, so Becky followed Juan out of the room to get a photo of her work. Addison noticed that Eleanor was off the phone, so she walked over to say hi. She hadn't seen much of her all week because of her lectures.

"How is your week going, Eleanor?"

"Just fine, Dr. Fischer. I was just trying to track down our order for more petri dishes. It was supposed to be here Tuesday, but we still haven't seen it. I was worried that it was lost in shipment or back-ordered or something. The distributor told me that it didn't make the weekend truck, but it was on the truck for tomorrow." She fiddled with her pencil while she spoke.

"Thanks for tracking that down. I know Becky has been using a lot of plates lately. Everything else okay?" Addison felt like Eleanor seemed nervous and quiet again.

"Everything is…good." She paused like she was going to say more and then shrugged.

"Okay. If you need anything, I'll be in my office. I have to write a few exam questions now that I'm finished lecturing."

Addison didn't check in with Laina since she knew that her experiment wasn't starting until after Anthony was finished. It bothered her that Eleanor seemed troubled again today *and* that Anthony had somehow messed up his reagents again. It seemed like he had turned over a new leaf in the last month, but now he was mixing up basic solutions wrong? She shook her head in frustration. Maybe he could get it straightened out and still save the experiment.

Chapter 48

Laina called Emmitt Thursday evening to update him with her experimental results. She had taken notes when observing Anthony's experiments and knew what values she should get with the control conditions if her system was set up correctly. She knew going into this that Emmitt's system might be more of a challenge than he was hoping.

"You couldn't get the baseline readings established? Are you sure you had everything set up correctly?"

"Yes. I took very detailed notes and I watched him do this several times. It always starts out the same."

"There has to be some way to manipulate it to get it in the right frame or level or whatever. Did you try altering the salt concentration?"

"I couldn't do that today. All of the chemicals are in the main lab and I made up my solutions before I got started. Someone might have gotten suspicious if I went back and made a new solution mid-experiment. I'll make a variety next week when I try again."

"What did you tell Addison?"

"I didn't tell her anything. Everyone was already gone by the time I cleaned up to leave. They asked me to lock up, which I guess means that they trust me." She let out an awkward giggle.

"Well, what are you going to tell her? You know she's going to look or ask when you see her tomorrow!"

"I'm just going to say that I must have had beginner's luck last week and couldn't patch a cell today."

"I thought you said that Addison could look at your data since she's the PI. She'll see what you did and know that something is wrong."

"I password protected my folder. Anthony told me that would keep everyone out."

"That seems like a short-term fix. She's going to ask why she can't get into your file."

"Maybe, maybe not. I think I can keep up the *I'm still learning* excuse for at least two or three weeks. It's not unusual for people to struggle with this."

"Someone might want to watch what you're doing if you have that much trouble!"

"I've got this *under control*, Emmitt. Chill. This was just the first try. Things rarely work on the first try."

"Except that in this case, they did work. They just don't work the way *we* want them to. I need to send some data over to *Apothecom* soon to keep their interests."

"I can send you some of Anthony's. Just call it raw data. They won't know. Or I could just adjust the numbers down to where they *should* be. I'll fiddle with it when I go in tomorrow and see if I can make the numbers look passable for *Apothecom*."

"How many lies are we going to compound onto this?" Emmitt threw up his hands in frustration.

"I don't know, Emmitt. How many have *you* already told? And for how long?" She ended the call before he could scream at her.

Emmitt threw his stress ball at the wall and swore under his breath. He didn't want any of his neighbors to call about excess noise or disturbing sounds, but he was really frustrated. He just needed one more thing to work. He did *not* need Laina to give him lip about it. He picked up the stress ball and started squeezing it again. Maybe he should go for a walk and try and brainstorm a solution to this roadblock. He didn't know a lot about patch clamping, but surely there was a way to make adjustments. He grabbed his keys and his jacket and left the apartment. He knew there had to be a solution that allowed this to work.

Chapter 49

Over the weekend, Addison stewed about the dismal ending to the week. Anthony's experiment was a waste. He never got the control run to work, so he couldn't make any other measurements with that out of whack. Eleanor was acting strange again but said that she was fine. She had always been so cheerful and easy-going, so it was disturbing for her to be this recluse. Laina hadn't had any luck patch clamping this week either, so that project was also at a stand-still. She wondered if there was a full moon that was wreaking havoc on her lab.

"You've been rather quiet all weekend. Want to talk about it?" Ryan asked as he sat down next her on the couch. Their kids had just left for youth group.

"No. I'm sorry. Ugh. I'm just frustrated. Is it that obvious?"

"You have seemed fairly distracted by your thoughts. I promise I won't try to fix it or offer solutions if you want to talk. I will just listen. Scout's honor." He held up his fingers to his forehead in salute.

Addison laughed. "I hope I didn't bring down the weekend for everyone. It was fun to go camping together again; it's just been one of those weeks."

Ryan waited to see if she'd continue.

"Eleanor is still not herself; it's like she's afraid to do something wrong, or I don't know. She says that she's fine, but her actions say that she is uncomfortable. Anthony completely wasted a week with his experiments, not to mention all the reagents. He either made up a solution incorrectly or messed up his transfection or forgot everything he's learned up to this point. Laina couldn't get a cell to patch this week either. She said that she broke a couple pipette tips and punctured some cells before she could get any measurements."

"Surely something went right?"

Addison shrugged and looked at the ceiling. "I guess Laina finally got a new fob that lets her in the building without a special song and dance."

"See? That's something."

"Juan has been really helpful getting Becky pointed in the right direction with her work too. I had to lecture almost every morning this week and that had me all out of sorts. Maybe I'm the one that's out of whack and everyone else actually had a normal week."

Ryan smiled. "I would never call you out of whack."

She squeezed his hand. "Thank you. I'm sorry if I was a Debbie-downer all weekend. On top of all the stuff at work, I feel like our time with Joe is slipping away. I can't believe he'll really be in Colorado next year while we're all still here."

Ryan grabbed her hand. "I know. It feels like we really need to maximize our time with him, but he's so busy. You weren't a Debbie downer. We had a great weekend. I could just see the gears in your mind turning things over whenever we were relaxing in the camper or by the lake."

"I'm not sure if I'm more frustrated that Anthony couldn't get his act together again or more worried that something is wrong with Eleanor. I wish she would talk to me."

"You could always call her. Invite her to lunch or something."

"I don't want to pressure her into it. I just want her to be herself or tell me why she feels like she can't."

"I guess you will just have to give her some time and space. She isn't just your employee; she's your friend too. I think she'll come around."

"Thanks. And thanks for getting me to talk. It's much better than keeping it all bottled up inside. I wonder if Taylor is serious about looking at schools in the Denver area. Joe seemed really hopeful that they could stay together." She sighed and gave him a hug. "Let's see what we can scrounge up for dinner before those starving kids get back home."

Chapter 50

On Monday, Addison sat down with Anthony to review his plan for that week's experiment. She double-checked the solution recipes that he was using and had him write down all of the reagents that he would be combining. She could tell by the look on his face that he was frustrated by the entire process.

"I'm sorry to make you do this, Anthony. I can see that you are frustrated. I just don't want you to waste another week like last week. It felt like you had really been making progress prior to that."

"I know Dr. Fish. I can't figure out what happened. I remade all of the solutions, but it didn't change anything. Maybe I messed up the transfection somehow. I haven't made a mistake like that in forever though." He put his hands in his lap and looked at the floor.

Addison sighed. "I don't want you to get discouraged. Maybe it was just an off week. I want you to double and triple-check everything this week. Be as absolutely methodical about every step as you can be. If it still happens, then we'll back track and see what might have changed."

"Okay. I will do my best. I hope it was just a fluke. Laina didn't have any luck either?"

"She said that she couldn't get a patch on a cell and that she broke too many pipettes trying to adjust the height with the microscope."

"That's too bad. I thought she would gain some confidence by working on her own this week. Hopefully, she isn't too frustrated," he said as he got up to leave.

"She seems pretty driven to get it figured out. I'm sure she'll get it to work in the next week or two." Addison mulled over the idea of asking Anthony about Eleanor, but decided it was too close to being lab gossip and kept it to herself. "Okay, well, good luck with this. I hope you realize that the end is in sight. You just need a few more good runs to pull this all together."

Anthony nodded and left her office. She picked up the phone

to call the lab. Maybe Ryan's idea to invite Eleanor to lunch wasn't such a bad one after all. It had been several months since they ate together.

"Hi, Eleanor. Are you busy for lunch tomorrow?"

"Tomorrow? I usually eat with the other techs on Tuesdays."

"Oh, I didn't realize. Is there a day this week that we could meet for lunch? My schedule is pretty free this week after being so busy last week."

"Well, I guess I could do Friday," Eleanor said slowly.

"Oh great! Friday it is. Is Santouits okay, or do you want to try some place new?"

"Santouits is fine."

"Okay, I'll swing by your desk around noon to walk over."

"Okay. Did you need anything else? I need to get back to these orders."

"No, sorry for interrupting. It's been such a long time since we went for lunch and I thought we could catch up away from the lab. I'll see you later." She hung up and wondered why Eleanor seemed so nervous. They had worked together for almost two decades and she had never seen her act this way. She pulled out her phone and texted Ryan.

Eleanor is still not herself today. I took your suggestion. Lunch on Friday.

Hope she will talk to you.

Thanks. Love you.

Love you too.

Addison opened up her email to catch up on anything she had missed over the weekend. She downloaded the journal article to read later in the week and saw her reminder to talk to Becky about putting her committee together. She wanted her to have her first meeting in January to keep her on track with her project and the graduate school's requirements. She knew that Becky still had two or three classes to complete before she would be in the lab basically full time. Addison sent Becky a quick email asking if they could meet one afternoon this week to put a plan together for her committee. If Anthony's experiment went well this week, he could possibly get his committee to meet at the beginning of the semester as well. Maybe he would actually graduate this year.

Chapter 51

Over in the lab, Anthony was waiting for Juan to arrive. Juan had started coming back in earlier because he was helping Becky with her project. He wanted to talk about his experiment with the more experienced postdoc before he did the transfection on Tuesday. He was hoping that Juan had seen something similar to what Anthony observed with his cells last week and could explain how to fix it. Laina was in tissue culture and Becky hadn't arrived yet either. It wasn't that Anthony felt like he had something to hide, but he did have some apprehension nagging at him. He hoped Juan could set his mind at ease.

"Juan!" Anthony called out when he saw the young man enter the lab. "Have a minute?" He looked over to see if he'd caught Eleanor's attention, but she seemed caught up with something on her computer and hadn't even noticed Juan walk in. Juan set down his bag and walked over to Anthony's desk.

"What's up?"

"I had something weird happen with my experiment last week. Let me pull up the raw numbers on the computer here." He clicked on his folder and found Thursday's date. The folder had fourteen different files in it. He opened several to show Juan at once.

"Okay, this was my first try. See how the control level is already high?" He pulled up another graph. "I changed out the solution and it's still high."

"Huh. These are our regular cells?"

"Yes. See here? I tried putting in mexipres to see if it would lower the elevated response and it just killed the cell."

"Did you try more than one dish of cells?"

"Yes, I tried three different dishes before I gave up. At that point, I was just pouring solutions down the drain for no reason."

"What did Dr. Fish say? She has more experience with this than I do."

Anthony squirmed. "I didn't really show her all of it. I just told her that something was off."

"Okay, let's take a step back. Was there anything—*anything* that was different from other times you've set up an experiment like this? Different media in the dish during the transfection? Extra DNA, less DNA? New cells?"

"No. Everything was virtually identical to what I did the last three weeks." He shrugged.

"I don't know, man. It almost looks like a different channel. You didn't add a potassium channel in there or something, did you?"

Anthony laughed. "I can barely keep up with one channel. Where would I find a different one?"

"I don't know. I'm just brainstorming ideas. The response you saw to mexipres is especially weird. I have read about cell death with mexipres somewhere. I'll try to see if I can find it for you before Becky gets here."

"Thanks, man. How is all that biochemistry going?"

"She actually caught onto it really fast, so I'm just double-checking her plans for her at this point. I think she's growing and purifying her proteins today and tomorrow for a big binding assay later in the week. Hopefully she'll get some interesting results."

"Well, I'm sure she's going to be here any minute. I need to get my stuff out for tissue culture so I'm ready when Laina finishes up. I let her start first since I'm trying to trouble shoot things here still."

Juan went back over to his desk while Anthony pulled his solutions out of the refrigerator. Anthony wondered if Juan still felt like Laina needed to be kept on a short leash. Maybe Juan had decided that she wasn't trying to manipulate them after all.

Chapter 52

Laina waited to pull up her data until everyone else had gone to lunch. She didn't want anyone to see what she was up to. She knew that Eleanor stuck to a strict thirty-minute lunch period so that she could start her commute before the rush hour traffic built up. She opened some of Anthony's files from the experiments she had watched him do so that she could mimic his data as closely as possible without actually copying it. Emmitt said that they just needed something to convince *Apothecom* that they were headed in the right direction. That would get the ball rolling and allow them to start recruiting volunteers for the drug trial.

Laina had told Addison that she hadn't gotten any data last week. Truthfully, she just hadn't gotten anything that she could share with the lab. She didn't know how familiar Addison was with the range of ion channels, but she didn't want to raise any red flags with the collaborating PI. Laina flipped back and forth between Anthony's data and her own. She pulled all of her data into a spreadsheet so that she could fine tune her numbers to look like his. On Thursday, she realized immediately that this wasn't going to be the walk in the park that they had hoped it would be. Rather than just give up on the experiment, she still ran through all the conditions that she had planned. She wasn't sure if the initial results would work for what Emmitt wanted, but having nothing was definitely not going to get them anywhere. It took a little finessing, but she eventually made her results look like Anthony's. She saved the graphs and sent them over to Emmitt just as Eleanor came back into the lab. Laina smiled and looked back at her computer screen. She saved all of the doctored files into a file that she marked as hidden. Then she removed the password protection from her folder in case Addison got a wild hair to look at Laina's trials from last week. She knew Emmitt was right when he suggested that password protecting her files would only arouse suspicion in the lab. The hidden file idea was a better option. She closed all of the files and grabbed her notebook to verify her transfection plans for next Tuesday.

Now that she knew how to adjust her results to look like the wild type system, she felt like she would be ready to try out their cells next week. The bonus was that next week was Thanksgiving, so almost no one would be around. She could work without anyone breathing down her neck or getting in the way. She had overheard most of the lab members discussing their plans for the holiday and knew that no one was staying past Wednesday morning. The department even had a little Thanksgiving luncheon planned for 11:00 a.m. that day. Anthony had told her that people usually eat and run.

Laina was still reviewing her experimental setup when she heard Addison coming down the hall. The woman's heels made a distinct clicking sound when she walked that was undeniable. Sure enough, when she looked up at the door, Addison walked in.

"I just wanted to let everyone know that it's fine to take off early next Wednesday. The university is technically closed from Thursday through Sunday, but they will send out an email mid-morning on Wednesday announcing early release or something to that effect. My son Martin's school is off all week, so he's going to be spending time here or with my husband Ryan. He'll be in my office the majority of his time here. If anyone needs me to take care of their cells over the weekend, just let me know. I'll be coming in on Friday morning for just a bit while my family is out Black Friday shopping."

"I can take care of mine. I'm not planning on taking much time off next week."

"Do you have someone to celebrate the holiday with, Laina? You're more than welcome to join our family." Addison offered.

"That's *so* kind of you. Actually, Anthony and Juan told me about a celebration that the postdocs and grad students put on together for anyone who doesn't have their own plans. I'm going to join that one."

"Great. I'm glad you won't have to celebrate alone. Anyone else? Happy to have anyone join us."

"I'll take you up on the offer to do my tissue culture." Anthony grinned.

"I'm not doing tissue culture right now, so you don't need to check on mine. I'll probably start cells up again after Christmas. Getting all my binding studies finished first." Becky responded.

"Okay. In case you missed the email, the department is requesting desserts from anyone willing to do some baking—or buying for Wednesday. No obligation, of course. I'm sure we'll have plenty of food as usual. Laina, the meal is held in the big conference room down the hall."

"I can show her where it is." Anthony offered. He barely caught Juan rolling his eyes behind his desk, but didn't mention it.

"Perfect. I'll be in my office if you need me." She turned around and walked away.

"If you have a minute, I can show you where that room is. You've probably walked past it a dozen times already." Anthony said to Laina.

"I just need to run to the ladies' room really quick and then I'm free. See you in a minute." She responded. Anthony watched her walk away.

Juan cleared his throat, breaking Anthony's stare. "What?" He asked, putting his hands in the air. He glanced at Becky and Eleanor to see if they were watching. Becky was busy with her notebook and if Eleanor was paying attention, she wasn't making it obvious.

Juan peeked his head around his desk. "We're *all* going to the Thanksgiving meal. Do you really need to give her a private tour of how to get there a week in advance?" He whispered.

"Are you jealous? Is that why you keep riding me for trying to be nice to her?"

Juan rolled his eyes. "Jealous? No. I'm married, fool. I just hate to see you looking after her like a lovesick puppy. She's an adult. She doesn't need her hand held by you or anyone else."

Sounds a lot like jealous *to me.* Anthony thought. "Forgive me for being kind. I'll try to cut back in the future." With that, Juan got up from his desk and walked over to where Becky was making notations in her lab notebook.

Laina stuck her head in the doorway, "I'm back and ready for my tour."

Anthony wondered if she'd really left at all when she used the word tour, but shook the thought from his mind. Juan was just making him paranoid. "Great. It's over on the north side of our floor." He said, pointing down the hallway.

"Does Addison always cover for the lab on holidays?"

"More or less. Sometimes Eleanor will, but she usually has a big family gathering for Thanksgiving, so that's probably why Dr. Fish is coming in."

"I'm kind of surprised that she doesn't want to go shopping with her family. They seem pretty close-knit."

Anthony laughed. "One thing you'll learn about Dr. Fish is that she *hates* shopping. Her youngest son does too, but he's half-addicted to video games and knows there are great deals to be had that day. Plus, she'll only be here for an hour or two at most."

"I figured that she would come on Saturday instead, especially since her kids won't have school and everything."

"She rarely comes in on a Saturday. She goes biking with her youngest nearly every Saturday morning. They basically have a race to the top of this hill every week."

"You sure know a lot about her family." Laina cocked her head at him in curiosity.

"I don't know what the lab you came from is like, but Dr. Fish has regular lab gatherings outside of work. We're kind of an extended family. Plus, Martin—that's her youngest—has had to come to work with her a few times when he doesn't have school. Juan and I both know him pretty well. I've been with Dr. Fish for—" he paused, not wanting her to know that he had been a graduate student far longer than most,"—a while, so it's easy to learn about both Dr. Fish and Eleanor's families."

"A *while*, huh?" Laina pursed her lips at Anthony in a teasing manner. "Taking the scenic route through grad school?"

Anthony blushed. "Something like that." He cleared his throat. "Here's the conference room. It's probably locked right now or I'd show you around. The doors will be open for the meal though. Are you going to bring a dessert?"

"I don't know. I guess I have about a week to decide. I'm not really much of a chef or a baker, so I would probably bring a store-bought pie if I brought something. How about you?"

"I always bring some pumpkin pie. It's almost impossible to mess that up." He said as they walked back to the lab.

"Well, I will look forward to sampling that, Mr. Wydrow." She said and licked her lips.

Anthony felt himself blushing again and tried to calm his emotions before his whole face was red. They had just reached the lab door and he didn't want Juan to see. "Thanks. It's usually a fun celebration. Some of our international students and postdocs will bring a cultural dish to share too. We have some multi-talented folks in our department." He cringed when the word *folks* left his mouth. *What was he, an eighty-five-year-old grandpa?*

Laina smiled. "Thanks again for the tour, Anthony. I appreciate it." She walked over to her desk and picked up her notebook.

Anthony was about to sit down and boot up his computer again when he saw Juan peek his head around the computer again. "Was it hot in the conference room?"

"What? No. It was locked. We didn't even go in."

"It's just, your face looks a little flushed, like maybe it was hot." He grinned.

"Hilarious." Anthony hissed back.

Neither man noticed Laina watching them smugly from the corner of her eye.

Chapter 53

L aina called Emmitt on Monday evening to see what he thought about the graphs she had emailed him. She knew he might still be grumpy from the conversation over the weekend, but needed to know if he wanted her to make further adjustments to the work. He picked up on the first ring.

"I looked at your graphs."

She waited for him to continue, but he was silent.

"And? Did you send them to *Apothecom*?" She asked even though she knew he hadn't. She had checked his tracker when she got home and knew that he'd looked at her email but that he didn't do anything with the data.

"If I send this, we're setting a precedent—"

"The *precedent* is already set, Emmitt. If we can't get a similar signal from what everyone thinks is the same, wild type channel, then there is no point in sending anything else. They will *know* that we're either A---incompetent or B—invalid or worse, C—fraudulent. This has to match or it's all irrelevant."

Emmitt ran his fingers through his hair. *Damnit. He knew she was right, but he'd never actually fudged data before.* "You're right. Of course, it has to match. I don't like doing it this way. I've never fudged data like this."

"Oh, come on, Emmitt. Like what you've actually done is somehow better. You said it yourself, we need *Apothecom* to get behind this if we're going to get our drug therapy on the market. You have a successful lab, but you could never fund this on your own."

"I know. I *know*! Fine. I'll send it over tonight and let you know when I hear from them. I already have the screening form typed up. Their admin sent me a template to follow when we first started interfacing with them."

Laina had seen the template, but Emmitt didn't know that. "Good to be proactive. How long does it usually take them to respond?"

"My contact usually responds quickly, but he'll have to run this by his team. I'm guessing they will allow us to start recruiting volunteers for the study, but say that the timeline for it is TBD pending the rest of our results."

"Seems reasonable. I'm running the experiment again this week. Next week is Thanksgiving, so I'll basically have the lab to myself. I can play around with some of the settings without anyone observing. Assuming I can repeat this in a way that won't make Addison suspicious, I'll send all of it to both of you on Friday. I'll get our own cells up and running over the holiday."

"Okay, but send it to me first. It's not that I don't trust you; I just want to be doubly sure that nothing looks falsified with what you've done."

"Fine. I'll be in touch." She ended the call.

Chapter 54

Rather than stress Anthony out by looking over his shoulder, Addison stayed out of his way on Thursday. She had already told him that regardless of his results, he had to present it at lab meeting on Friday morning. Maybe someone else would have an idea of where he'd gotten off track. She kept to her office all day, catching up on email and getting ready for her meeting with Becky that afternoon.

When she arrived on Friday morning, she had an email from Laina waiting in her inbox. *At least Laina was able to get her experiment to work.* Addison thought as she opened the attachments. Laina had basically repeated Anthony's control experiments. It was a necessary step before using their own cells. She needed to show that she could replicate the process before testing a new system. Addison clicked through Laina's graphs and thought they all looked good. It gave her hope that Anthony's experiment had gone smoothly too. Maybe everything was back on track after a brief hiatus last week. She put her computer to sleep and grabbed a notebook and pen to take notes at lab meeting.

When she arrived, Anthony was already hooking up his laptop to the projector. She couldn't tell if he was anxious or excited and could hardly keep from asking him if he'd worked out the kinks from last week. Soon, everyone else arrived and he pulled up his power point presentation.

"Well, everyone, here we are again." He said as he started the presentation. Addison blinked when he pulled up his first graph. It wasn't at all what she expected. The signal was much higher and the slope of the response was different too. *What the hell?* She thought. *Our lab newbie made this work yesterday and he's blundering yet another experiment?*

"I'm not sure what went wrong, but Dr. Fish wanted me to show you my results regardless of how confusing they are." Addison heard someone choke on their beverage, but didn't look to see who it was. She still couldn't believe that Anthony was spinning his wheels again.

"I have run these control experiments at least one hundred times before and I have never gotten results like this. If anyone has any idea of what I'm doing wrong, please, I'm begging, enlighten me." His shoulders sagged.

The other two PIs asked the same questions that Juan and Addison had already asked. No one had any new ideas of how his experiment was so different. They all agreed that it was almost like he was doing a completely different experiment. The meeting ended earlier than usual since no one else had anything new to offer. Addison knew that Anthony was frustrated and didn't want to berate him for it. She sat down with him after everyone else left to brainstorm a solution.

"I know you don't want to hear this, but I think you need to thaw new cells and try again in two weeks. You weren't going to do an experiment next week anyway with the holiday taking up half of the week."

Anthony ran his fingers through his hair. "I can't imagine that it's the cells though. They worked just fine two weeks ago."

"Well, you amplified your DNA again recently, right? Did you check it to make sure it didn't rearrange or something?"

His shoulders slumped further. He never did the extra intermediate steps unless he absolutely had to. "No. I just assumed—" He bit his lip. "I'll check it this afternoon. If it's wrong, then I'll redo that again at the beginning of the week."

Addison nodded. "Okay, hopefully it's just something simple like that. I know you're frustrated. We're going to get this back on track. This is our bread-and-butter experiment. I could do it in my sleep if I had to. We'll figure it out. Don't worry."

She left him to gather up his things and shut down the projector. She hated seeing him so dejected even though she was feeling the same way. *How in the world could his experiment have gone so haywire when Laina's was close to an exact replica of what he usually does?*

Addison stopped by the lab to see if Becky had heard back from any of her potential committee members. Everyone except

Laina was at their desks when she walked in. She walked over to Becky's bench.

"Any update on the committee?"

"Yes! I am just waiting for one more confirmation and then I'll have my five-member team." She smiled. "Also, my binding assay went *really* well yesterday. Do you have a minute to look at it with me?"

Addison pulled up a free chair and sat down next to Becky. They discussed her next steps and the possible direction she could take based on her preliminary results. It was encouraging to see Becky so excited about her project. When she got up to go back to her office, she realized that Laina still wasn't back.

"Has anyone seen Laina?"

"She said that she had to take a phone call from her mom and left straight from lab meeting. I'm not sure if she's coming back or not." Eleanor said.

"Hmm. Hopefully, everything is okay. Still on for lunch today?"

Eleanor nodded. "Looking forward to it."

Addison smiled and thought, *"Are you, though?"*

Chapter 55

After lab meeting ended, Laina rushed out of the building with her phone, mumbling some sort of excuse about her mom calling. *If they only knew!* She thought. She dialed Emmitt as soon as she was out of the building and willed him to answer even though it was still relatively early on the west coast.

"Laina? I wasn't expecting a call from you this morning."

"We might have a problem."

"Just one?" He said awkwardly, even though inside he felt panicked.

"I think that dweeb Anthony might have snatched our channel construct."

"What?! How is that possible. It's locked in the freezer except for when you're using it."

Laina sighed. "On Tuesday last week, I had just pulled all my samples to thaw on ice when that fool from the admin office called to tell me that my new fob was ready. He said that I had to come sign for it right then or I wouldn't get it. No one but Eleanor was in the lab at that point, so I literally ran down the stairs to get it. Unfortunately, the admin guy was super chatty as though I might be interested in giving him the time of day and it took way longer than it should have for me to get the fob from him. By the time I got back up to the lab, Anthony was in the tissue culture hood doing his own transfection."

"That doesn't mean that he took the construct. I don't understand."

"Okay, you know how he has to give lab meeting every week?"

"Yes."

"Well, just now in lab meeting he put up his results from yesterday and his control runs look *just like mine*."

"That doesn't necessarily mean that he took the construct. Maybe this is good news. Maybe something else is different in the lab and the issues you have been having getting our channel to behave like the wild type are related to his issues."

"Or maybe he stole my DNA construct and won't admit it."

"I don't think we can safely jump to that conclusion yet. Give it another week and let's see if the results line out on their own. If we're in the same place at this point next week, then we can brainstorm about how to mitigate this."

"*Mitigate? Are you fu—*"

"Easy, Laina. You must keep your temper in control."

"Thanks for the tip, Captain America. This could blow up in our faces. What if they sequence it? What then, Sherlock?"

"Again, you don't even know that they *have* it. What if you find a way to somehow get it back and it turns out to not be what you think it is? And what if you get caught trying to get it back? What then?"

"I already sent graphs to Addison showing her how *well* everything worked yesterday. She's going to be suspicious."

"She has no reason to suspect foul play. This student of hers, Anthony, is a loose cannon. She knows that he makes mistakes and is sloppy. I'm sure she is not in any way thinking that we've been trying to hide something from her. Relax."

"I think we need to get ahead of this, Emmitt."

"We're ahead of it by being aware that it *could* be an issue. We cannot overreact. Stay cool, Laina. Do not do anything rash. Understand?"

"Fine. We'll do it your way for now. I'll keep you updated." She ended the call even though she knew he was wrong. She had seen the exact response in her own experiment that Anthony had put up on the screen. What were the odds that he didn't take her channel?

Chapter 56

A
ddison thought Eleanor seemed more relaxed as they walked from the elevator to the café. Maybe she just had something going on at home that had been distracting her and now it had resolved. Addison hoped that her cheery personality would come back soon.

"It's been way too long since we've gotten lunch together." She said to Eleanor.

"It has been a few months. We've both been fairly busy with getting Laina settled and everything else. Thanks for inviting me out. I really like this café too."

A waitress came over and took their orders. Both women had eaten there enough times that they knew what they wanted without looking at the menu. Addison wouldn't really consider herself a regular at the restaurant, but she knew several PIs who ate there almost daily for lunch.

"I never followed up with you about Gary's DNA screening. Did anything come from that?"

"Well, sort of. Just this week he was contacted about a new drug trial for people with mutations like his. Of course, he wouldn't find out if he was getting the placebo or the real thing until it was over."

"That's exciting! Did he say who was conducting the trial?"

"He did, but I can't remember. I'll have to ask him and let you know. I think he was pretty set on doing it."

"Good for him. He's really proactive about his health. I admire that."

Eleanor smiled. "He is. He loves to tell people about our lab and what we do even though he doesn't completely understand it."

"We should make him a shirt or a hat that says *number one fan* or something like that." She laughed. "How is everything else going? I've talked your ear off about the kids, but haven't gotten to hear about your own family. Anything else new?"

Eleanor picked up her napkin and fiddled with the hem. "Oh, not much really. Everyone is doing well and staying busy."

Addison noticed that Eleanor's mood had shifted and wondered if she was still bothered by something. "Sometimes boring is nice, right?"

Eleanor looked up, but didn't seem relaxed. "Yes," she said slowly.

"Is everything okay, Eleanor? I feel like I upset you somehow."

"Oh, it's nothing. Really. I'm just...distracted."

"Is someone bothering you in the lab? You can talk to me. I don't want you to be unhappy at work. We're friends. Please, how can I help?"

Eleanor continued to fiddle with the hem of the napkin. She looked around the dining area and chewed on her lower lip. "It's not that. It's just---" she stopped speaking. Addison waited, trying to keep from interrupting Eleanor's thoughts.

"It's just that...well, I have been getting these notes." She grabbed her purse and pulled out some scraps of paper. Addison instantly thought of the weird note she had received weeks earlier. She took the notes from Eleanor to read them.

Don't trust the Strydent people.

The Strydent lab has skeletons in their closet. You've been warned.

Watch your new postdoc like a hawk.

"Oh Eleanor! This must have felt very threatening. When did you get these?"

"I have been getting one every few days or so in my mailbox since the week that Dr. Hibber, um, Laina, arrived. At first, I thought that someone was just trying to stir up drama, but then I kept getting them. I know you knew Dr. Strydent from high school and that you trusted him, so I didn't want to concern you about it. Why shouldn't we trust them, though?"

"I can't think of a reason, Eleanor, but I didn't stay in touch with Emmitt after high school graduation. Do you have any idea who could be leaving the notes?"

"I don't. I was hoping that whoever it was would talk to me directly, but no one has. I've just been collecting them in my purse.

I didn't know what else to do. I'm sorry."

"There's no reason to be sorry, Eleanor. You have done nothing wrong. I got a note too, right after I submitted the paperwork for the collaboration, but I haven't gotten any since then. I'm not sure what to make of it either. Like you said, we have no reason *not* to trust Emmitt and Laina. Thank you for telling me. I'm not sure what the best course of action is. I suppose I will have to lend a more critical eye to anything unusual that happens from this point."

Eleanor nodded. "I should have told you sooner. It feels much better to talk about it than to hide it from you. I will let you know if I get any more notes."

They finished eating their sandwiches and then split the check. Addison was glad that Eleanor had opened up to her, but the news that she was receiving warning notes too was troubling. She wished whoever was sending them would stop being so clandestine and just talk to them. Her mind flashed back to the secretary's face when Addison submitted the request to collaborate with Emmitt. It couldn't be Sheila, though. The handwriting wasn't at all close to anything she had seen the woman write. Until she could figure out who it was, she needed to think about what would make someone be so wary of Emmitt's lab. She would have to get some input from Ryan. He was good at critical thinking and problem solving.

Chapter 57

When Addison and Eleanor got off the elevator, they saw Anthony carrying a gel back into the main lab. Addison wondered if the gel had revealed any answers to his experimental struggles. He hadn't seen them step off the elevator, so she followed him over to his lab bench. No one else was back from lunch yet.

"Anything interesting?" She asked when she caught up to him.

"No. It looks just like it should." He showed her the photo he had taken of the gel. She had looked at the same image enough times to know that it was correct.

"It's possible that a mutation incorporated somewhere other than the places we check with this test. You know, we have a DNA sequencer in the lab. We could run it through that and see if there is a mutation. If it comes back as the wild type, then we'll have to look elsewhere."

"I haven't used the sequencer before. Is it straightforward?"

"More or less. I think Eleanor can probably help walk you through it."

"I would be happy to, dear," Eleanor said from her desk. "Just let me get my things put away and I'll meet you over at the common bench."

"Thank you. I'll go get the construct from my box. How long does it take to get the sequence?"

Addison looked at her watch. "We probably won't get a sequence until we come back on Monday. Eleanor, can you remind me where the primers for the channel are?"

Eleanor met her gaze. "Sure. They're in the lab freezer." She pointed to the regular refrigerator by Juan's desk. Anthony left the room to get his sample from the deep freezer next door.

"Eleanor, I know that the grant we used to pay for the sequencer requires that we submit any sequence to the public database, but let me analyze it first before we do that. I don't want to put an errant sequence in that system without understanding where it came from."

"I understand. Should I email it to you?"

"Just save it in your folder on the network. I can access it from there on Monday. I might try to look at it over the weekend if I get a chance."

Before they could discuss it further, Anthony came back with his ice bucket. Addison locked eyes with Eleanor for a moment before walking towards the door.

"I'll leave you both to it. If anyone hears from Laina, let me know. I just realized that I don't have her phone number. I guess I can check with Emmitt and see if she's okay or if she needs anything. At the very least, he can get us her number."

"Oh, I have her number," Anthony said. "I can shoot her a text."

Addison blinked to conceal her shock. "Thank you, Anthony. Let me know if she needs anything." She turned to go back to her office, passing Becky who was probably on her way back to the lab after lunch. Addison wished that they could get a sequence back before the end of the day, but the sodium channel was too big to finish by then. She wondered if Anthony had just gotten unlucky and ended up in a random mutation or if something else was happening. Laina kept all of her DNA constructs locked in that freezer, so it seemed rather unlikely that Anthony would have been able to get his hands on it. Still, even if he had taken her construct, it should still be the wild type. It didn't make any sense that it would have a different response than they were used to seeing. Plus, Laina's experiment was normal, so it couldn't be the construct. She texted Ryan when she got back to the office.

Today has been a crazy day. Even more bizarre than last week. Is everything okay?

Yes. Just...weird.

Addison spent the rest of the afternoon trying to concentrate on her upcoming grant renewal, but her mind was constantly going back over various scenarios that could explain Anthony's results. Whenever she had a new idea that they could check, she jotted it down on her notepad. Hopefully, the sequence would shed some light on the mystery. She didn't have many other ideas to fall back on if it didn't.

Chapter 58

Ryan had dinner ready when Addison got home. Joe's football season had ended the previous weekend when they lost in the divisional round. Even though she knew Joe was disappointed about the loss, Addison was ready for a break from weekly football games. Of course, basketball practice had already started, so it wouldn't be long before he had games twice a week. Martin was spending the night at Joel's house to celebrate the start of Thanksgiving break and their older kids had both made plans to see a new movie at the local theater.

"So, tell me about this crazy day."

"You wouldn't believe it. I'm not sure where to start. Anthony's experiment still bombed, but Laina's didn't. Eleanor is getting borderline threatening notes from some mystery person—assumably someone in the department, and Laina had some sort of family emergency right when lab meeting ended. She never came back, but Anthony heard from her that she was fine. She'll be back at work on Monday."

"Eleanor is being threatened?! Did you report it?"

"Let me clarify. Someone has been leaving notes in her mailbox warning her not to trust people from Emmitt's lab. I told you about the note that was slid under my office door a few weeks ago, right?"

"Yes, but when you didn't get any more, I just assumed it was somebody trying to play a dumb joke. Did Eleanor show you the notes she received?"

"She gave them to me." Addison pulled them from her bag to show Ryan. "I mean, no one is threatening any kind of bodily harm or anything."

Ryan looked through the notes and shook his head. "They are strange. Does Emmitt have history with anyone besides Dr. Watt?"

"I mean, not that I know of, but that doesn't mean that he hasn't worked with someone else. It's a big department. Who knows?"

"I think we can assume that if Dr. Watt had an issue with Emmitt or his lab, he wouldn't have approved the collaboration."

"Agreed. I wonder if there is anyone still with his staff that had interactions with Emmitt back then. Maybe a long-time technician or research professor?"

"Could be. Do you think Eleanor should ask some of the other techs and see if they know more about the people that came to the department with Watt?"

"I'm not sure if she would do it. The notes really put her on edge. Zenia might know. I'll ask her next time I see her."

"What do you think is going on with Anthony? It seemed like he'd really gotten back on track."

"It really did. I'm fairly puzzled. We're sequencing the DNA of the sodium channel construct that he has been using the last two weeks. If it comes back normal, then I'm not sure what to test. Laina's experiment looked just as it should. It wasn't even an experiment; she was just repeating our controls to make sure that she had the process figured out. It looked completely normal."

"I'm sure you'll figure it out. Let's watch a movie and see if you can distract your mind from all of this for an evening. The lab will still be there on Monday."

"I guess I'm off the hook for biking tomorrow morning since Martin is over at Joel's. Maybe we can actually sleep in on a Saturday."

"I'm going to hold you to that."

"Wait, are your parents still coming on Tuesday?"

"Oh, yeah, they are. Guess we've got a house to clean this weekend." Ryan sighed and turned on the TV.

Chapter 59

Emmitt continued to stew about his conversation with Laina over the weekend. She had already overstepped by putting the tracker bug things—*what did she call them*—keys on the Fischer lab's computers. He wasn't very knowledgeable regarding technology, but she even admitted that they were illegal. He felt like she was repeatedly making snap decisions that would get them into trouble if he didn't get her under control again. He had always been very methodical and deliberate with his decisions regarding the lab and his project. He picked up the phone to call her again.

"Yes, Emmitt?"

"I need to make sure that *you* understand that we are not going to act on any of your thoughts or opinions about Anthony's results. We are walking a tight line here, Laina, and you're really making it a challenge."

"I'm making it a challenge? Unbelievable. I'm just trying to keep you from writing your own death warrant. You started this charade."

"You need to tell me before you formulate any plans or chase some wild hare idea that you don't even have proof exists!"

"I do have proof! I saw his data."

"No actions, Laina. If we overreact, we will never get through this."

"I still think we need to be proactive, but I guess this is still your circus, so we'll do it your way." She ended the call.

Emmitt didn't feel any better. He tried to think of a reason to call Laina back to California, but that would just slow things down with *Apothecom*. He couldn't send anyone else because no one else was good enough. He picked up his stress ball and tried to will a good idea into his mind.

Chapter 60

Laina rolled her eyes as she went over her conversation with Emmitt. She could almost guarantee that he was wrong. He was always so arrogant, so unable to see or hear anyone else's opinion. Anthony took her sample and she knew it. Maybe she could ask him for it back in an innocent way. She could tell him that she hadn't amplified her own construct yet, and ask to borrow whatever he was using. She wondered if that would make him suspicious that she was suspicious. If he gave her some of his own sample, that wouldn't get her anywhere either.

She drummed her fingers on the table and kicked her foot trying to figure out a solution. Emmitt didn't believe her that the kid took the reagent, but she knew in her heart that he did. The only way she could convince him that he took it would be to get it back and sequence it. Emmitt would never allow that. It would just be more evidence of his deceit. Laina knew they would start to inspect each of his reagents to troubleshoot his struggles and eventually land on the channel construct. She needed to get it back before they could do any more tests with it. This was going to require some outside assistance and Emmitt just didn't need to know about it.

Chapter 61

Addison got to work early on Monday with Martin in tow. She let him bring his iPad to play some video games while he was at work with her. After getting him set up in her office, she walked over to the lab to see if Eleanor was in yet. She was really anxious to get a look at the sequence to see if it solved the mystery of Anthony's lab troubles.

Eleanor was already at her desk and working at the computer. She had some purchase orders in a stack that she was logging into her filing system. The lab had several standing orders for frequently used materials, especially solutions that they used in tissue culture with their cells. Addison noticed that Laina was also in early. She wasn't at her desk, but her messenger bag was draped over her chair. Addison guessed that she was already setting up her cells for the week.

"Hi, Dr. Fischer! How was your weekend?"

"It kind of drug on. Martin spent the night at a friend's house on Friday, so we didn't get to do our weekly biking adventure at the park. Ryan's parents are coming on Tuesday, so we spent most of Saturday cleaning up the house to their standards. I am really ready to be back here." She laughed. "Have you pulled up the sequence yet?"

"I haven't. I was just entering all of our recent purchase orders into the system so that they could get paid. I can take a break and look at that now."

"I don't want to interrupt your process. I'll check the folder later this morning. Thanks." She left the main lab to go back to her office. Martin was supposed to be reading his book for half an hour before he did any gaming, so she hoped he had listened to her instructions. While he had several games on his iPad that he enjoyed, he also liked playing some of the older games on her desktop computer. She had promised to take him to lunch for hamburgers since he had to hang out in her office all day rather than be outside with his friends.

When she got back to her office, Martin was sitting in her

rotating office chair, moving it back and forth while he read. She didn't know how he did that without getting dizzy or sick. It made her dizzy just watching.

"I see you've made yourself at home, as usual. Could I have my seat back, please?"

Martin reluctantly pulled himself from the cushioned chair and sat down in one of the stationary chairs in her office. He barely pulled his eyes from the book when he moved, but somehow didn't trip over anything in the process. He sat sideways in the chair with his legs draped over one of the arms. She shrugged and logged into her computer. She was just about to open her email when her phone rang.

"Hi Eleanor. What's up?"

"I just saved the sequence into my folder. Did you want me to look through it or just leave it for you to analyze?"

Addison thought for a moment before answering. "Let's both look it over and see if we find the same result."

"Okay. I'll let you know when I'm finished." Eleanor responded, knowing that she wouldn't get through it as quickly as her boss.

Addison had a shortcut on her desktop to the lab's common folder, which allowed her to easily access each of the lab member's sub-folders. She clicked it open and quickly found the sequence file that Eleanor had saved. She could copy the sequence into a program that came with their sequencer to have it screen for mutations. This was a much faster option than going through it base by base. The computer that Eleanor had in the lab also had the application installed. Addison knew that it was virtually impossible for them to get different results, but wanted someone else to review it with her nonetheless. Because the DNA sequence of the sodium channel was so long, it would take a few minutes for the program to scan through it. She looked through her emails while she waited for it to finish. The only relevant email she had was from Dr. Watt's secretary reminding the department about the Thanksgiving meal on Wednesday. Addison deleted the rest of the messages and set a reminder in her phone to pick up a pumpkin pie from the deli on her way home the next day. She knew Ryan's mom would happily make one for her, but hated to ask as she was also making most of the Thanksgiving meal for their family too. Her computer chirped with a notification. The program had finished analyzing the DNA sequence. She mentally crossed her fingers even though she wasn't sure what she was hoping for.

The application identified one mutation in the sequence. Addison scrolled over to its location to see if the mutated base would cause a change in the amino acid sequence. Even though she had been working in biological research her entire adult life, she didn't have all of the amino acid sequences memorized.

"Hey, Martin—"

"Yes, Mom?" He asked without taking his eyes off the page.

"Can you reach that yellow folder that's on the shelf behind you?"

Martin stuck his finger in his book to mark his place and then turned around to look for the yellow folder. He passed it over to her.

"Thanks, Dude." She said as she took it from him.

"What's in the folder?"

"It has all the base code triplets for the twenty amino acids. I need to look one up."

"Why wouldn't you just Google it?"

"Because this is how I do it. Come here and look." She waited for him to put his book down and come to her desk. "You like computer coding, so maybe this will be interesting to you. Each amino acid has two to six combinations of base pairs—the A-T-G-C letters that *code* for it. We ran a DNA sample through our sequencer over the weekend and it reported a mutation in one base. Just because a base is changed doesn't mean that the amino acid will change."

"Okay, that makes sense. Did yours change?"

"Well, the wild type—that's the original sequence—has a triplet of AGG, which codes for arginine. *Our* new sequence reported *GGG*, which codes for?" She let him look through her printed list of codes to find the correct amino acid himself.

"Pro-line." He said the second syllable with a long "i" sound.

"Pro-*lean*." She corrected him.

"So, it is a mutation!"

"Yes, it certainly is."

"Is that a good thing?"

"To be perfectly honest, Martin, I'm not sure. It answers one question but raises many more. Let me show you the difference between the two amino acids. We also have to look at where the amino acid is within the bigger structure of the channel. Arginine is a positive charged amino acid."

"Like a proton?"

"Sort of like that. Some of the amino acids are positively charged, some are neutral, and some are negative."

"What is proline?"

"Great question, my little scientist! Proline is neutral. It's also a lot smaller than arginine." She showed him the simple chemical structures that were also in her yellow folder.

"They look very different. Does the mutation make a big change?"

"It might. We're just learning about it. I need to look some things up and see if I can find out some more about it before I can answer that question well. Why don't you get back to your reading?"

"Okay, Mom. Thanks for the cool biology lesson." She ruffled his hair and then turned back to her computer. She opened the publication database to see if the arginine-proline mutation was documented. Before she could type in her query, her phone rang again.

"Hi, Dr. Fischer, it's Eleanor. I got a mutation in position 655. Looks like an A to a G."

"I got the same, Eleanor. I was just showing Martin what it means. Let me know when Anthony gets in. I want to talk to him about it. This is obviously what is causing his troubles with his experiment. Hopefully, it will set his mind at ease that he hasn't lost his touch or something."

"Will do. Talk to you later." Eleanor hung up. Addison went back to searching publications that cited a mutation in the sodium channel. She wasn't familiar with this particular mutation, so she didn't think it was one that had been well-studied. When Anthony arrived, she was going to have him look at the structure map of their channel to see where the mutation was located. She also needed him to set aside any of the DNA he had amplified with the mutation so that no one else inadvertently used it in their experiments. Ideally, she would like him to put it in a completely different box and clearly label it, but experience told her that he'd just put a red dot on it or something and move it to a corner of his box. She sighed and rolled her eyes. She would personally watch him move it out of his working box.

Chapter 62

When Laina finished dividing out her cells into new dishes, she returned to her desk to outline her experiment for the week. She was still on edge about Anthony's results from lab meeting and wished she could secretly figure out if he had taken her construct. She knew Emmitt thought it was just a fluke of the lab, but he hadn't seen the images. Laina was certain that the cretin had stolen some of her sample while she was out of the room. Proving it would blow their cover, so she had to figure out a way to get it back without arousing suspicion. She couldn't stay late and look through all of his boxes. Nothing was labeled in any coherent manner, so she'd never know what to take from him. She figured that he must have taken a few microliters from her ice bucket, which was why she hadn't realized anything was missing. It *was* possible that he'd used all of it after the last two weeks and didn't have any left.

She had heard Emmitt mention that Anthony had a history of leaving his samples out overnight in an ice bucket. Maybe she could find a way to make it look as though he had been careless with reagents again. Still, she couldn't do it herself because he would definitely deny being responsible for the loss. If they reviewed the building entrance history, her fob would reveal that she was the only one present when it happened. She needed to find someone else to sabotage the samples.

"You look deep in thought." Anthony startled her.

"Oh! Hey! Sorry, I was trying to decide if I wanted to add any conditions to my experiment this week." She lied. "How was your weekend?"

"It was okay. I'm still pretty frustrated by the results from the last two weeks. I can't figure out what I'm doing wrong."

"Sorry to interrupt, dears. Anthony. Dr. Fischer asked that you call her." Eleanor interjected.

Laina turned back to her computer while Anthony picked up the lab phone. She tried to eavesdrop on their conversation, but she could only partially hear what he was saying. After he hung up the phone, he logged into his computer and started typing. She wondered what Addison had asked him to do, but didn't want to be nosey. Before she could come up with a reason to walk past his desk, she heard Addison coming down the hallway from her office. Laina grabbed her lab notebook so that she could use it as a screen to keep them from seeing her stare.

"Hey, Anthony—did you get the structure pulled up?" Addison asked as she walked over to his desk. He slid his chair over to the side so she could see the screen easily too. Laina wished she knew what they were discussing. Addison was pointing at the computer screen and gesturing with her hands while Anthony listened. Laina could only guess as to what she was saying to him. After a few minutes, they both got up and left the room. Laina wondered if she could casually eavesdrop in the hallway under the guise of answering a personal phone call. She decided it was worth a shot and grabbed her cell phone from her messenger bag. She couldn't quite hear everything they were saying, but caught some of it.

"...samples you have left from when you amplified the DNA last. Label ... Here, ... work. ...different box... so we don't mix them up on accident. Then check with Juan to see if he has any wild type left from his last set of experiments. You can use that for the time being."

Laina held her phone up to her ear and turned away from the doorway when she heard Addison's steps coming toward the hallway. She made sure to speak up as Addison passed so that she knew Laina was on the phone. Based on what she had overheard, she wanted to run across the street and call Emmitt right then, but knew her hasty exit the previous Friday was already a bit suspicious. She would have to wait and call him in the evening.

Emmitt had told her over the weekend that he was granted permission to start recruiting volunteers for the drug trial, but had to keep specifics to a minimum since no start date had been announced yet. Each person interested in volunteering for the study had to undergo a DNA screening. The study would be done with a double-blind where neither the participant nor the doctor administering the drug therapy knew if they were getting a placebo or the real deal. However, Emmitt had made a special request that he be able to select all the participants based on their DNA screening results. He made the request saying that he was more familiar with the mutations of interest and agreed to only select volunteers that had the relevant mutations. It would be a very specified study, but then the gene therapy they were developing was for a specific group of people with specific mutations. The therapy wouldn't be meaningful without the mutations that Emmitt had studied for the last two decades. On the one hand, Laina was surprised they were giving him so much control over their drug trial. She knew that he had a lot of connections in the world of scientific research and probably knew the right person to ask.

Chapter 63

When Addison got back to her office, Martin was seated in her office chair clicking around on her computer. He hadn't even looked up when she entered the room. She knew that she had logged out before she left to meet with Anthony and gave Martin the side eye, knowing that he had hacked into her computer.

"Okay, little raccoon, confess. I know you hacked my password."

"Mom! I didn't hear you get back." He looked at her with wide eyes.

"I take it you finished your reading for today?"

"Yeah, I put in my thirty minutes. By the way, your password is terrible. I got it on the first try."

She narrowed her eyes at him. "I do love taking criticism from my favorite sixth grader, but what is wrong with my password? I followed all of the constraints that the university requires. The IT department gave it a *strong* rating."

"You used your birthday for the number and your and dad's initials for the letters. How is that considered *strong*?"

"I guess they didn't realize that the master of all password breaking skills would ever be a risk to their system. What are you doing to my computer right now? This doesn't look like *Solitaire*."

"Okay. Do you remember when I was telling you about the new tracking program that had been discovered?"

She didn't, but he talked about computers and video games so much, she figured he had mentioned it at some point. "More or less. Why?"

"I found one on your computer. Look." He turned the monitor to face her and pointed at the screen.

"For the moment, let's pretend like I've never used a computer before and I have no idea what you're talking about." She said, wondering what in the world he was trying to show her.

"It's okay if you don't remember, Mom. I found one of those tracker keys on your computer. The ones that people attach to emails without you realizing it. You open the attachment and the key gets added to your device without you realizing it. The file is hidden unless you know what to look for, so it's virtually undetectable to the layperson."

"And there's one on my computer?! Surely our anti-virus software would have caught it."

"No, Mom. The anti-virus software won't find this because it doesn't look like a normal virus or bug. It's a completely different kind of code. I'm sure they will catch up and be able to find them soon, but it's beyond all of the normal spam-ware and anti-virus firewalls. Do you want me to turn it off? I can do that, but I need to read some more about how to remove it before I try to do that."

"I don't know. Can you see when it was added? Was it added by someone with network access here, or is that not necessary?"

"It usually comes from an email, though someone could add it directly if they have access to your machine."

"No one else has access to my office. Not even the custodial crew. We put our trash out for them to take on Tuesdays and Fridays, so they don't have to enter the offices." Addison racked her brain, wondering what attachment she had opened that had given some stranger access to her computer. Thankfully, she never did any online shopping from her work computer, so her credit card and bank information should still be secure. "I should probably let IT know about this, right?"

"Wouldn't it be *more interesting* to find out where it came from first?!" Martin raised his eyebrows at her. "I can figure this out for you, Mom. This is a walk in the park."

"I'm going to call your dad and see what he thinks. I really think I should call IT and alert them to this. What if it's infected other computers in the department?"

"That's not how it works, Mom. It only affects the computer where the download originated."

She turned her head sideways in confusion. "What?"

"Okay. Someone sent you an email with an attachment. You opened the attachment and downloaded it. The key was hidden in your system. Now if you were to forward the email attachment to someone else, then it could also get into their system—but only if they downloaded the attachment too."

Addison got her cell phone out of her purse and called Ryan. It went straight to voice mail. She didn't really know what she wanted to say in the message, so she just hung up. She started to send a text but then realized the tracker could be on her phone too.

"Could this tracker thingy be on my phone too?"

"I haven't read about them being designed for cell phones yet. I can look if you want me to."

Addison handed him her phone and watched as he pulled flipped through various screens, occasionally searching for something on his iPad, then looking back at the phone. After a few minutes he gave it back to her.

"I can't find anything on it, Mom. Either you didn't open the attachment on your phone ever *or* it can't embed into the operating system of a cell phone."

"Okay. I'm going to text your dad in case he sees the missed call and gets worried." She thumbed off a text saying that everything was fine, but she had a question to run by him when he had a minute.

"Do you want me to turn the key off? It's not hard."

"Yes. No. I don't know. See if you can figure out when it showed up and maybe that will help me figure out where it came from in the first place."

Addison sighed. She really didn't have time to deal with people messing with her computer. What was she doing that was so interesting someone wanted to keep tabs on it? She immediately thought about the mysterious notes. Maybe whoever was sending the notes had found a way to watch her computer and keep tabs on Emmitt's lab? She wasn't sure if she should report this to Emmitt too. She didn't have any intellectual property of his on her computer. The only things she had looked at from his lab were part of the public domain and accessible to anyone. Maybe she should call Emmitt and see if this had ever happened to him. She didn't want to spook him out of continuing with the collaboration though. It had gotten off to a good start and could really give her lab a boost in the long term.

"Whoever made this really knows computer code. They've hidden the time stamp. I can probably still find it another way, but it will take me longer." Martin told her.

"Let's take a break from it for now. I'm not doing anything suspicious or illegal, so I can't imagine that whoever is trying to eavesdrop on my work life is paying that close attention. I need to get some more work done before lunch. I'll let you look some more tomorrow, okay?"

Martin nodded and relinquished her chair. He pulled out his iPad again and a set of headphones. Addison inwardly celebrated that he had remembered headphones. The background music that played with his video games was not conducive to a relaxed work environment. Hopefully, Ryan would call soon and she could get some advice about how to proceed regarding the tracker key.

Chapter 64

Anthony waited outside at one of the picnic tables for Juan to join him for lunch. After learning that his construct had a mutation from Addison that morning, he wanted to bounce a few hypotheses off of Juan before he prepared for his next experiment. Even though he knew Juan hated eating outside because of all the bugs that were constantly swarming around the over-filled garbage cans, Anthony had suggested the outdoor meeting place so that no one would interrupt them. Anthony waved Juan over when he saw his friend walk outside into the courtyard behind their building.

"What did you do that we needed to meet outside in secret?" Juan asked, setting his lunch on the table.

Anthony sighed. Juan was always so direct. "Can't I just enjoy an innocent lunch outside with a friend?"

"I'm not buying that for a minute. You've been a ball of anxiety for over a week and it can't just be because your experiments bombed. I've seen that happen to you enough times to know better."

"Hey! I am frustrated by the experiments, but you're right; there is something else. I need you to keep this between us though. At least for the time being."

"Laina asked you out and you don't know which shirt goes best with your only pair of non-jeans?"

"No—"

"Laina said that she'd go to dinner with you if you do all of her tissue culture for a month?"

"Stop. No. Nothing like that. The other day, I got to the lab and there was an ice bucket on the bench. I had a simple transfection planned with just a couple things. I was *going* to get my own DNA samples out, but then there was this ice bucket…"

"And you took some of the samples in it."

"Not exactly. I took a little bit of one of the samples. You know, I just put a little in a new tube and stuck it in my own ice bucket. I took a few microliters. It was not noticeable."

"Whose ice bucket was it?"

"It was Laina's."

"Shoot, man. Their stuff is patented and locked up. Why would you *do* that?"

"It was there. I was there."

"Didn't you still need to get your little alpha9 out of the freezer anyway?"

"Yes. And I could have just grabbed one of my tubes at that point, but I hadn't diluted my new sample and put it in separate tubes yet. So that was going to take extra time and the tissue culture hood was available right then…"

"So, you took it. I guess she didn't miss any of it, so it seems like you're in the clear. What's the problem?"

"The problem is that my experiment was messed up, man. Everything was wrong. The last two weeks have been a huge bust. Dr. Fish has been helping me troubleshoot what went wrong, including sequencing the sample over the weekend. It has a mutation."

"Wait, your new sample, or the sample you *borrowed*?" Juan used air quotes.

"Laina's sample. It says wild type on it, but it has a mutation and it has totally changed how the channel behaves."

"Do you think they know about it?"

"I don't know. She sent Dr. Fish results that looked like our normal control experiments. What did she do that made it work for her, but not for me? Have you ever heard of a construct mutating *during* the transfection process?"

"I can't think of anything off the top of my head. It seems unlikely."

"Dr. Fish thinks that I used my own sample from my recently amplified stock and that it incurred a random mutation at that point. She told me to label anything that I had left and make sure I set it aside so that I didn't accidentally use it again."

"That's why she told me that you needed my left-over channel DNA. She thinks you're out of wild type."

"Yeah, and if I tell her that I'm not because it wasn't ever my sample, I'm going to look like an irresponsible twerp again. She thought I had gotten past that and I don't want to disappoint her, but I feel like she should know that Laina is using a mutated sample."

"I hear what you're saying. I know you don't want to tell her and I understand why, but I agree, she needs to know. Laina needs to know too."

"I do not want to tell Laina. She would be pissed at me."

"You don't have a chance with her. I promise. She's going to be angrier the longer you wait to tell her."

"Probably so." Anthony ran his fingers through his hair. "Do you think I can wait until next week?"

"You at least have to tell Dr. Fish this week. Let her decide how to proceed once she knows the whole story."

Anthony dropped his chin to his chest. "I really screwed up this time. I don't know what I was thinking. I'll tell her tomorrow. I need to build up my nerve to do it."

"Okay. You know you have to do it, though, right?"

"Yes. And I'll do it. It just sucks." He sighed. Maybe this would be enough to scare him into being more responsible.

Chapter 65

When Laina got back to her apartment, she pulled out her laptop to check her various trackers. She hoped maybe Addison or Anthony had emailed someone about whatever they had talked about that morning. She knew something was wrong with Anthony's reagents since Addison had talked to him about them next to the freezer. She knew Emmitt would tell her not to jump to conclusions, but she was seriously worried that the Fischer lab had stumbled onto their secret.

She logged into the laptop and opened her software program. She had labeled each of her keys after the person whose computer had that tracker. Even though they all had the same code, she was able to designate any information into different folders based on where it originated. She opened Anthony's first. His web browser search history was fairly meaningless. She already knew that he had looked up the structure of the sodium channel, but he didn't do any other searches to indicate why. She closed his folder and opened Addison's. The tracker on Addison's computer indicated that she had accessed the lab network folder a few times as well as her email account, the computer's settings, and some sort of application that Laina wasn't familiar with. She scrolled through the emails, but none of them mentioned anything about Anthony. She looked to see which folders Addison had accessed within the network. For some reason, she hadn't accessed her own at all, but had opened up Eleanor's.

Laina decided that there couldn't be anything interesting in Eleanor's folder. It was probably just purchase orders or something useless like that. She wished she could have heard more of Addison and Anthony's conversation.

"Emmitt."

"Laina. How did the day go?"

"It was stressful. Something is going on and I'm trying to get to the bottom of it. I still think Anthony stole some of my sample. Addison was having him look at the channel structure today and directed him to pull some of his samples and set them aside. I think they know, but I can't find proof of it yet."

"I don't know why you think that. Addison is very blunt and cuts to the chase. If she thought something was off, she would say something."

"I don't know. Not if they already don't trust you. We just need to get it back. What if they sequence it?"

Emmitt ignored her question. "Did Anthony admit to taking it?"

"I can't very well accuse him of it, Emmitt. I need to find someone to steal it back. The building logs a record of whoever is entering or exiting the building whenever you use your fob. I can't go in after hours and take it. They'll know it was me."

"You're right. I think for now, just stick with ignorance. If he confesses to taking it, act surprised about the mutation and make a show of calling me, worried that we've introduced a mutation."

"We have another problem. I reported *typical* channel responses from my experiment last week. How do you explain my construct working normally for me, but not at all for him? I just need to get it back before they sequence it or something."

"I think the path of caution is the right one, Laina. We can't make desperate maneuvers or we'll lose control of the situation. We don't even know that there's a situation."

"I do. The signal he got from the channel, *our* channel, was identical to what I was seeing. He used the construct, Emmitt."

"You said yourself that you don't have proof. You haven't seen it in his hands or heard him say that he used it. Let's just relax and *proceed with caution*." Emmitt wrung his hands and swiveled his head around the room to find his stress ball. He couldn't believe that Laina was trying to blow this for him.

"I'll be in touch. You're wrong on this, Emmitt. This is going to bring us down." She ended the call and tossed her phone onto the couch. *How could he be so stupid? They needed to get ahead of this, not watch it drown their livelihood.*

Chapter 66

"I'm sorry that I missed your call today. We're swamped this week trying to get everything shipped out before the holiday weekend. What's going on?" Ryan asked when Addison and Martin got home.

"I found a tracker key on Mom's work computer!" Martin announced proudly.

"What? A what?"

"Does no one pay attention to me?"

"It's that thing he was talking about the other day. It tracks keystrokes or whatever. He was reading about it in his nerd magazine." Liv said from the living room.

"It's not a *nerd* magazine! But thanks for listening." He turned back to Ryan. "Someone put a tracker on the desktop computer in Mom's office. I found it while I was working there today."

"Working, mhmm. I see. What does this mean?"

"I'm not sure. Martin couldn't find when the tracker got onto my computer today. I told him that he could look again tomorrow. I can't figure out who would care about what I'm doing so much that they want to keep track of it." She raised her hands in the air.

"Let's go for a walk. Maybe some exercise will help us brainstorm some good ideas." Ryan suggested.

Addison almost protested, but then realized that Ryan didn't want the kids to hear the whole conversation. They hadn't told the kids about the strange notes she and Eleanor had received and didn't want to alarm them. Going for a walk would give them some privacy. At least the weather was nice. She shrugged back into her jacket and followed Ryan out the door.

"When will you be back?" Martin called after them.

"Ten minutes tops. We'll get started on dinner after that." Ryan responded as he was pulling the door closed.

"Have you considered that the same person leaving these strange notes is also the person that put the tracker on your computer?"

"I have, but Martin told me that the tracker must have been

hidden within an email attachment that I opened. I was hoping he could find a time stamp on the key, but he said that it was hidden. I think he might be able to find it if he has more time, but I'm not sure. Should I report it to IT or the department?"

"I'm not sure. My knee-jerk reaction is yes, you should report it, but since we don't know who could have sent it, we don't know if telling the department will alert them. They might do something more drastic."

"*More* drastic? What could be more drastic?"

"I don't know. I'm brainstorming here. If Martin can't crack the code by next Monday, then I think you need to let someone know."

"I hate the idea that I would lose my computer for possibly weeks or more because of this. It's so frustrating."

"Well, hopefully our little computer genius can save the day tomorrow." They had circled the block and were coming up on their house again. Addison squeezed his hand and rested her head on his shoulder.

"I sure hope so. Thanks for talking this out with me."

When they got inside, Liv and Joe were already cutting up some vegetables for a salad. Martin had his headphones on and was rapidly pressing buttons on the video game controller.

"Thanks for getting the salad started. Dad said he was going to grill steaks tonight, so this will be perfect to have alongside it." Addison said to her two older children. "How was practice today, Joe?"

"It was hard. They've really been making us run at the end of practice. Not everyone plays football and half the team is out of shape. Our first game is next week, so Coach is trying to make up for lost time."

"I keep forgetting to ask you, has Taylor heard back from any of the schools she applied to?"

Joe smiled. "Yes! She got a really good scholarship offer to DU, uh, Denver University. It's really close to Mines."

"Oh, that's great, honey! I remember you saying that was one of her top picks for schools in Colorado.

"How is play practice going, Liv? Has everyone learned their lines?" Ryan asked their daughter.

"It's about fifty-fifty. I'm trying not to be frustrated by people that haven't learned theirs yet, but it's hard. I have really had fun painting sets, though. It's cool to be involved on both sides of the show."

"Oh good. I'm glad you're getting to experience all of it. We are really excited to go see your play next month. Mom already bought all of us tickets for opening night. I'm going to go get the grill fired up."

After dinner, Ryan told Martin he had dibs on the TV to watch Monday Night Football. The Falcons were playing the Packers. Addison started falling asleep before half time and offered her apologies to Ryan and Joe. She encouraged Martin to get to bed on time so that it wasn't too hard to wake up in the morning.

Chapter 67

Addison and Martin arrived early again on Tuesday. She logged into the computer and told him that she was going to go check in with Eleanor. She showed him how to call the lab if he needed her.

Eleanor was entering more purchase orders when Addison got to the lab. No one else was in yet. Eleanor set the purchase orders aside when she saw Addison walk in.

"Gary got accepted into that study I told you about. They haven't announced a start date yet." She grabbed her purse and pulled out a sticky note. "The study is being done by a company called *Apothecom*."

"That sounds familiar for some reason, but I can't place it. I'll look it up."

"He's real excited about it." She smiled.

Before they could continue, Anthony walked in. He had bags under his eyes and looked like he hadn't slept well. Addison wondered if he was still stressed out about his experiments. She thought finding the mutation would help ease his mind, but apparently not.

"Hi, Dr. Fish, uh, could I talk to you for a minute?" He was fidgeting with his hands and looked uncomfortable.

"Sure, Anthony. Martin is in my office right now, but we can talk by your desk unless you'd like to go somewhere else."

"My desk is fine." He walked over and set his bag over the back of the chair.

Addison pulled up a chair. "How can I help?"

Anthony sighed. "Before I start, I just want to apologize for disappointing you again. I know I said that I would do better and I was doing better, but—that's not the point. I'm sorry. Two weeks ago, when I got to the lab, Laina's ice bucket was on the bench. I had already filled my own ice bucket, so I, uh, saw that she had the sodium channel in her bucket...so I took some and put it in my own tube rather than getting my own sample out. It was lazy and irresponsible and I'm sorry. I shouldn't have done it."

Addison's mind was reeling, but she didn't want to alarm Anthony. "Thank you for being honest with me. Is this the sample that I had you move to the other box last week? How much do you have left?"

"Yes, just a couple microliters. I didn't take very much." He looked at his feet.

"Don't talk to Laina just yet. I want to think about the best way to let her and Emmitt know. They have been fairly adamant about keeping their reagents separate from ours, so I'm not sure how they will respond to this." She told him.

"Should I throw it away? I added a red dot to the tube to remind myself not to use it."

Addison mentally rolled her eyes at his lazy labeling system. "Okay. Make sure you keep track of it for now. The good news is, once you start using your own reagents again, your experiments should be back to normal."

Anthony gave her a half-hearted grin. "Yeah, that's true. I'm sorry if I messed all of this up for you, Dr. Fish."

"It will be okay, Anthony. We'll figure it out." She squeezed his shoulder and got up.

"If this experience doesn't scare me straight, there's probably no hope for me." He said, half-joking.

"There is *always* hope for you, Anthony. You're a good scientist, you just occasionally make hasty decisions that are not always in your best interest."

Addison walked back to her office wondering what else Anthony's confession indicated. *If the mutated sample was actually Emmitt's construct, then where did the mutation come from? Why did Laina's experiment look like a normal, unmutated channel if she used the same construct? Could Anthony have mixed up samples? Did all of this somehow relate to the mysterious notes??*

Martin was busy clicking away at her computer. He had a DOS window open and was scrolling through lines of text while intermittently switching to the screen with files and folders. He had his iPad next to him and was occasionally checking it before returning to her computer. She wished she knew what he was doing.

"Find anything?" She touched him on the shoulder, making Martin jump. He was wearing his headphones and must have had some music playing.

"You scared me! I think I'm close. I just need to go back a little further. I found the code where it's sending information out. I just need to back track to where it starts. It's been at least a few weeks."

"Is there not just a start to the file it created?"

"It didn't create a file, Mom." He still hadn't looked away from the screen. She decided to let him keep working instead of interrupting the process. She felt like all of this was connected but wasn't sure how the pieces fit together to make it all make sense. Since she couldn't use her computer, for the time being, she grabbed her laptop out of her bag and set it up on the edge of the desk out of Martin's way. She wanted to look up the trial that Eleanor had mentioned.

She pulled up the *Apothecom* website and found the page that listed their drug trials. They had a link for current trials and those still accepting applicants. She chose the latter and scrolled through the results. She wasn't sure what trial Gary might have applied to, so she used the search option to find anything relevant to blood pressure. They had two trials, but one mentioned that applicants would need to have their DNA screened for mutations. She figured that must be the one that Gary was doing. Addison tried to remember why *Apothecom* seemed so familiar to her. It wasn't a major pharmaceutical company. She knew she had read something about them recently, but she just couldn't place it. She closed the browser and moved her laptop to the side. She needed to think through Anthony's revelation that he'd used Laina's construct. What did it mean that it had a mutation? Emmitt had said that the reagents had to be stored in a locked freezer because of patents and requirements by his legal team. What if none of that was true? She hated to suspect her high school classmate of dishonesty or worse yet, fraud. She was having a hard time coming up with an honest explanation, though. Maybe she would have a chance to talk about it with Ryan that night. Until she knew for sure what was going on, she wanted to get the sample out of Anthony's box so that no one else mistakenly used it. She left Martin with his search and went to move the sample to one of her boxes.

Chapter 68

L aina had only been in the Atlanta area a little while and hadn't made any friends, or even acquaintances for that matter. She needed to find a way to get the reagent back that Anthony stole without anyone thinking that she took it back. Emmitt thought they should play this conservatively and just keep tabs on what people were doing and saying before turning to more drastic measures. Laina disagreed. They needed the reagent back before someone figured out what it was and sent this whole charade crashing down. She couldn't believe that Emmitt wasn't more upset, but he was always such a controlled individual. Maybe he was able to hide his fear over the phone.

While living in Los Angeles, Laina had created an alias for herself within the dark web. She had worked especially hard to keep this persona completely separate from her real identity. She even had a disguise, should she ever need to meet someone. She had told Emmitt that she took computer classes to keep up with her coding skills, but in reality, she had learned most of what she knew through her contacts on the dark web. *As though a real computer class would teach you how to hack into your co-workers' files,* she laughed to herself.

Laina pulled out her tablet that she only used for accessing the dark web. She needed to post a request for someone to get one of the other lab members' fobs. Addison's would probably be the easiest since Laina at least knew something about the woman's weekend schedule. She'd find someone to swipe her fob from her vehicle while she was at the state park with her kid. She composed her request and posted it onto the message board of one of her groups. They simply knew her as Lorraine: the raven-haired woman with green eyes. Surely one of the members lived in the Atlanta area and would be willing to bend the laws of society a bit to make a little cash. She waited for someone to respond, tapping her foot impatiently as the seconds ticked by. She knew Emmitt would be incensed if he had any inkling of what she was doing. Before she could have second thoughts, a response popped up on the screen. Someone with the handle E-rock was interested in her proposal. She quickly accessed his profile, even though she knew that other people were just as likely to lie about who they really were as she was. If she had more time, she would have done some sort of deep dive to figure out who this guy really was, but time was not her ally right now. She looked over *E*-rock and discovered his name was Eddie. He was a big, muscled-up guy with a shaved head and dark, almost black eyes. He had a few barbed wire tattoos on his arms that you could see in his photo. He left a phone number for her to contact. She pulled out her burner phone and sent a text.

Hey. It's Lorraine. Have time to make a little cash this weekend?

She only had to wait a few seconds for the meathead to respond.

Always. What can I do you for?

She gagged at his juvenile joke.

Ha. U wish. I need you to get something out of a car for me.

B&E? 4 how much?

What's your rate?

$200 cash up front.

I can do that.

$200 more when I get you the goods.

Fine.

What am I looking 4?

She described Addison's car and where it would be parked on Saturday morning. Anthony had told her about her weekly bike ride at the state park with her son. She also knew that the woman kept her little bracelet with the fob on it in her car. A little trick to keep from forgetting it when she went to the lab. Laina gave him a time window to be watching and waiting for Addison to arrive with the bikes. She wondered if he was a regular at this sort of thing or if he usually connected people with other criminals. She didn't really care; she needed to get this done before things got more out of control. He should have plenty of time to take the fob and get out of the park before they got back. She knew Eddie wasn't dumb, even though he looked like some sort of muscled-up meathead. He quickly realized that the state park required you to pay to enter the park and upped the fee to cover the expense. She told him to text her after he was out of the park so that they could make plans for him to drop the fob for her somewhere. Once she had the fob, she could go into the building at night and it would log her in as Addison. Then she could enter the lab and find the sample before anyone started getting suspicious of it. Most likely, Anthony wouldn't even realize that she'd taken it because he was such a mess with reagents anyway. Then they could get back to finishing these experiments for *Apothecom*. She wasn't going to tell Emmitt about her plan. She'd just get the reagent back and everything would be on track again.

Chapter 69

By lunchtime, Martin still hadn't tracked the emergence of the key onto Addison's work computer. He had scrolled back through almost two weeks and the entries seemed to go on forever. Ryan's parents were arriving later in the afternoon, so if he didn't figure out when it originated by the end of the day, Addison would have to consider turning her computer over to the IT people. Since no one was going to work over the holiday weekend, she decided that waiting until Monday would be fine.

"Why don't you take a break and we'll go get something fun for lunch? Your pick." Addison said to Martin.

"I feel like I'm really close, Mom."

"I know, Dude. The computer isn't going anywhere though. It will be here after lunch."

"Okaaaay." He said, drawing the word out. He put the computer to sleep and got up from her comfy chair. "Let's go to the Asian place up the street. They always give me extra fortune cookies."

Addison smiled. "Lead the way, my little worker bee." She followed him out the door and made sure her office was locked before she walked away. The Asian restaurant was only about a five-minute walk up the block, so she wouldn't have to pull her car out of the parking garage and find parking near the restaurant.

They were about halfway to the restaurant when her cell phone rang. Emmitt was calling.

"Hi, Emmitt."

"Addison! Are you busy? I just had a quick update about the project."

"I'm on my way to lunch, but I can spare a minute or two. What's up?"

"Just wanted to let you know that *Apothecom* approved our request to begin recruiting volunteers for our study. We've already had several sign up."

"That's where I've heard that name before. I think my lab

tech's husband might be on the list. I won't give you his name in case you need to keep the double-blind standard or stay unbiased or whatever."

"Of course. It seems like things are going smoothly for Laina. I'm looking forward to her getting to use our cell line with your system down there. I think we could really see some exciting results."

"Me too. Well, we've reached the restaurant, so I have to let you go. Thanks for the update." She ended the call. She wondered if she should have mentioned the mishap with the reagent. Normally, she would have alerted a collaborator about an unexpected mutation immediately, but since they didn't want her lab using their reagents, it made it more complicated, as did the mysterious notes. She wished that she knew what the best path forward was in this situation.

Martin ordered chicken strips, which Addison found hilarious given that he'd requested a restaurant that specialized in a completely different cuisine. *It's all about the DESSERT*, she thought. She was enjoying getting to spend some extra one on one time with her youngest son. Maybe she could get the other two to spend some time with her at work over Christmas break. Martin updated her on his progress and tried to dumb down the computer language to her level, but the long and short of it was that he didn't have an answer for her yet. He wasn't sure how long it would take to search for the origin with his current method, but he did have a backup idea if it started to take too long. She changed the subject to his Christmas wish list. He was always thinking about what video game he *needed* next, so it was easy to shop for him.

"You know, Dad's birthday is coming up after Thanksgiving. What should we get him?"

"How about a *Mines Dad* sweatshirt?"

"That's a great idea, Martin! He will love having something like that. I'll look for one on my laptop when we get back."

"You know, Mom, I was just thinking. What if I tricked the tracker?"

"What do you mean?"

"What if I give it access to view what looks like your daily activities, but it's really just seeing the same two or three days over and over again?"

"Oh, like a video loop."

"Yes! Like that, but with code. Whoever is keeping track of you won't notice right away and I'll have your machine set up so they can no longer get access to your entire drive."

"Okay. Let's do it. Ready to get back to work?"

Martin nodded. Addison paid their bill and they walked back to the university. Martin felt confident in his plan to keep Addison's hacker at bay. When they got to her office, he immediately sat down and started typing and clicking.

"First, I set up a screen, so they couldn't see what I've been up to. Otherwise, we'd just be wasting our time here."

"Carry on. I'll take your word for it."

Addison busied herself ordering Ryan's birthday gift. Normally, she wouldn't do any personal shopping at work, but she felt a little hamstrung by not having her work computer available. After she ordered the sweatshirt, she went back to the *Apothecom* drug trial website. It had an application link as well as a summary of the study. The trial was going to use a gene therapy approach to target a mutation in a small protein—Addison guessed it must be STABL—and correct it to wild type. It reasoned that the mutation decreased the interaction between cardiac sodium channels and the small protein leading to poor ion exchange and subsequent high blood pressure. If the mutation was corrected, the channel would operate normally, and the patient's blood pressure should drop to the normal range. Patients would need to receive the treatment at a medical facility and have their blood pressure monitored continuously. They would have to stay overnight for observation and then wear a blood pressure cuff that would keep a record of changes in their blood pressure. Addison clicked on the associated risks tab. Most of the things on the list were standard for any treatment. It included information on the study done in mice who contained a similar mutation. The gene therapy was 98% successful in correcting the mice's blood pressure within one month. No fatalities occurred in either the placebo or gene therapy groups. It seemed like a solid study, yet something bothered Addison. If she hadn't started a collaboration with Emmitt, she would have assumed that everything in the study was above board. She wondered if Emmitt knew that Laina was working with a mutated construct and why they would be trying to pass it off as wild type. It didn't make sense.

"Mom. Mom!" Martin startled her from her thoughts.

"Sorry, honey, I was just tossing ideas around in my head. What's up?"

"I'm finished. I just need to restart the machine to have everything take effect."

"Alright, let's do it."

Her computer restarted quickly and soon brought up the login screen.

"You should change your password. There's a decent chance that whoever's been watching knows what it is."

"Fine. It's really a pain to remind myself that I changed it. *And* then also remember what I changed it to when I log in."

"Use the sentence trick."

"The what?"

"Take a memorable sentence—*my amazing and handsome son Martin is a computer genius*—for example, and then just use the first letter of each word. *M-A-A-H-S-M-I-A-C-G* then change the *I* to a 1 and put an exclamation point on the end. It's brilliant, right?"

"Where do you learn such things?" She tussled his hair.

"It's pretty standard. You just can't use a sentence that you say *all* the time or people could guess it."

"Fair enough." She used Martin's suggestion and updated her password. Hopefully, she wasn't setting herself up to be locked out later. Maybe she could put the sentence in her phone as a backup. She looked at her watch. It was getting close to four in the afternoon.

"Why don't I check in with the lab and then we'll head home? I think Dad is picking up Grammie and Pop soon."

"Yay! I hope they brought cookies." He started packing up his stuff while Addison went over to the lab.

Chapter 70

J uan stopped Anthony in the hall on their way to the department's Thanksgiving luncheon. He motioned for him to follow him into the men's room. Eleanor had asked Becky to help her get her pies from the breakroom and Laina had just entered the women's restroom.

"This is weird, man. It feels like two high school girls needing a buddy to use the bathroom." Anthony said to Juan as his friend checked to see that all of the stalls were empty.

Juan rolled his eyes and put his index finger to his lips as he checked the final stall.

"Did you talk to Dr. Fish? About the sample?"

"Yeah, I told her yesterday morning. She said that she would handle talking to Emmitt and Laina." He looked at his feet. "I guess I probably blew my chance at a postdoc with them."

"Probably, but I don't know if you'd want one."

"What? Why?"

"About a week ago, I was here later than usual helping Becky map out her binding site. I hadn't checked my mailbox in a few days, so I went by the mailroom on my way out. Right as I was walking in, I saw this guy putting something in Eleanor's box. I thought it was strange because they always bring the mail in the mornings."

"Who was he?"

"I'm not sure what his name is, but when I got a look at him, I recognized him from Dr. Watt's lab."

"What did he leave for Eleanor?"

"I almost didn't look because it could have just been something that got put in the wrong box by mistake, you know?"

"Right, but we're having this conversation, so it must have been *something*."

"It was a scrap of paper that had *Don't trust the Strydent lab* or something like that written on it."

"What? How would someone here know Laina or Emmitt? They're from California!"

"I'm not sure, but I do remember Dr. Fish mentioning that he was one of Dr. Watt's former grad students. Maybe this guy was a lab assistant or something."

"Oh, maybe so, but what does it mean? Why shouldn't we trust them?"

"I don't know, but I'm guessing it has something to do with that sample you used. Didn't you say it had a mutation?"

"Yeah, I thought that was weird. Why would they have a mutated channel labeled as wild type if it wasn't?"

"I don't know, but something isn't adding up."

"Well, we'd better get over to the luncheon before someone realizes we're missing."

"We'll talk more later. Not at work though. I'll text you later."

They exited the men's room and walked quickly over to the conference room.

Chapter 71

Laina had still set up her experiment for Thursday even though it was Thanksgiving Day. She was joining Anthony for the student and postdoc celebration at two, but had plenty of time to work before then. She was hoping that she could figure out how to tweak the system while no one was around. She had made several solutions to try until she found one that made her channel mimic the wild type.

She got everything set up quickly and then pulled pipettes for the experiment. She needed to repeat the control experiments before Emmitt would agree to start using their cell line. She had already thawed the cells on Tuesday so that she would be ready to experiment with them in two weeks. This assumed that everything went well with this experiment, which she was bound and determined to make it go well. She had considered looking through Anthony's boxes while she was the only one at the lab, but knew if they couldn't find it over the weekend, she would be the one to be blamed since no one else was in the building on Thanksgiving Day. She planned to leave it in an ice bucket overnight on Tuesday next week, making it appear that Anthony had carelessly forgotten to put it away after his transfection that day. The sample would be ruined and would have to be thrown away. He was such a mess; he probably wouldn't be able to say if he'd done it or not. She'd just need to keep it hidden for a few days in her freezer.

She sat down in front of the microscope to start the experiment. She felt confident that she could get the system working as it should before she needed to clean up and go to the luncheon. She had several hours to make various adjustments. She was already mentally planning her next phone call to Emmitt to tell him the good news. She could almost hear him congratulating her and telling her how lucky he was to have her alongside him in this ground-breaking scientific project. She knew when she got this project completed that he would have no choice but to consider her an equal and include her in any accolades he received from this point forward. She peered through the eyepiece and lowered the pipette to the first cell, silently begging it to function as she wished.

Chapter 72

Addison was really looking forward to biking with Martin after a rather stressful week. The fresh air and exercise always lifted her spirits and cleared her thoughts, plus she enjoyed some one-on-one time with her youngest child. Biking was one thing that they could share and enjoy together. She had spent a few hours at the lab the day before, trying to work through the mystery of the mutation they found along with the strange notes she and Eleanor received. She wasn't sure if she needed to report something or even what she would report if she did. She still wasn't totally confident about using her desktop computer, so she brought her laptop with her to read some papers while the solutions warmed up in the water bath. Normally, she left the laptop at home on the weekends because she didn't have any meetings that she needed it for and could use her office computer for anything else. This was probably why she had left the laptop in her office when she went home for the day. Luckily, the lab was not too far out of the way when they drove to the state park. Martin was not thrilled about the extra stop, but she promised that she would be in and out. She pulled up in front of the building in one of the restaurant's twenty-minute parking spots.

"I promise I'll be fast. Sorry for the detour, Bud. It's easier to stop on the way out than it is to come back this way on our way home. There will be more traffic later because of the football games today."

Martin sighed. "I know. See you in a minute, Mom. I've got you on a timer." He held up his wrist.

She laughed and walked quickly up to the building, swiping her fob to enter. Since virtually no one else was in the building, the elevator opened as soon as she hit the call button. She rode it up to eight and strode over to her office. The laptop was in its bag, right where she'd left it the afternoon before. She knew that it was probably just as safe in the office as it was at home, but didn't want to be without it for the rest of the weekend. Ryan's parents were leaving after lunch, so she no longer had to be the hostess and could get some work done. Addison grabbed the laptop and locked her office behind her. Martin was holding up his wrist and pointing at it when she got back outside.

"How did I do? Was it a new world record?"

"I don't think any records were under any threats with that time." He grumbled.

"Sorry again. Now we're all ready to go biking." She tossed her fob and ID into the open console. Then she swung the SUV out of her short-term spot and headed back to the highway.

"I think I have a good chance at beating you up the hill today. I saw how much turkey you ate on Thursday and for leftovers yesterday. All of that tryptophan is going to slow you down, make you tired."

"Sure, sure. I think I'm on a seven-week winning streak right now. I'm ready to make it eight. All of the *protein* that I ate made me stronger and faster."

"Okay, Bruh."

"Mom, please. Don't *bruh* me."

Addison laughed and continued up the road to the state park. It was usually fairly deserted this time of year, partly because it was getting cooler out and partly because most people were home watching football games. After showing her annual pass at the ranger station, she pulled around to their usual parking location. Only two other vehicles were in the lot: another dark SUV like hers and a white sedan. The SUV also had a bike rack, which made her wonder if they would run into other bikers on the path. Martin helped her remove their bikes from their own bike rack. She buckled her helmet into place and tried to give his a jiggle to make sure it was secure. She was just climbing onto her bike when she heard a motorcycle racing down the road towards them.

"I hope that guy isn't planning on riding up to the top behind us. He seems a little out of control." She told Martin.

"Isn't the path for non-motorized vehicles only?"

"Not everyone follows that rule, but hopefully he will. There is a road next to the path for cars and I guess motorcycles to use, but you access it from the main road."

"Well, either way, I hope you're ready to lose."

"Says the one who isn't on his bike yet." She clicked the lock button on her key and pulled her bike around him towards the path.

"Hey! No head start!" Martin shouted as he jumped on his bike to catch up.

Chapter 73

E ddie pulled out his phone to call *Lorraine*. He had seen a mom and her kid riding their bikes out of the parking area when he pulled into it, but didn't know which vehicle was theirs. The two SUVs looked nearly identical. He didn't want to waste his time in the wrong one, nor did he want to get caught by the other park visitors as he was digging in their car. She didn't answer, so he left a voicemail.

Hey Lorraine. Two dark SUVs are up here at the park. Which one is hers? The Ford or the Toyota? They both have bike racks. I'm going to start with the Ford. It's easier to break into. Call me back as soon as you get this. I don't want to waste my time on the wrong vehicle!

He walked over to the Ford and scanned the area to see if anyone was in the vicinity. There were signs for several trailheads nearby, but no one that he could see coming on any of the paths. He peeked into the window of the driver's door to see if anything about it would identify the owner as the woman Lorraine wanted the fob from. The vehicle was a pigsty. Receipts and papers were all over the floorboards and the passenger seats. He also spotted a baby seat in the back row as well as several empty food wrappers and fast-food cups. *This looks like a busy mom's car if I ever saw one*, he thought and pulled his tools from his cargo shorts. The lock popped easily and he dug around in the console for the fob that Lorraine said would be there. After a few minutes of sifting through random pens and more receipts, he decided it wasn't there. He had no desire to dig through more garbage, so he locked the door and closed it.

Before walking over to the other SUV, he checked his phone. Lorraine had sent him a text.

I don't know. It's dark-colored and big. It probably has a sticker for the university on one of the windshields.

He walked around to the front of the Toyota and looked at the windshield. Sure enough, there was a parking sticker in the bottom left corner. He smacked his forehead, wishing he'd thought of that before he pawed through the garbage in the other car. *Gross, she's gonna owe me extra for that.*

The Toyota was spotless compared to its Ford counterpart. In addition to the university parking sticker, the vehicle also had a state park sticker on the windshield. Eddie looked around again and listened for anyone coming up one of the trails. He thought he heard footsteps, so he quickly walked back over to his motorcycle and pretended to busy himself with his saddlebag as they approached. Half a minute later, three people emerged from the woods and walked towards the white sedan. He didn't look up and hoped they wouldn't speak to him either. Luckily, they got into their car quickly and drove away without paying any attention to him. He waited for their car to get out of sight before pausing to listen for sounds from the trails again. It had only been four minutes since he had left the message for Lorraine, so he should still have plenty of time to find the woman's fob and get out of the park. When he felt confident that no one else was coming, he walked back over to the Toyota.

Popping the lock was a little more challenging, but luckily, he knew how to get the door unlocked without setting off the vehicle's alarm. His cousin had the same model and frequently locked his keys inside. He carefully popped the lock and eased the door open. There was a messenger bag that probably held a laptop in the front seat. He mulled over taking it along with the fob. He could probably get the hard drive wiped easily and resell it for a quick $500 profit. First things first, though, he needed to find the fob. The console only had two items: an ID badge and a fob with a little coiled bracelet connected to it. He grabbed the bracelet but left the ID badge. He was just closing the door and turning away from the vehicle when he heard voices again. He forgot about the laptop and casually walked away from the vehicle towards his bike, putting the visor back down on his helmet so that no one could see his face. He stuck the fob bracelet in his pocket and started the motorcycle up without looking to see who was coming on the trail. With any luck, he could get Lorraine on the phone and deliver the fob this afternoon. He could use some extra cash and planned to push her for extra for ignoring his call. He drove out of the park and a mile down the road to the gas station before stopping to call her again. This time she picked up.

"I told you to text, not call. Did you get it?"

"I got it, but I had to dig through a garbage-car first. That's gonna be an upcharge for you. It was disgusting."

"We agreed on a price, Eddie."

"Well, *Lorraine*, maybe next time you'll answer the phone when I call or maybe know a little more about the car you need me to break into! It's an extra $50 or I'm tossing this fob and you're shit out of luck."

"Damnit, Eddie. Fine. Where do you want to meet?"

"Bar on 37th Street. I'll see you there at two o'clock." He hung up, pleased with his bargaining skills.

Chapter 74

Laina threw her burner phone onto the couch. Trusting criminals to be honest was never wise, but she didn't know the first thing about breaking into a car. She ground her teeth until her jaw hurt and stomped across the apartment to get a glass of water. She was glad that she hadn't told Emmitt about her scheme to get the sample back. She just needed to get the fob from Eddie and then hopefully never see him again. *Who did he think he was, extorting money from her just because he had to move around a few pieces of paper in a vehicle that was clearly not the right one?!* She was glad he didn't know her real name or where she lived or even what she really looked like. Investing in green-tinted contacts and a decent raven-colored wig had been one of her better decisions.

It had taken her nearly all morning on Thursday, but she had finally found a solution that allowed her to mimic the Fischer lab's system. Emmitt didn't really celebrate Thanksgiving either, so she had called him after the university gathering to tell him about her success. He wasn't as excited to hear about it as she had expected him to be. It didn't matter. In two weeks, she would be completing experiments with their cell line and paving the way to a big payout from *Apothecom*. She just needed to get their sample back from Anthony before they got too suspicious about it. She knew without a doubt that he had taken it and used it. *Little thief.* She wished she could further sabotage his work for making her have to go to all this extra trouble with Eddie.

Laina drummed her fingers on the counter as she planned out her next move. She would retrieve the sample early tomorrow morning. She also needed to get Addison's fob returned so that she didn't suspect that someone had stolen it. She didn't want to get Eddie to put it back; he was already a loose cannon that should never have been trusted. Maybe she could leave it somewhere that made it seem like it had just been dropped by accident. She looked at her watch. She had about two hours until she needed to meet Eddie. She grabbed her laptop and pulled up her app that stored the tracking information from her little keys. She started with Emmitt's since she hadn't checked on his activity in the past week.

He had sent an email to his contact at *Apothecom* with some of her data a week ago. The rep had gone back and forth with Emmitt on how to proceed with the trial as well as the enrollment process. They could only include people in the trial who had the known mutation, so everyone needed to have their DNA sequenced before they could sign up. *Apothecom* didn't want to include that as a perk with the trial, but not a lot of people had gone to the expense of having their DNA sequenced, so they hadn't had a lot of volunteers apply yet. It looked like Emmitt was looking into applying for a last-minute grant that would cover the DNA sequencing costs for interested applicants. She decided to give him a call so she could find out more. He answered on the first ring.

"Yes, Laina?"

"Emmitt. Have you thought any more about my data from this week? Do you think it will help light a fire under *Apothecom* and get this drug trial started sooner?"

"I think the data looks good, Laina. I told you that. It's just, well, we're not getting as many applicants for the study as I had hoped. People are applying, but not all of them know if they have the mutation, so we're looking at the cost of providing DNA sequencing if you sign up for the study."

"*Apothecom* is okay with that extra expense?"

"No, they aren't. The population that's affected by this condition is already on the smaller side. That makes the study less desirable in terms of profit and loss for them. I put in an application for a short-term grant that could cover the extra expense on our side. I should hear back in the next week or two."

"What are our next steps? Is the project in jeopardy?"

"Oh no. Nothing like that. I would like to be able to show them some striking results from your work in Atlanta soon. I think it will bolster their confidence in our project."

"I'm working as quickly as I can, Emmitt. I'll be testing out our cells the week after next. That should really help move things along."

"Great. Keep plugging ahead. We're really close here, Laina."

"I'll keep you posted, Emmitt." She ended the call. He sounded more optimistic than the email conversation looked. Laina wondered if he had talked to their rep and discussed other things that she wouldn't be able to spy on with her tracker key. She really needed to get some results that would keep *Apothecom* interested in the project.

Chapter 75

Martin rounded the corner back into the parking area and shook his left fist in the air.

"Victory, victory! That's eight in a row, Mom!"

"You got me again. Great ride, Dude."

She looked around the parking lot and noticed that their car was the only one left. They hadn't seen the motorcyclist on the trail, and she wondered if he had come to the trailhead parking area by mistake. She and Martin had only been biking for about half an hour, so whoever he was, he hadn't stayed long. She unlocked the SUV and opened the hatch so that she and Martin could sit and drink some water before they packed up the bikes again. She rode with a little fanny pack that held her wallet, cell phone, and keys. She pulled out her phone to let Ryan know that they would be headed back to town soon.

"Hey! We're just cooling down in the back with some water before loading up the bikes again. How is your morning going?"

"My parents are gathering up their things and we'll be going to the airport soon. I thought about offering to let Joe drive them instead of me."

"Not a bad thought!"

"By the way, I was just thinking, did you look at Gary's mutation relative to that mutation you found via Anthony's laziness?"

"Oh, you know what? I never did go back and look at that. I need to remember to look into it. Remind me again when we get home."

"Okay, see you soon. Love you."

"Love you too." She ended the call and turned to Martin. "Should we get these bikes back on the rack?"

"Probably so. I think that's a job for the loser, though."

"Oh no you don't! This is a team effort or you can ride your bike all the way back home." She laughed as she slid out of the SUV.

They put their helmets into the back of the vehicle first. Then,

Martin helped her lift both bikes onto the rack and secure them in place. Addison double-checked that the cables were secure on both bikes before getting into the driver's seat.

"Are you sure that I can't sit in the front seat?"

"Are you suddenly thirteen years old without me realizing it? Where did the time go?"

"Oh, c'mon, Mom. It's a short trip."

"It's a no. Buckle up, Buttercup." He slouched his shoulders and put his seat belt on.

"Mom, will we still get to go see Joe play football next year?"

Addison looked into the rearview mirror at Martin. "We probably won't make it to every game, but we'll try to catch as many as we can. Maybe we should join a frequent flyer program."

"It will be weird not seeing him all the time."

"I'm going to miss him too. It will be weird not having him around all the time. He'll still come home though—at Thanksgiving, and Christmas, Spring Break."

"I wish he could go to school here."

"I know, Dude. He picked the right place for him, so even though we're going to miss him, we need to be happy for him too."

"I'm not making any promises." Martin sighed and blew his hair out of his face. Addison hadn't realized how much Joe's college decision was affecting him. Maybe she would encourage Joe to spend some time one on one with Martin over Christmas break.

Chapter 76

Laina dressed in dark jeans, black boots, and a hooded rain jacket to go over to the lab early on Sunday morning. After debating with herself, she had ultimately decided to wear her *Lorraine* disguise again in case one of the cameras caught her entering the building. She didn't plan to look up towards any of the cameras and hoped the large hood would cover most of her face while also looking like normal attire for a possibly rainy day. Luckily, it was a relatively cool morning, so she wasn't getting hot wearing the rain jacket. She hoped to be in and out of the building within ten minutes.

As she expected, all of the lights in the hallways were off when she stepped off the elevator. She kept Addison's fob on her wrist for the time being, hoping that the bright yellow bracelet would remind her to slide the object under the office door before she left. She shuddered as she remembered having to deal with Eddie the previous afternoon. He was such a sleazebag. She had taken the hottest shower she could withstand after she got back to the apartment. If she hadn't needed the fob so badly, she would have taken a chance at breaking his jaw with a punch to the face.

Laina walked quickly to the room with the deep freeze. She was trying to behave normally, so she turned the lights on instead of using a flashlight to look for the sample. She pulled the sleeve that held all of Anthony's boxes and withdrew the one she had seen him using recently. Remembering his nearly useless labeling system, she cursed under her breath when she didn't recognize the little symbols on any of the tiny tubes. She tried to remember what he'd told her he used to indicate that the sample held DNA for the sodium channel. *Two parallel lines!* She knew that her sample would be in a smaller tube with a small volume because he had already used what he'd taken from her twice and he hadn't taken a noticeable amount in the first place. She pulled tube after tube, but none of them that were small were labeled with his channel symbol. *He couldn't have used all of it because I heard Addison tell him to keep it separate. Keep it* separate. She closed the box and pulled the one below it. None of the tubes in that box were small nor were any of them labeled as the channel. She ground her teeth and looked in the next box. Her frustration grew as the number of boxes she looked through increased. *Where was the damn sample?!* She tried to calm herself down by slowing down her breathing, but she could feel herself starting to panic. If the sample was missing, that meant that they knew something was off about it.

Laina checked her watch. She had already been searching the freezer for fifteen minutes, much too long. She put the boxes back and closed the lid, formulating a new plan. Just as she was reaching out to press the call button for the elevator, she noticed the yellow bracelet and pulled her hand back. She moved quickly around the corner to Addison's office and pulled the bracelet off of her wrist. Thankfully, the bottom edge of the door was not flush with the carpet inside the office. She pushed the bracelet into the office as far as she could with her thin fingers, then pulled out her driver's license to give it a final nudge into the room. Satisfied that it would look like it had been mistakenly dropped on her way out of the office, Laina retreated back to the elevator. She needed to call Emmitt. She didn't care that it was three o'clock in the morning in California. Things were getting out of hand at a rapid pace.

Laina grabbed her cell phone as she re-entered her apartment. She let the phone ring to his voicemail and hung up. She hit redial and willed him to answer. *Now was not the time for beauty sleep, Emmitt! Wake up already!* She hit redial a third time and he answered in a groggy voice on the second ring.

"Emmitt! We've got problems." She said as she pulled off her wig.

"Laina? What time is it?"

"Emmitt! Pay attention. I went over to the lab this morning to get the sample back. I was worried that they would sequence it."

"I told you not to worry about that. To not make a big deal out of it so that they wouldn't make a big deal out of it. What are you doing? Doesn't the building log your entry?"

"Don't worry about that. I found a way around it. Now listen—"

"You found a way *around* it? Are you breaking and entering now? How is this staying *incognito*?"

"Would you shut up and listen already?!" She paused, daring him to challenge her again. "I went to get the sample back because I was worried that they would sequence it. Anthony was having tons of trouble with his experiments and they were trouble-shooting the cause. Sequencing a DNA construct is not out of bounds for them. I went early in the morning when no one else would be there, but I looked in all of his boxes. It's not there."

"Maybe he used everything that he took."

"No. I heard her tell him to set it aside. He still has some. I don't know what to do, Emmitt."

"Have you checked your *big brother spy system* to see if she's mentioned a mutation to anyone?"

"I haven't seen anything that looks like she had it sequenced, but the fact that they have moved it is really bothering me. We need to do something, Emmitt!!"

"And what exactly do you suggest we do, Laina? Throw all of their samples out? Burn down their lab? Hire a muscle man to threaten them about being nosey?"

"Are you serious right now? A muscle man? What does that even mean? What do I do if they ask about it? Do I pretend not to know? Do I tell them to call you?"

"If they were going to ask you about it, they would have already asked you about it. I can't believe you let someone get their hands on one of our constructs. You had *one* job, Laina." Emmitt was getting more irritated by the second.

"*One job? ONE job?!* I had way more than one job, Emmitt. I had to drive all the way down here *by myself*, put up with this ogling grad student that couldn't be lazier, and try to learn a completely new system in just a few weeks. Do not put this on me."

"I can't talk about this right now. I'm too angry. I need to think it over and figure out what should happen. *Damnit, Laina.* This was supposed to be easy." He ended the call. Laina threw the cell phone at the couch and swallowed a scream. How was everything falling apart?

Chapter 77

Eleanor returned to the lab and heard the phone ringing. She quickly snatched up the receiver.

"Fischer lab."

"Oh, Eleanor. Thank goodness you answered! I'm locked out downstairs. I couldn't find my fob this morning. It wasn't where I usually leave it in my console. Maybe Martin was fiddling with it or something. Could you come let me in from the catwalk?"

"Definitely, Dr. Fischer. I'll be right down." Eleanor grabbed her keys with her own fob and walked over to the elevator. Addison was waiting by the double doors to the catwalk when she got off. She swiped her fob at the door and pushed it open for her boss.

"Good morning!"

"Thank you so much, Eleanor. I can't believe that I've lost my fob."

"I'm sure it will turn up. Did you have a nice Thanksgiving?"

"We really did. How was yours?"

"It was perfect. We had lots of family and fantastic food. Everyone brought their favorite dish. Even my brother Robert brought Jell-O, which I'm pretty sure is the only thing he knows how to make." She laughed. "Gary told everyone about the clinical trial that he signed up for. He's really looking forward to it starting, they emailed him last week to say that it's going to start on December *first*!"

Addison nodded, remembering that she wanted to look up Gary's mutation and compare it to the mutation they had discovered in Laina's sample. She didn't want to worry Eleanor about the trial until she knew more. Even if the mutations were identical, it didn't necessarily mean that Emmitt's lab was doing something wrong. It could be a coincidence. She realized that she had kind of zoned out of the conversation when the elevator dinged to indicate they had arrived on the eighth floor.

"...really hopeful that he'll get the actual treatment and be able to have normal blood pressure. All of the background on the study sounds very promising."

"That would be fantastic, Eleanor! Wait, did you say December first?"

"Yes, December first." Eleanor looked at her funny, but then continued. "He did say that if the study is successful, that he will get the treatment for free after the trial ends. It's usually two years, though, I think, unless the preliminary results are overwhelmingly good."

"I think that's how it works, but I've never been in a clinical trial before. Thank you again for letting me in. I guess I'll have to put in a request for a new fob if I don't find my old one today. So frustrating."

"It's not a problem at all. See you around."

Eleanor entered the lab and Addison continued down the hallway to her office. She unlocked the door and pushed it open with a bit of a struggle. Something was caught under the edge of the door.

"Oh, it's my fob!" She was thrilled to see it but couldn't imagine how it had fallen off her wrist and gotten wedged under the door. She retrieved it from the floor and slid it back onto her wrist. *One less thing to do today,* she thought.

She set her things down and logged into her computer. She wanted to look up Gary's mutation and compare it to the one they found. Eleanor had given her a printout that had all of his mutations listed. Addison grabbed the folder that she had put it in and sat down to look through it again. She ran her finger down the list of known mutations until she found the cardiac sodium channel: 655 A to G. *That sounds familiar,* she thought. She opened her sequencing app on her computer and found the file she had created from Laina's sample. *Same mutation.*

Addison sighed. It seemed like too big of a coincidence to be just a coincidence. She had talked with Ryan about how to approach Emmitt with the news of the mutation. It felt awkward because she would have to confess that her lazy grad student had swiped one of his patented samples. On top of that, she was questioning her old classmate's ethics if he knew about the mutation already. She wasn't looking forward to the conversation and was glad it was too early to call the west coast for now. If he did know about the mutation, then she was also going to have to break the news to Eleanor that Gary did not want to participate in the clinical trial. She hadn't realized that the trial was set to begin before the end of the week. If Emmitt was hiding one thing, he could be hiding more and that could be hazardous for those participating in a clinical study. She was about to grab her lunch to put into the refrigerator when someone knocked on her door.

"It's open," she called out. Anthony and Juan entered.

"Hi, Dr. Fish. We, uh, need to talk to you about something."

"Okay, what's up?" Addison asked, hoping no more catastrophes were coming.

"Can we sit down? This might take a few minutes." Juan asked. Addison moved her bags that she had set down onto her chairs when she entered earlier.

"Here's the deal. Several weeks ago, Juan was here late and noticed a guy leaving a note in Eleanor's mailbox. He thought it was a little strange for someone to be doing that at the end of the day, so he looked at it."

"It was a really strange note, written on a scrap of paper. It said not to trust the Strydent lab, but nothing else. I didn't know who the guy was, so I couldn't ask him about what he meant. I kind of let it go until Anthony told me about taking Laina's sample and subsequently learning that it was mutated. It seemed really fishy when you considered the weird note."

"Juan and I decided to figure out who the guy was and get him to talk to us about what he knew. I mean, Laina has been nice to us and everything, so we didn't have any reason to think that she'd be trying to pull one over on the lab or something."

"We knew that Dr. Strydent had been a student in Dr. Watt's lab, so we started with his people. A lot of them had signed up to attend the postdoc and grad student Thanksgiving meal, so we figured that was our best chance of me seeing him again. Laina would be there too and we didn't know if she would know him or not. We decided that one of us would be with her all the time so that she didn't get suspicious of us eyeing the group."

"Juan didn't really want to miss his family's Thanksgiving celebration, so we got to the meal early, hoping he would see the guy when he first arrived. As luck would have it, the note-writer did arrive early. He walked in at the same time as Juan and me. He didn't realize who we were right away, so we were able to talk to him casually before asking him about the note. Laina didn't get there until right when the meal started, which was convenient. We were able to talk to Trevor—that's the guy's name—and get his story before she even arrived."

"Trevor used to work for a neighboring lab when Strydent was first starting his own lab in California. He and a classmate had both taken positions as lab techs at the university there. His friend started in the Strydent lab. He had hoped to get some experience before going to graduate school himself. He wanted to be more than just a lab tech for his boss, you know? He wanted to show him that he understood the work and could contribute to it. Just a few weeks into his position, he started getting curious about some of the things Strydent was asking him to do *and* asking him *not* to do. Strydent told him not to order any of the generic reagents; they used a lot of in-house things that actually cost more to maintain than it did to just order pre-made stuff.

"The lab does X-ray crystallography, right? Okay. Trevor's friend started reading some background information on how the technique works, but also about protein-protein interactions. He knew a little bit from his undergrad degree, of course. Strydent had identified the binding regions on both the small protein and the channel. When the lab tech was looking at the make-up of the site on the channel and comparing it to the small protein, he was kind of surprised that they bound as well as Strydent had reported. Again, he wanted to be seen as involved and intelligent, not just a lackey. When he brought his questions to Strydent, the man got upset—almost angry even. Trevor said that Strydent didn't say anything that was out of line or concerning but that his friend could see it in his eyes—Strydent was scared by the questions. About a week later, Strydent called him into his office with *exciting* news. He had recommended him for a graduate student program at a rather prestigious school on the west coast. He was already pre-accepted and started classes the next week. They had even found housing for him. Trevor said that his friend—Mike—felt like he was being put into some sort of reverse Witness Protection program."

Addison listened to their story unfold and realized that her upcoming conversation with Emmitt was probably not going to go well. She contemplated going to Dr. Watt first before confronting Emmitt. Ultimately, she would have to report this to Dr. Watt, so she supposed the timing didn't really matter.

"Oh goodness. Did Mike go to the graduate program?"

"He did. And he has been really successful. Initially, he was only slightly suspicious of the graduate school offer, but the longer he was away from that lab, the more he realized that Strydent was trying to get him away from his data."

"It is all very strange. Thank you for telling me. I am going to have to confront Emmitt about this. I'm sorry for dragging our lab into this, even if we're only on the periphery of it. I know it's probably been unsettling for everyone. I had no idea that they were up to anything untoward or unethical. I'm going to be meeting with Dr. Watt, hopefully today. As long as we are up front and transparent about everything, I don't think there will be any effect on the lab. I will keep you in the loop. I'm not sure if Laina is in yet today or not, but don't mention this to her. I don't want some sort of crisis on top of this already awkward situation."

Juan and Anthony nodded and left her office. Addison looked at her watch. It was almost 6:30 a.m. in California. She grabbed her lunch and tried to decide if she should call Emmitt first or Dr. Watt. She couldn't believe that what had started out as such a promising opportunity to collaborate was coming down in flames around her. As she rounded the corner, she almost bumped into

Zenia.

"Oh, sorry about that. I wasn't watching where I was going." She apologized.

"Not a problem! Deep in thought again?"

"It's a story too long to tell right now, but yes. Maybe one day I'll feel like sharing." She gave a half-hearted smile. Zenia nodded and continued on her way.

Addison took a deep breath before unlocking her office door. It felt like she was about to cross the point of no return. Even though she knew it was the right step, she still dreaded taking it. She unlocked the door and sat in her office chair. She would have liked to call Emmitt first, but knew that for her lab's sake, she needed to speak with Dr. Watt before she told Emmitt anything. She picked up her office phone and called his office. Sheila answered immediately.

"Hi Sheila. It's Addison Fischer. Is Dr. Watt available? It's *very* important."

"He does have a few minutes free right now. Should I connect you?"

"Actually, I'm coming to the office. I need to talk to him in person. I'll be there momentarily. Thank you." She hung up and grabbed her laptop on the way out the door. She wanted to be able to show Dr. Watt all of the evidence and not just talk in hypotheticals. She needed to stay in front of this before it brought her down too.

Chapter 78

Addison was impressed with how quickly Dr. Watt responded to her revelation. He immediately called someone he knew within the *Apothecom* company and requested that they put a hold on the work with the Strydent lab. He also recommended that they not respond to any requests from Emmitt until the impending investigation was completed.

"Thank you for taking this so seriously, Dr. Fischer. I'm equally shocked by all that was happening right under my nose for all of these years. I never would have pegged Emmitt as dishonest—yes, he was always pushing to be the best, the top student, all of that, but he worked hard. I wish I could go back in time and, I don't know. I just feel partially responsible for not knowing about the mutation when it was first discovered."

"Thank you for your support in this rather awkward situation. You couldn't have known about the mutation. Not everything was fully digital back then. I'm sure it was easy to delete files and shred printouts without anyone realizing it had happened. What else do you need from me?"

"Let's see. I'm going to need Laina's notebook. I asked Sheila to put in a call to the chair of Emmitt's department out in California. I haven't met him before, so we might not connect right away. We're going to need to secure that freezer somewhere that Laina cannot access it. Also, any data files that she has created need to be locked so that she can't alter them in any way. Now, you said that she put some kind of virus on your computer?"

"Yes, it's a digital tracker of some sort. Honestly, I don't fully understand it myself. My son is a computer nerd and discovered it during Thanksgiving break. He was, um, playing solitaire or something while I was at a lab meeting..."

"Ha ha ha—I have children and nieces and nephews. I know how curious they can be. Don't worry about him using the computer. I'm glad he found the tracker bug thing." Dr. Watt laughed.

"Thank you. Anyway, my son said that it records all of my

keystrokes as well as what files I access, email applications, everything. We currently have it sort of locked out of working right now. He put it in a loop or something." Addison shrugged.

"I have no idea what that means, but don't delete it. We will need to include it with the other evidence. Unfortunately, that means you will lose that computer for quite a while. We can set you up with a different one for the time being. I'll get Sheila to take care of it. You and I need to fill out a report for the Ethics Board. They will handle getting all of Emmitt's papers flagged and probably pulled."

"Okay. Do we do that today or do you need to talk to California first?"

"I would really prefer to speak to Emmitt's boss first as a professional courtesy. Let me check with Sheila to see if she was able to reach his office." He picked up his office phone and pressed a button.

"Hi Sheila. Were you able to talk to anyone in California?" He paused and listened.

"Oh good. What time did they say...oh, okay then! He's calling me or? Okay, okay. Just connect him as soon as it rings. Thanks, Sheila." He hung up the receiver.

"Sheila was able to reach the department chair, a, um...," he looked at his notebook. "Dr. Peregrine. He should be calling any minute."

Dr. Watt's phone began ringing just as he finished speaking. He picked up the receiver again and then pushed another button. A man's voice came through the speaker.

"Is this Benjamin Watt?"

"Yes, sir. This is Ben. Dr. Peregrine, I presume?"

"Yes, please, call me Mark. How can I help you, Ben? My secretary said it was urgent that I return your call."

"Well, I have some unfortunate news to share with you, Mark. This is not going to be a pleasant call."

"Unfortunate news? Please, proceed."

"It's come to my attention that Dr. Emmitt Strydent has been falsifying data and publishing falsified results. One of my PIs recently started a collaboration with the Strydent lab and, through a series of events, discovered this mess.

"What?! Emmitt? The Emmitt Strydent? He's the top of his field. Surely, this is some sort of misunderstanding."

"I'm sorry, Mark. I've seen the evidence and it's undeniable. We're going to have to file a report with the Ethics Board."

"I can hardly believe this. Emmitt is the gold standard here by which everyone measures their success. How did I miss this?"

"Don't be too hard on yourself. This actually originated in my own lab many years ago, when Emmitt was a graduate student. I wasn't aware of it either. He's done a very good job of covering it up."

"Should I call our legal team? I've never had this happen before."

"I can't really advise you on your course of action, Mark. I'm sure you understand. Our department will be filing the report later today."

"I understand, of course. Thank you for contacting me first. We will cooperate in every way that's needed. I don't want our department to lose funding because of one person's misguided judgment."

"Exactly. If we think of anything else that we need, we'll be in touch. Thank you, Mark." Dr. Watt hit a button and ended the call.

"Do you want to do a conference call with Emmitt? We can do it right now from my office line."

"I think that would make it a bit easier, yes, though I would rather call him from my office. I'm a little concerned that if he sees a different number that he'll get spooked, you know?"

"That makes sense. Lead the way." He stood up to open the door for her.

"Thank you, Dr. Watt. This has all been such a nightmare. It's a relief to know that I have your support and leadership moving forward."

"Of course! You have done all the right things with this. The department will have your back every step of the way. I need to ask Sheila to contact campus security in case Laina comes over and tries to destroy any evidence. I'll be in your office shortly."

Addison nodded her thanks again and smiled at Sheila on her way out of the office. Sheila was on the phone again already. Addison could only assume that untangling Emmitt's web would be a time-consuming process. She had two missed calls from Emmitt that she ignored. She wanted to call Ryan, but knew that she had to get the call with Emmitt over with first.

Addison unlocked her office and arranged one of her extra chairs for Dr. Watt to sit near her desk and the phone. She sat in her office chair and took a few deep breaths to calm herself down while she waited for Dr. Watt to join her. She thumbed off a quick text to Ryan to let him know that Watt was supporting her and her lab in the whole debacle. She'd just put her phone away when Dr. Watt stepped into her office. She had Emmitt's office number on a post-it note above her computer and dialed it from her office line. She put the call on speaker so that Dr. Watt could hear everything. Emmitt answered on the second ring.

"Addison! What do you need?" Emmitt asked cheerfully.

Addison took another deep breath. "Well, Emmitt, I don't really have a gentle way to approach this, so I'm just going to say it. A few weeks ago, my grad student reverted to his opportunistic ways and *borrowed* some of Laina's sodium channel construct."

"What? He broke into her freezer?!" Emmitt raised his voice slightly.

"No, he saw it in an ice bucket and needed to do a transfection. The sample was right there, so he took a few microliters and put them in a new tube. I'm sure it didn't actually save him any time, but this is a bad habit of his. Unfortunately, his next two experiments were completely different than anything we have ever seen in our lab. We did some troubleshooting that ultimately led to us sequencing the construct. At the time, he hadn't told me that it was Laina's. He was embarrassed about taking it and didn't want to get into trouble. When we got the sequence back, we found that it was mutated—"

"Can you even trust him to tell you the truth about which sample he used? Maybe he messed up his own sample and didn't want to be blamed for that mistake."

"Please don't make this harder than it already is, Emmitt. I *know* about your first lab tech too. Another employee in our department shared that story with my postdoc over the weekend. How far back does this go, Emmitt?"

"Addison, let me explain. I'm not a monster or anything. It was just a simple oversight. It's not hurting anyone."

"It can, Emmitt! You're starting a clinical trial with real people who think you're trying to help them!"

"I'm not going to hurt anyone. I would never. Just let me tell my side before you throw me to the wolves. As I told you, I chose to study *STABL* in graduate school. I isolated the protein and sequenced it. I already knew that it interacted with the ion channel—Dr. Watt had identified it. I could have started with Watt's construct for the ion channel, but I wanted to go from scratch—I wanted to be innovative. I had so many big dreams, Addison. I isolated the channel from a sample the lab had received from a patient. Keep in mind, this was before everyone sequenced everything all the time. I purified it and crystallized it with and without *STABL*. The crystal structure was virtually identical to Watt's published structure, so we assumed it was fine. I made this big discovery about how *STABL* regulates the channel. It was big news in the science world.

"About a month before I defended my thesis, our lab got its own sequencer. Watt encouraged all of us to try it; he knew it was going to be a standard piece of equipment in labs one day. For fun, I sequenced the channel that I'd isolated from that patient's sample—the one that I was still using. It came back with a mutation from what had been identified as wild type. I thought it must have been an error, so I ran it again, but, of course, it didn't change. I was so afraid that this would upend my defense. The mutation was in the binding region that I had identified. I would have had to start over and do more crystals and more binding studies. I would have lost my two *Science* papers."

"Emmitt, you can't cover that up, though. It started as an innocent mistake. Now it's a huge lie and coverup. People could die if you go forward with this!"

"Addison, relax. I was never going to just fix one thing with my gene therapy treatment. I was going to fix both. I have an *in* with the registration manager. I'm screening everyone for both mutations. No one with just one mutation would get the therapy. I know that isn't safe. I'm not a monster, Addison!"

"I can't ignore this, Emmitt. Don't you see? You won't be the only person screening the registrations—the *patients*. In theory, your treatment will be prescribed by doctors at some point. You can't send out a memo and say that you have to approve all users. It doesn't work that way. You have to know that."

"Addison. Wait. You have to give me a chance to tell my side. You can't just tear the rug out from under me here."

"Emmitt, we called you as a professional courtesy." She paused.

"WE?! Who else is on the line?"

"I am, Emmitt." Dr. Watt answered. "We've already contacted Peregrine. It's over, Emmitt. I wish you would have come to me all those years ago. It wouldn't have been a big deal. We have already started the process of notifying the ethics board and we'll be contacting the police as well."

"You're *reporting* me? Addison. C'mon. Let me be the one to handle this. Don't throw me under the bus."

"Throw you under the bus?! Emmitt! This is my lab. You have to know how important this is to me. If I don't report this, I could lose my lab, my position here at the university. I would never be able to publish another paper."

"That's exactly what you're doing to me. How is that okay?"

"*I didn't lie, Emmitt!* That's on you. This is not a minor misunderstanding. We spoke to a friend of *Mike's*. I know all about how far you've gone to keep this under wraps, not even mentioning everything you and Laina did here. I probably can't prove it, but I know you were tracking my computer usage. I'm getting that shut down ASAP."

"I didn't do that. That was all Laina—"

"You've sent people away from your lab, you've created your own cell line that carries your *secret* mutation, you published falsified data. You even have your own animal model with the mutation. Imagine what you could have discovered if you had been honest from the first moment? Your discovery was no less meaningful with the mutation. But you've now influenced the entire field with your lie."

"Wait, back up...*You found Mike?!* Oh, it was that damn guy in the photo. I *knew* he looked familiar. This is all his fault."

"No, Mike's friend found us. He happens to work here and was anonymously warning us not to trust you. My postdoc and grad student tracked him down though and he was more than willing to tell us what he knew. I just wish someone had told us the whole story before we got involved at all. Now, we have to go." Addison ended the call. Her hands were trembling with anger.

"I had no idea that he was capable of such deception. He always just seemed very motivated and intelligent." Dr. Watt said to her.

"I grew up with him. He had us all fooled, I guess. Will campus security come to your office or the lab?"

"I asked Sheila to send them to your lab. You should probably head over there, while I get the ball rolling on some of these other tasks. This is going to be okay for you, Addison."

She smiled and followed him out of her office, locking the door behind her. Two campus security officers were walking up to her lab as she turned the corner to the hallway. She was glad that she was arriving at the same time.

"Dr. Fischer?" One of them asked.

"Yes." She motioned for them to enter the lab.

Eleanor raised her eyebrows when she saw the two uniformed officers enter. Addison looked quickly around the room and saw that everyone but Laina was present. She hoped that she could ease their fears with a few quick statements.

"Everyone, if you could gather round for just a moment." She waited as the other three approached Eleanor's desk. "These two officers are with campus security. I can't tell you the entire story right now, but we've done nothing wrong—we are not in trouble. Unfortunately, the same cannot be said for Emmitt and Laina.

"These two officers are going to need our cooperation as we get a few things sorted out. Please save anything you have open on your computers. I promise, we will not be sidelined from our work for too long, okay?" She turned to the officers, indicating that they could explain what they needed.

"I'm Officer Statin and this is Officer Hanes. Right now, we're just going to *babysit* your lab space until the police can get here. We also have a gentleman from IT that will be joining us to resolve an issue with your computers. Don't worry, he assured me that all of your data would be fine. Dr. Fischer?"

"Yes?"

"We need you to get a freezer of some sort—they said you'd know what we were talking about—and take it over to your office. Can someone grab your boss a dolly to get that rolled out of here? Will it fit in your office?"

Addison nodded as Anthony jumped up to retrieve the dolly from the custodian's closet. She saw her lab members' eyes filled with fear and wished she knew how to reassure them. Hopefully, Laina would not arrive before they were able to clear out of the lab.

mmitt threw his stress ball at the wall and knocked a framed certificate to the floor causing the glass to shatter. He ground his teeth together and stifled the urge to growl. He couldn't believe that Addison was besting him again. This could *not* be happening. He paced the room, trying to decide what to do first. Should he call Laina and warn her? Try and pack up his binders and run? Call everyone in the lab and tell them to take a personal day? He pounded his fist into his other palm. *Laina. Maybe she could stop this or lessen the severity of it.*

"I'm just about to go to the lab, Emmitt. What's the problem?" Laina answered rudely.

"Laina! Laina! Listen to me!" He hissed.

"God, Emmitt. Are you finally seeing what I've been telling you for a week? Calm down."

"I will not calm down. We're going down in flames. Addison knows. She *knows*. The whole thing. She knows about the mutation, about how I have fought tooth and nail to cover it up. She's turning us in."

"Correction. She's turning *you* in. I'm just another innocent bystander in your house of lies, honey." Laina said in her best southern accent.

"Oh no you don't. You're in just as deep as I am. You aren't walking away from this unscathed."

"Actually, I think I am. In fact, I think I'll call your friend at *Apothecom* and fill them in now."

"How do you—you bugged me too?"

"Of course, I did, Emmitt. I was flying blind over here. I needed to know what you knew."

"You're not innocent, Laina. You doctored those results. Addison knows that I've never used that software. You can't talk your way out of that. And—Addison found your tracker. They can never put that on me."

Laina paused. "I can tell them that you threatened to fire me if I didn't meet your demands. I'm an *orphan*, remember? People will pity me. I'm clean here, Emmitt. You're all on your own." She ended the call.

Emmitt took a deep breath and mentally screamed. He dug behind the desk for his stress ball. *How infuriating!* Laina was just as guilty as he was at this point. She never reported anything either. She encouraged him to push things to the next level. She wanted that Nobel Prize and money as much as he did. He would make sure she went down with him.

Hadn't she said that she faked her way into the building over the weekend? She must have had help. She put one of those damn BUGS on my computer. How dare she?! I can get her arrested for that. I have proof on my own computer. I'll report her to our IT department and she won't weasel out of this.

Emmitt paced around the office. He couldn't decide if he should call IT first or *Apothecom*. Maybe the pharmaceutical company would see his side, see how valuable his project is to the country—to the world! They would probably fight to protect it and him. It was *his* project after all. They couldn't freeze him out. They needed him. He scrolled through his contact until he found the number for Steve, his friend at *Apothecom*.

"Steve! How are you? It's Emmitt, by the way."

"Oh, Dr. Strydent. Yes, hi. Um, I can't really talk right now. Maybe you could call at another time? Things are really busy here today. I could forward your call to my secretary. She might be able to squeeze in some time for you later tomorrow. Apologies!" He ended the call.

What the? Does Apothecom *already know? Did Laina call him first? Has Addison moved that quickly?* The questions kept circling in Emmitt's head. He felt betrayed. He was going to change people's lives with his gene therapy. Everyone was missing the point. He never wanted to hurt anyone. He would protect them; he could manipulate any system. Surely, they would be able to see that if they just gave him a chance to explain.

Chapter 80

Laina debated about going to the lab and feigning ignorance or just gathering her things and driving away. On the one hand, she could probably get away with saying that she didn't realize anything was wrong. It would give her a chance to possibly remove the tracker keys from the computers before they confiscated those as *evidence*. *Evidence against EMMITT,* she thought.

If she just drove away, she would have to start over completely. She wouldn't be able to work in science after working with Emmitt so closely for the last five years and change. She wouldn't be considered trustworthy. She would have to go back to school, get a new degree, and make a new name for herself. She had been so close to making it big with Emmitt. They got greedy trying to go in with *Apothecom*. They should have just stuck with doing basic science. It didn't matter now, unless she could clear her name.

She could testify against Emmitt. Tell the review committee or ethics people, or whoever it was, everything and bargain for immunity. Or whatever. She had to get those keys off the computers first. She could possibly do it remotely, but only if no one was on the computer while she was trying. She grabbed her laptop and logged in quickly. The machine booted up, but flashed the battery symbol at her.

Damnit! I forgot to charge it after I used it over the weekend. Where is the stupid cord? She fished around in her bag until she found the charging cable and plugged it in. She would have to give it an hour or two to charge before she could try taking it over to the lab or it would die before she finished shutting all the keys down. Maybe she would get lucky and no one would be using their computers right now. She could just access the keys remotely and remove them before anyone knew she was responsible. Then she could login to Emmitt's computer and plant the coding files that would lay the blame at his feet. She just had to get into these computers first.

She logged into the system and decided to start with Anthony's computer first. He would be the least likely to be using his computer at any given moment. She clicked on his file and a red X popped up: ACCESS DENIED. *Did that dweeb change his password?* She tried again and got the same message. *Fine. I'll start with Juan instead.* She hovered her mouse over Juan's file, but it said that the machine was currently being used. She balled up her fists in frustration and clicked over to Becky's next. ACCESS DENIED! *What was going on? Did everyone change their passwords today? She didn't have time for this!* Eleanor's computer was also in use. She couldn't plant the evidence on Emmitt's computer if she couldn't access it.

She opened her file from Emmitt's computer. He was on the computer at the moment too. She wondered if he was trying to find the key. He was too clumsy with technology to have any idea how to find it. If he would log out, she could just put the files on there now, assuming she could get access to their machines. Maybe the tracker had logged the keystrokes for the new passwords. She opened Becky's first and clicked around to see what she had accessed that morning. Her email, her calendar, and social media were the only things. There was no evidence that she had changed her password, so why was her file locked? Surely, the timid, mousy, blonde girl did not know how to find and block Laina's tracker key. It must be something else. The keys were undetectable, though Emmitt had said that Addison knew about them; her geeky son must have found it. *She* would have to go into the lab with her laptop and one by one, delete them from the different machines. She checked her phone for the time. It was 10:30. She would have to give her laptop at least another hour to charge. Maybe if she went over at noon, everyone would be at lunch. Then she could quickly remove all the trackers and alter their coding files to look like they came from Emmitt.

This all depended on them believing that she wasn't involved, that she was coerced. They might not let her into the lab, but she had to at least try. She had given almost fifteen years of her life to science and research. She needed to stay in the game. It was time to sweet-talk these southerners. She set an alarm for 11:55 while she planned her course of action.

Chapter 81

Officers Statin and Hanes had requested that Addison and her lab members clear out of the lab space for the remainder of the day. Frank was able to access everything on their computers with his administrative login, so they didn't need to stick around to provide passwords. They said that they would get in touch with them when the police arrived. They weren't sure if everyone would need to be interviewed or give a statement, but asked that they stay on campus until they had more information. Addison decided a trip to the coffee kiosk would be a nice distraction. She phoned Sheila to let her know where they would be if anyone needed them. She sent Ryan another text letting him know that she would be free to chat soon.

The five colleagues lined up to place their orders with Addison in the back. No one spoke as the shock of what had just happened settled on each of them. Becky wrapped and unwrapped one of her blonde curls around her finger repeatedly while Anthony continually ran his fingers through his hair. Addison started to speak, but couldn't find the words that would help them relax. After she ordered and paid for everyone's coffees, she walked over to the table to join them.

"I'm just going to give Ryan a quick call to let him know what's happened and then I'll be right back over." They nodded as she stepped aside.

Ryan answered on the first ring.

"Ad! What's happening? It's after eleven o'clock already. Is it okay?"

"It's still happening, but we're okay. The lab is okay. I'm okay. We're all a bit shell-shocked and getting coffee together while IT collects evidence off of the computers. The police are supposedly on their way too. It's a lot."

"Dr. Watt was on board with your approach? He's behind you in this?"

"Yes. He's great. He was as surprised as I was, but he's already talked to Emmitt's boss, the pharmaceutical company, and has started the ball rolling on the ethics report." She sighed.

"I can hear the emotional drain in your voice. I'll let you get back to your lab people. I'm sure they are equally zapped. Call me when you can. Love you."

"Love you too." She ended the call and walked back to the table. They were all still sitting in silence.

"Does anyone have questions? I can't promise that I'll have answers, but I'll do my best."

Addison navigated their questions as well as she could. They were all mostly worried that they would have to start over with their projects or join a different lab. She assured them that everyone's project was fine. Juan's paper was still fine and unaffected by all of the morning's discoveries too. It might be a day or two before they could get back into the lab and work again, but they would not lose their projects or their progress. Everyone had just started to relax when Addison's cell phone rang.

"This is Addison Fischer."

"Dr. Fischer. This is Officer Statin. We've heard from the local police station that the officers will be arriving shortly. They would like to speak with each of you, but not in the lab. Is there an office or conference room available that could work?"

"We can use the one connected to Dr. Watt's office. They will probably want to talk to him too."

"Have you heard from Dr. Hibber this morning?"

"We have not. She had recently started coming in a little later to offset her schedule from another lab member's. It kept them from getting in each other's way. She is usually here by now, though."

"We have her local address from her personnel file, so we passed that onto the police in case she doesn't show up here."

"Okay, well, we were just downstairs grabbing coffee together. We'll head up to Dr. Watt's office area now."

They finished off their coffees and walked silently back to the elevators. Addison hoped the interviews would be quick and easy.

271

Laina strode down the hall from the elevators for the lab. She wanted to appear confident and natural, even though on the inside her stomach was tied in knots that she would fail and everything would be over for her. She mentally shook the thought from her mind. *No, I've worked too hard. I can make this work too.* She decided to start in the postdoc lounge, where she could log in to the network and see if anyone was on the various computers. She had to go around the long way, so that she wouldn't inadvertently run into someone in the hallway from the lab. Laina quickly thumbed in the entry code on the door and peeked inside to see if it was empty. *"Luck must be on my side finally,"* she thought as she stepped inside. The room was vacant. She quickly pulled out her laptop and started logging into the network. Laina checked each of the lab members' computers: only Eleanor was currently logged into hers, which meant that she was in the room with the other computers. She'd have to access each computer's file through the network instead of directly from the machines themselves.

Laina's fingers flew over the keyboard as she pulled up Juan's network folder first. His password hadn't changed, so she knew she could get into his file without any issues. She entered his password and scrolled down to where she'd hidden the tracker. She keyed in the instructions to delete it from the file, but an error message popped up. She was about to do it again, when there was a soft knock on the door.

"Just a moment!" She called out, wondering who would knock and not just enter. She started to key in the instructions again, when the door opened revealing Juan and one of the department's security guards.

"Juan! Good morning, er, afternoon, I guess it is. Is there some sort of problem?"

Juan bit his lip and looked at Laina with hard eyes. Before he could speak, the security guard put up a hand.

"I need you to take your hands off the keyboard and stand up, away from the laptop."

"What?! It's my laptop. What are you talking about?" Laina felt her stomach start to churn. Something felt very, very off.

"Please don't make this any harder than it already is. I need you to come with me. Your colleague will collect your laptop."

"He most *certainly* will not. I have done nothing wrong. This is my personal machine. It's not the department's. Why are you treating me like a criminal?" Laina looked up at the guard with wide, scared eyes. She desperately wanted to look at the screen to see if she'd gotten the file deleted but couldn't risk it yet.

"Please, just stand up and do as I said," the guard repeated calmly.

Laina sighed and stood up. She couldn't believe that they knew anything at this point. There's no way they could have found her trackers. The guard stepped out of the doorway, allowing Laina to exit as Juan stepped into the room behind her. He picked up the laptop and turned it around for the guard to see.

"Just like Frank said, she was in my network drive, trying to delete something."

Laina felt her eyes go wide in horror but tried to remain calm. She could talk her way out of this. She just needed to turn on the charm and tell them how Emmitt made her do it. The guard directed her down the hallway back towards the lab.

As she turned the corner into the lab, her heart sank. Another security guard was standing next to her desk while that geeky IT guy, what's-his-name, was typing away at Eleanor's computer. She glanced towards the spot where the little freezer sat, but it was empty. She was too late. She tried to casually, silently turn on her heel to leave when she felt a hand on her elbow.

"Oh good, you're here." An unfamiliar voice spoke to her.

Laina turned her head and saw another officer at her side. The other guard had disappeared. The new one was over six feet tall with thinning hair and bright blue eyes. Her eyes widened further in fear. Time to plead her innocence and ignorance!

"Who are you? What's going on?" She asked helplessly,

hoping to seem weak and vulnerable.

"My name is Officer Statin. That's Officer Hanes. We need to speak with you regarding your work with Dr. Emmitt Strydent."

"With Emmitt? Has something gone wrong? I don't understand." Laina looked around the room and realized it was empty of familiar faces, save the IT guy. She took a deep breath and looked up at the tall officer.

"Oh, from what Frank tells me, you understand *very* well." Statin motioned over to *Geeky* at the computer. "Why don't you have a seat while we wait for some of our other *friends* to get here."

He pulled out a cell phone and thumbed off a text to someone. Laina sat down in the nearest chair frantically trying to think of a way out. She needed someone to help her. Not Emmitt. He was definitely enemy numero uno right now. She needed to tell this officer something to convince him that she had done nothing wrong. Who could she call? Laina started to pull out her phone, but Officer Statin cleared his throat.

"No phones right now. Policy. Sorry. If it's too tempting, I can hold onto it for you."

"Why are you treating me like a criminal? I haven't done anything!" She cried.

"Sorry, ma'am, but I can only follow the rules I've been given. Just sit tight. I'm sure they'll be here any moment. They were just about to head over to your apartment—oh, look! Here they are now."

Her apartment? What? Why would—

"Laina Hibber?" She nodded. "You need to come with us. You're under arrest."

Laina melted into a puddle on the floor, sobbing real tears.

Chapter 83

"Wow, Mom! They really arrested her? Like the real police?" Martin asked excitedly.

"Now, Martin. It isn't kind to celebrate someone's hardships." Ryan started.

"But sometimes you get what you deserve!" Joe shouted. "She tried to ruin Mom's lab. Good riddance."

Addison waited for them to stop before continuing. "Yes, yes, the real police, Martin. Like we told you, it's illegal to hack into other people's computers and files. The department had to press charges once they learned what she had done. Luckily, we have a pretty decent IT guy and when I told him what you told me about the tracker keys, he knew exactly what to do."

"They had put them on more than one computer?"

"Every computer in the lab, except Laina's had one."

"So that's five counts."

"What?"

"Five counts. She did it five times, so five counts of the charge, whatever it's called."

"Oh, yes. I suppose it will be five counts. She had her laptop with her too, so they confiscated that along with her phone. When they searched her apartment, they also found a burner phone and said that they found even more damaging evidence on it."

"A *burner phone*?! This is like a real crime novel, Mom! Why would she have a burner phone?" Liv asked.

"I'm not sure, honey. They said there was evidence that she tried to pay someone to break into my car, which would explain how my fob was missing from the car this morning. I can't believe that was just this morning. They also found a black-haired wig and colored contacts, possibly some sort of disguise to hide her identity from the other guy."

"A secret identity! Wow, Mom. Are you going to be on the news?" Martin asked.

"I don't think so, sweetheart. They said that she wore this wig and probably the contacts when she entered the building in the middle of the night. She was trying to get something out of the freezer, but whatever it was, she didn't find it. Most likely, it was the sample that Anthony took a few weeks ago. I tucked that away into my own box, just in case. NIH confiscated it, along with all of her reagents and her notebook."

"What will happen to Emmitt?"

"You know, I'm not sure. It will probably take some time to figure everything out. Dr. Watt said that Emmitt's lab was shut down by NIH for now. They've put a hold on his grants and took all of his notebooks from the last two decades. I don't think he'll be arrested, but he probably won't do any more research. I spent the afternoon filling out a report to the Ethics Board with my boss. It's been a busy day. I'm exhausted."

"I can imagine, Mom. Joe and I made dinner tonight and it's going to come out of the oven any second now." Liv smiled.

Addison hugged her as the timer on the oven sounded. "Thanks so much. What a kind thing to do."

"We knew you were stressed out, Mom. We could all tell. I'm sorry that your collaboration didn't work out. I know you'd been really hopeful about it." Joe said.

"Thank you, Joe. I was really hopeful. I guess it was just too good to be true."

"Wait! What about Eleanor and Gary? Did you get him out of that trial?"

"I spoke with Eleanor and she immediately called Gary. He called *Apothecom*'s helpline right away. They told him the trial was on hold, but agreed to remove him from the list. I'm so relieved that the trial never got started—it was supposed to begin on December 1. Apparently, Emmitt was just using our lab to perpetuate his lies. He thought he could get the data they wanted without anyone realizing something was off. I can't believe I'm saying this, but for once, I'm glad that Anthony is such a lazy student. If he hadn't taken Laina's sample, we never would have known. She'd altered her own results to look like ours and probably would have continued to do so. Emmitt thought he could keep his finger in all the pies and control the clinical trial so that no one had life-threatening reactions. It's all very shocking."

"But also reassuring that there are standards and regulations in place to keep all of us safe," Ryan said. "Now, who's hungry? Martin even set the table for us without being asked. Miracles abound!"

About the Author

Leslie A. Piggott lives in the Austin, Texas area with her husband and their two children. She is a scientist-turned-mom who received her doctorate in Biomedical Sciences from the University of Texas Health Science Center at Houston. In addition to writing, she also enjoys running marathons, quilting, knitting, singing in the church choir, and watercolor painting. She has previously published two watercolor and poetry books, both in 2021: Poems in the Pandemic, and Art in Words. This is her first novel.

www.ingramcontent.com/pod-product-compliance
Lightning Source LLC
Chambersburg PA
CBHW010737130726
47899CB00015B/3301